MY NEEDS,
YOUR NEEDS,
OUR NEEDS

MY NEEDS, YOUR NEEDS, OUR NEEDS

Jerry Gillies

DOUBLEDAY & COMPANY, INC.

GARDEN CITY, NEW YORK 1974

ISBN: 0-385-01749-9
Library of Congress Catalog Card Number 73–83634
Text Copyright © 1974 by Jerry Gillies
Poems Copyright © 1974 by Judy Altura
Printed in the United States of America
First Edition

To my mother, Minnie Gillies, for allowing me the freedom to grow, encouraging me to put words on paper, and demonstrating how very remarkable women are.

CONTENTS

ACKNOWLEDGMENTS

This book wouldn't have been possible without the many people who contributed so much to make it happen, both personally and professionally.

Bonnie Cousins has always been there when needed, and has been the perfect love-partner throughout the writing struggle, offering much in the way of common-sense comments and helping to audition many of the exercises.

Special thanks go to three very special couples. Dr. Bart Knapp and Marta Vago, for their warm friendship, generous advice, and many hours of interviews that helped form the core of several chapters. Nena O'Neill and Dr. George O'Neill, for their co-operation and encouragement, despite a hectic schedule, and for *Open Marriage*, an inspiration to anyone writing about love relationships. Marc and Rachel Shane, for providing many insights, being a joy to know, and turning me on to rolfing as a sharing experience. These six people are beautiful examples of how synergy and growth really work in a relationship, and I am proud to have them as my friends.

Judy Altura has to be one of the warmest women in the world, as evidenced by her poetry, which plays such an important part in setting the mood for all twenty chapters.

Carole Altman has been a delightful friend and partner, as well as a remarkable psychotherapist and encounter group leader.

For their willingness to share so much in our personal interviews, I am deeply grateful to Dr. Daniel Malamud, Dr. Edward Askren, Dr. Denis O'Donovan, Dr. Freyda Zell, Dr. Herbert Otto, and Roberta Otto.

Biofeedback scientists have been especially kind in granting interviews, and include most notably: Dr. Johann Stoyva,

Dr. Tom Budzynski, Dr. Elmer Green, Dr. Marjorie Toomim, Dr. George Whatmore, and Dr. Edmund Jacobson, for his important work on relaxation. Also, Adam Crane, for getting me involved in biofeedback in the first place.

A man can't write a book on relationships without incorporating a lot of what he's learned from women. All of the following have been good friends, and most helpful in teaching me the female point of view. A warm hug to Susannah Lippman, Kaye Erhardt, Ann Hardy, Pat Nugent, Lenny Dash, Jane Rossin, Stephanie Hirsch, Barbara Hoke, Lois Gross, and Noreen Fox. A double hug to Randie Levine for her expertise in the world of publicity.

Jeff Saks has been an important sounding board and a valuable source of material. Dr. Bernard Aaronson has provided much information on chanting and consciousness. Stephanie Sladon has made a major contribution as my staff programmer at Miami-Dade Community College. Jim and Peg Reilly have been an inspiring couple to watch in their growth process.

Emily Coleman is a great group leader and friend, and her vitality and spontaneity have helped spark many new ideas in interpersonal communication, including a number of those in this book.

Two men helped guide me on the path that led to this book. Edward Karr is the kind of teacher everyone should have the good fortune to experience. Harold Phillips did much to convince me that there were greater aspirations than to become a network newscaster.

Julie Coopersmith has been much more than I ever expected an editor to be, and I thank her for using a light whip.

Agents Malcolm Reiss and William Reiss really helped me put it all together.

A special debt of gratitude is owed to a most unique organization, the Association for Humanistic Psychology. Many of the people who contributed their ideas and energy to this work were first contacted at national conferences of AHP.

Most of all, this book is the result of the many workshops

I've conducted, and Love Potential classes I've led, at growth centers and universities throughout the nation, for the Together Circle in New York, the Biofeedback Institutes in New York and Miami, and Cornucopia in Miami. To the hundreds of good people who have attended and participated, thank you for allowing me to share your learning and growing process with my readers.

Jerry Gillies
Miami, Florida
1973

LOVE POTENTIAL

I will not burden you
with all my needs.
In short:
I love you so,
I will protect you from my love.
Judy Altura

This book is largely based on a single premise: that each of us can increase our capacity to love and be loved.

This love potential can be activated. All it takes is a willingness to explore the possibilities. No one can tell you what you are feeling in a love relationship, only you know this. To begin to more fully realize your own love potential, you have to start to examine those feelings, and become aware of the dynamics of what is really happening as you interact with a love-partner.

Love Needs

A love relationship consists of the two people meeting, fulfilling, communicating, and sharing needs. Their individual needs and those of the relationship.

Few people know all their needs, fewer still understand them, and even fewer can communicate them. To know and understand our needs, particularly the needs of our love relationships, we have to examine and evaluate our priorities. These priorities are the agenda that determines which of our needs are most important. This agenda is often a hidden one, and so it's not surprising that a lot of confusion surrounds the needs we have in a love relationship. Quite a few individuals find themselves in the wrong relationship with the wrong person, trying to fulfill the wrong needs.

Considering we almost always enter a relationship to meet our needs, it's ironic how often we ignore them, how rarely we even think of love in terms of these needs, and how easily we misinterpret them.

The first step is, of course, to identify and become aware of our needs. Since we often send out an emotional smoke screen, we have to find a way to plunge through the camouflage. There are many directions you can take, and this book could be considered a road map of the possibilities.

All of the exercises, techniques, and learning experiences in this book are designed to help you understand and communicate your needs, the needs of your partner, and the needs of the relationship itself. It is not a question of MY NEEDS+YOUR NEEDS=OUR NEEDS. These are three separate entities. They may often parallel each other, but they may also conflict. Most problems in love relationships involve these conflicting needs. Often the individuals in a relationship aren't even aware of the conflict until it's too late. Early examination and sharing of the three sets of needs can avoid much pain and remove many obstacles to a fulfilling relationship. It quite often is simply a matter of making a hidden agenda an open one.

This is an action-oriented book. Taking action is the only way to facilitate growth in a love relationship. In this context the action involves dozens of exercises in communication and awareness. These exercises or experiences are only teaching aids, designed to guide you as you discover your own best path. The techniques sometimes set up contrived or simulated situations, but in many ways these involve more reality than our actual life experiences. This is true because we can often suspend our conditioning and role-playing more easily in a contrived exercise than we can in the "real world."

These exercises are important because they enable individuals and couples to choose new perspectives, and see more of what is really happening.

Risk and Responsibility

Of course, you have to make a personal commitment to take the risk and the responsibility. The risk is that you will change. The responsibility is for your own actions and feelings. If an exercise doesn't seem right for you, you must take the responsibility to discard it. If something does seem to provide insight, you must take the responsibility for seeing that you make full use of it.

In other words, this is not a series of sacred concepts that have to be regarded as gospel. There is an occupational hazard in psychology that could be called the "messiah complex." It is a statement, either explicit or implicit in words or attitude, that says:

"I am your leader. Everything I say is important to you and can change your life, if you only have the good sense to understand and appreciate it. I know what is best for you. I know the only true path to enlightenment. Only I can really teach you how to reach fulfillment and bring joy into your life. Only I can solve your emotional problems. My methods are the best, and completely negate any other system ever conceived."

The exercises in this and other chapters are not the only answer. If, however, you try them, and select those that especially appeal to you for further exploration, there's a good chance you will accomplish something. If nothing else, you will have a good time, either alone or with your love-partner. It's a lot more entertaining than a movie or a cocktail party.

Some of the exercises may make you feel silly, and even this can serve a useful purpose. Your experience may be pleasant, it may be enlightening, it may be sad, it may even make you angry. But it will be real, at least for that moment, if you honestly enter into it and stay in touch with what is happening to you.

Experiencing is living, whatever the experience. There are, however, some things that get in the way. Expectations, for example. If you begin an exercise with the expectation that it will profoundly change your life or give you a peak experience, you'll either be disappointed or create your own pseudoexperience through self-hypnosis. Even an expectation that an exercise will be fun to try may get in the way of the experience. One suggestion may be to say to yourself:

"I am going to try this and see what happens. I will examine it only after experiencing it."

Pace Yourself

There are a lot of things to experience in this book. Enthusiasm is energy, and like energy it can be conserved and made to last longer. The exercises are not meant to be tried all in one week. It almost seems to be an integral part of human behavior that as soon as we discover something new we tend to go overboard. Self-awareness and sensitivity and honest communication are all the rage now. The encounter group groupie is a sad side effect of the human potential movement. More than one individual or couple has discovered new insights and communication links in a group session, and rather than put it to use and savor the experience, they have rushed off to another group experience. Spacing and timing are all-important in the growth process. Learning to fully experience. You need time to absorb and reflect on what has happened. In our accomplishment-oriented society, it sometimes seems that getting there fast is more important than how much you enjoy the trip.

Only you can choose the right pace for you. When you stay aware of what is happening at a feeling level, you should know when and if speed is getting in the way of the learning experience.

One possibility might be for you to read through the book, and then select the exercises you want to try first. They are not in any particular order, though in some chapters the exercises follow a natural progression. Another alternative, and perhaps the easiest one, is to slowly work your way through the book, trying exercises as they appear.

If you don't have a partner, you might ask a friend to join you, or work alone, perhaps with a tape recorder so you can listen to your own feelings.

Role Review

What are your respective roles? How do you describe yourselves to the world? As husband and wife? Boy friend and girl friend? Roommates? Lovers? Do you see your relationship as having an identity that can be labeled? If you're not married, do you find it difficult to come up with a role title? If married, do you take the easy way out and merely address each other as husband and wife, mates, or spouses?

Discuss the role you have been using. Check out your feelings at being placed in this particular category. Repeat the following sentence to each other several times, coming up with as many different answers as possible: "I like being your (role title) because ———."

Notice that almost all such labels include the possessive pronoun. How important is it that you possess each other, that you be each other's undisputed property? Discuss this.

New Role Titles

Throughout this book, couples will be referred to as lovepartners. How do you feel about that designation? Can you discuss and agree on a new name for your respective roles?

How would you like to be introduced by your love-partner? While thinking about this, try to stay in touch with the reality of what you mean to each other. This doesn't mean you can't have fun with it. Some new role titles picked by couples:

SNUGGLER
CUDDLING COMPANION
BEAU and BEAU-ess
LOVABLE
LOVE OBJECT and SEX OBJECT
WARM SPOT
LOVING FRIEND
LEADING WOMAN and LEADING MAN

See if you can't come up with a few new role titles to choose from.

Role Identity by Gender

Many of the manipulative acts that emerge in love relationships are attempts by the partners to assert their masculinity or femininity, according to preconceived notions of how men and women are supposed to act. Getting in touch with real facets of your masculinity or femininity can clear up some of the confusion and animosity.

Sit across from each other and close your eyes. Each partner start becoming aware of your gender, in fact chant it over and over to yourself as you try to feel it. MAN. MAN. MAN. MAN. WOMAN. WOMAN. WOMAN. WOMAN. When you each individually feel ready, open your eyes, start chanting your gender aloud, and make eye contact with your partner. Move closer and join hands, still chanting your respective genders. When you each feel ready, change it to a mutual chant of LOVE LOVE LOVE LOVE LOVE LOVE LOVE.

Discuss what this felt like, and whether any part of it

made you feel uncomfortable. Were you able to identify with your own gender?

The Gestalt Prayer

Fritz Perls, the father of modern gestalt therapy, stressed individuality and a strong sense of self in his work and in his now famous prayer:

I DO MY THING, AND YOU DO YOUR THING.
I AM NOT IN THIS WORLD TO LIVE UP TO YOUR
  EXPECTATIONS
AND YOU ARE NOT IN THIS WORLD
  TO LIVE UP TO MINE.
YOU ARE YOU AND I AM I
AND IF BY CHANCE WE MEET, IT'S BEAUTIFUL.
IF NOT, IT CAN'T BE HELPED.

These lines have probably been reproduced on more posters than any ever written, or five sixths of them have. It is probably indicative of our happy-ending fetish that most of the posters have eliminated the last line.

Your reaction to this prayer can provide a strong indication of how dependent you might be in your current relationship. Do the words make sense to you? Do the ideas expressed seem valid? Of the millions who pay lip service to these words, few have really examined what they mean. Few have examined them at a feeling level. Do you feel a person advocating this philosophy would lack warmth or compassion? Do you resent the lack of a sentimental or romantic theme? Would you honestly want to be involved with someone who wholeheartedly lives by these words?

The Gestalt Prayer deserves more intimate attention than it has received. Word by word attention. Each of you say the prayer, one line at a time, to your partner. Start with the first line. First one, then the other partner recites it, then discuss your feelings before going on to the next line.

I DO MY THING, AND YOU DO YOUR THING.

What does this mean to you? Can you relate it to the way you now react to each other? What are each of your "things"?

I AM NOT IN THIS WORLD TO LIVE UP TO YOUR EXPECTATIONS

If your partner says this to you, and means it, has he or she let you down?

AND YOU ARE NOT IN THIS WORLD TO LIVE UP TO MINE.

Does this line feel any different, as you say it, than the preceding line did?

YOU ARE YOU AND I AM I

Which of the two statements in this line is easier for you to say and feel? Which do you believe the most?

AND IF BY CHANCE WE MEET, IT'S BEAUTIFUL.

What does this line mean to you?

IF NOT, IT CAN'T BE HELPED.

Can you really agree to this? Can you be this philosophical about your relationship? Do you think the poster companies are right in leaving this last line off?

How did sharing all this feel? Did it change your attitude toward the prayer? Had you ever read it before? If so, how has your feeling changed?

How would you feel about a completely opposite statement?

WE DO OUR THING TOGETHER.
I AM HERE TO MEET ALL YOUR NEEDS AND EXPECTATIONS
AND YOU ARE HERE TO MEET MINE.
WE HAD TO MEET, AND IT WAS BEAUTIFUL.
I CAN'T IMAGINE IT TURNING OUT ANY OTHER WAY.

Try repeating these lines to each other, one at a time. Does this feel more or less comfortable to say than the Gestalt Prayer?

If you can't accept the Gestalt Prayer with open arms, it doesn't mean that your relationships are all doomed to failure. It may be that this philosophy just doesn't meet your needs. Taking responsibility for yourself also means being able to say "Bullshit!" whenever you come across something that doesn't feel right, no matter who said it.

Four Basic Guidelines

1. Take responsibility for yourself.

Recognize how many times you blame externals for what happens to you. For example, look at your past relationships and why they ended. Explain the reason in one sentence. Does the sentence start with "I"? If not, see if you can't change it so that it does. Instead of something like, "He didn't understand me," or, "Men just don't understand me," try, "I seem to choose men who don't understand me," or, "I couldn't seem to make myself understood."

2. Be aware of your feelings.

Children always seem to know what they are feeling. Sad. Happy. Angry. Thus they can more easily and honestly express themselves. It takes only a split second to ask yourself, "What am I feeling right now?" If you would do this before starting any kind of communication with a love-partner, you'd save a lot of wasted energy and misdirected emotion.

3. Have a sense of commitment to the relationship.

This is not to provide your partner with a feeling of security, or to make an unrealistic declaration of permanence or exclusivity. The commitment is to growth and honesty, and to declaring that when you are both together you are both there, emotionally as well as physically.

4. Be able to honestly share what's happening when it's happening.

Staying in the here and now isn't easy, but try to note how

many times you dwell on the past or the future. Before sharing anything together, be able to say to yourself, "I am here." Be able to tell your partner what you are really feeling. Communicating your fantasies or your façades isn't really communicating, though it may provide useful information if you are aware that they are fantasies and façades.

It can be stated even more simply, in a single sentence:

BE AWARE AND ABLE TO HONESTLY SHARE YOUR AWARENESS

Honesty as the Best Love Policy

Few of us are totally honest with ourselves or others. We are brought up in an insidious atmosphere that could be called, at best, "kindly dishonesty." As children we see our parents practice all sorts of supposedly innocent deception. Aunt Harriet is a bore and mom and dad discuss her irritating habits at great length before her visit. But all is sweetness and love when she actually arrives. Not only have mom and dad set us a fine example, but we have been made unwitting accomplices to the deception. Can you remember back to your childhood and recall for each other some of these learning experiences in dishonesty?

Much dishonesty is described as courtesy. We don't tell our hostess the meal practically gags us. It just wouldn't be polite. So we lie. It's just a little white lie, and it does make her feel good. So, of course, she goes right on making lousy meals. After all, doesn't everyone tell her how wonderful they are?

Honesty is a very important factor in encounter groups, and many people attending these groups are shocked when other group members tell them they have an irritating habit or unattractive feature. How can this be true, and if it were true wouldn't their friends have told them about it?

The next time you are tempted to treat someone kindly

with a little white lie, particularly a love-partner, ask yourself if you aren't really just taking the easy route and avoiding confrontation. It's once again a question of taking full responsibility for yourself.

Of course, the building of trust has to parallel the increase in honesty. Telling something that you've been repressing to someone you don't trust can be an unhappy exercise in masochism.

As you go through the experiences in this book, for instance, be able to say, "I don't think I can share that with you at this moment." And if your partner says this to you, be able to respect that decision. If you feel this prerogative is being abused, then be able to discuss your feelings in that area.

In Nena and Dr. George O'Neill's book *Open Marriage* a lot of the emphasis is on honesty. We asked the O'Neills whether they saw dangers or risks in being honest with your love-partner.

DR. O'NEILL: Well, as long as the honesty isn't brutal honesty, and I think if you're talking about initiating our concept of "open trust" early in the relationship, the chances are that there will not be much of this. The idea is to communicate with tenderness and a preamble of the fact that, "This is the way I want you to know I really feel."

NENA O'NEILL: Right, and you can use honesty for manipulation, in the same way you use other things for manipulation. I certainly think there are dangers in that area. So, you have to do it with, as George says, tenderness, and with care and concern for the level at which the other person is, and also with an awareness of how you are using the honesty and for what purpose.

DR. O'NEILL: You can't force anybody to do anything. I think that's the basic rule. So you've got to say, "Look, this is the way I feel, and hopefully you feel the same way, or understand how I feel, and let's see what we can do with that." Anything else takes the big risk of not being anything more than manipulation, and not getting anybody anywhere in a love relationship.

So, much of the answer seems to be in how you use the honesty, what your feeling is toward your love-partner as you are being honest, and your motivation in being honest.

A fear that a lot of people share is that, once they bare their souls to a love-partner, the joy of discovery will be gone. You will know everything there is to know, and boredom will set in. This is ridiculous. By opening up the communications network, you expand the horizons of your relationship and make it less vulnerable.

Trying to maintain the mystery by withholding information can be a painful self-defeating effort. It can be compared to the efforts of the maiden who holds on to her virginity until she's fifty, and then wonders why no one wants this precious gift. Holding on can mean stagnation. Letting go can mean growth.

Dr. Bart Knapp, a noted psychologist, and his colleague, psychotherapist Marta Vago, emphasize the need for honesty in their extensive work with couples. But they have comforting words for those who feel this can end the mystery and excitement. Dr. Knapp says, "If each person is moving and changing, what you knew yesterday may already be changed today. The mystery is still there. You can never know all. The individual and the relationship are both changing."

Marta Vago agrees: "Assuming that one can know all is assuming that the person or the relationship is going to be static. If you have any two human beings who are growing and changing, there is no way on earth that they'll know everything about one another."

The best way to learn how much honesty you feel comfortable with is to try some. You might pick a one-day period, and try being totally honest with your love-partner, sharing every real feeling you have. If your partner feels ready, it can be a reciprocal exchange. Then you can both share how uncomfortable or painful the effort may have been, and whether you feel better about each other after making these disclosures.

You may already know how much honesty you are willing to try, but what you can't possibly know is how much your partner can handle. We often underestimate each other's capacities and capabilities in this area. Sometimes it is self-serving to do so.

Martin and Ginger and Nancy

Martin often says that his wife, Ginger, just couldn't take his being honest about his affair with Nancy. Martin is a psychologist working for a major university, and Nancy is a therapist at a drug rehabilitation center. Both are "into" growth and encounter, and had met in an encounter weekend Martin was leading. Nancy is divorced and living alone. Martin lives with Ginger, whom he professes to love very much. Ginger doesn't know about Nancy. She isn't "into" growth, and Martin doesn't really encourage her to be, other than making a half-hearted attempt once in a while to persuade her to try an encounter group. Nancy is a very open and honest person, and is deeply disturbed over Martin's not telling Ginger about the affair. She has broken off the relationship twice over this issue, but Martin is persistent and persuasive, and they do have strong affection and attraction for one another. Martin says Ginger can't handle the truth, and he cares for her too much to want to hurt her feelings that badly. Nancy feels it is Martin who can't handle the confrontation because he's afraid he'll lose Ginger. Nancy sees Martin as emotionally weak on this point. Martin feels guilty whenever he returns to Ginger after being with Nancy. Ginger seems to be perfectly happy in her ignorance of what is really going on.

So, Nancy has Martin, Martin has Nancy and Ginger, and Ginger has Martin and their home and a new baby. The main problem for Martin is that he is personally and pro-

fessionally committed to the concept of open honesty, and
realizes only too well his hypocrisy. He is living a major lie,
though he is open and honest in most other respects. There
is no way he can ever feel good about the times he is open
and honest, when he knows he isn't sharing what is really
happening with the one person to whom he is supposedly
committed. Martin not only wants to have his cake and eat
it, too, but he doesn't even want the cake to know he's also
eating the icing.

What are Martin's alternatives?

1. He can keep it up, trying to alleviate the guilt feelings,
   and just enjoy his two women.
2. He can tell Ginger everything.
3. He can give up Nancy without telling Ginger about
   her.
4. He can give up both women and retire to a monastery.

With the emotional merry-go-round Martin has been on,
it's not unlikely the fourth choice would seem a logical one.
Seriously, it's a very confusing problem, though not a very
unusual one.

With Martin's dedication to honesty, there seems little
chance he can ever have any self-respect if he doesn't tell
Ginger. What he would really like to do is be perfectly
honest and still keep both women. Of course, he's pretty well
destroyed that possibility by maintaining the deception for
two years. He says he is holding back because he doesn't
want to hurt Ginger. Actually, while he can say his relationship with Nancy has been honest and important in terms of
growth, at a gut level he feels like an old-fashioned philan-
dering husband, and he is afraid to tell Ginger he isn't the
devoted spouse he's been pretending to be. He says he's
afraid her weakness will cause an emotional collapse, and
he's sincere in saying this, but he also fears that she *will*
have a lot of emotional strength, enough in fact to be able to
remove him from her life if she finds his deception intoler-
able.

Martin's hesitation is the height of arrogance, since as

long as he avoids the confrontation, he is withholding from Ginger the right to make a vital decision. He is fulfilling some of his additional needs with Nancy, but giving Ginger no opportunity to fulfill any she might have. It's a modern version of the old double standard.

All three people involved in the situation are basically decent, loving people. They want to do only what is right and good for themselves and their loved ones. Keeping this in mind, examine the problem. How would you react to it? Can you identify with the feelings Martin has? Can you identify with Nancy and Ginger? What would you do if you were Martin?

Of course, if Martin and Ginger had started out with an open and honest relationship, the situation would never have developed.

You cannot hold back the truth without shutting down some of your capacity to give and receive love.

One of the beautiful aspects of being in a sharing love relationship is the opportunity it provides to let yourself be vulnerable to another person. We hold ourselves in so tightly all through our lives that it's not surprising that we can achieve an ecstatic sense of release by letting down all the barriers for someone we love.

Honesty is perhaps the best tool for building a fulfilling relationship. It can be a dangerous tool, but not if you obey some simple safety regulations.

PASSIONATE PRIORITIES

We are
A moment of strength
In too many muted hours.
Judy Altura

The Unlearning Process

The happy couple is becoming an endangered species. Drastic measures are needed to protect the love environment. It has to be a highly personal crusade, with each of us individually agreeing to make the effort, and work on eliminating the fears and restrictions that prevent us from fully opening up to another person. There is only one way to unlearn the negative conditioning and remove the fears. That is to venture forth, at our own pace, and confront those fears, reassuring ourselves that it doesn't have to hurt to be vulnerable, that it can feel good to let go, that we are really capable of feeling and enjoying more. This unlearning process may take a lifetime, but the rewards are in the trying rather than the reaching of any final goal.

Checking It Out

Each of you prepare three lists. Do this individually, without comment or conversation until you are finished.

1. MY NEEDS.
2. YOUR NEEDS.
3. OUR NEEDS.

Before starting your lists, make certain you understand the difference between them. The first one is a list of the things you think you need to make you happy. The second list is your opinion of what your love-partner needs to be happy and fulfilled. It's important to be as honest as possible. If you feel your partner needs you to be happy and fulfilled, then say so! The final list is composed of those things you think the relationship needs to make it a good one.

Make the lists as complete as you can. Start now.

After finishing your lists, show them to each other, share and discuss your thoughts and feelings.

Some possible questions you might ask each other are:

"Did anything on my list of my needs surprise you?"

"Did I leave out any of your major needs?"

"Do you think I have any needs that I left off my list?"

"How would you feel if my list of your needs was somehow made official, and you had to live by it as a permanent guide?"

"How would you feel if my list of our needs was the one we both had to use as a guide for our relationship?"

Honest sharing should give you a pretty good idea of your current agenda. Now comes the tough part: deciding whether you are willing, able, and really want to change anything on your list of priorities. First, you have to decide which priorities involve the biggest investment on your part. These are the ones that should be examined most closely.

Let us say, for example, that you've been married for twenty years. Obviously, this is a major investment on your part. You must have home and family as a very high priority, as something very high on your list of needs. Or is it really on your partner's list? Only you can decide whether you're ready to challenge that priority.

Harold

Harold held a blue chip stock for twenty-one years. During that time it hardly increased in value at all. It paid Harold a fair interest rate, and it maintained a steady level during bad times, but it never took those exciting leaps and bounds that signify a glamour issue. Harold changed brokers. His new, younger investment counselor told him he was being too cautious. He was advised to take some money out of the old faithful blue chip company and try for some profits. Harold was nervous and upset. He dreaded going to see the new broker. He put off making a decision. Finally, Harold decided to go back to his old broker, keep his old stock, and try to put aside the fleeting thoughts he had had of easy riches.

Was Harold wrong? For Harold, not necessarily. While new financial gains would have seemed attractive, they would have made Harold uncomfortable. All the time he'd be making money, he'd also be remembering the past twenty-one years, and the possibility that he could have been making money all along. It would be a repudiation of what he had assumed was wise and cautious action on his part. It just wouldn't be satisfying. And, of course, there would be the chance that he'd lose some of his investment. So, why take a risk?

This is precisely why many people stay together after many years of marriage. It's just too big a risk to try for anything better, and even getting something better might not feel that good.

You have to decide whether it's worth the risk to try changing any of your major priorities. Whether it's worth re-evaluating those needs. If you are miserable right now, the choice is probably an easy one. But if you are fairly satisfied and comfortable, the risk just might not seem worth it. No psychologist or counselor can tell you whether any such change is worth the risk, nor can this book. It's a personal decision that can be based only on what you are feeling right now about any particular priority.

Where Are We Now?

Before working on any effort to change something, we have to know what it is we want to change. So, in the effort to move your relationship in new directions, you must first examine where it has been, where it is now, and where it seems to be going.

Discuss together the following points:

Where are we now?
Where have we been?
Where are we going?
What would we each like to change?
What are we each willing to change?

Discuss these issues as long as you'd like, but don't expect to reach any definite conclusions. You are starting a process, not taking a quick cure. Contrary to what many people believe, love is neither an illness nor a medicine.

Love as Medicine

Look at all the answers a group of men and women came up with when asked to complete the sentence "Love will bring me ———."

"Companionship."
"Security."
"Fulfillment."
"Contentment."
"Satisfaction."
"Joy."
"Ecstasy."

"Appreciation."

"Peace."

"Release from tensions."

"Growth."

"Completion."

"Respect."

"Freedom."

"Accomplishment."

"Maturity."

"Happiness."

"Radiance."

"Closer to God."

"Comfort."

"Self-esteem."

"Energy."

"Warmth."

"Responsibility."

How many of these would appear on your list? Can you see what a burden love has to carry?

"Unhappy? Take a love pill! Insecure? Take another one! Anxious, incomplete, unfulfilled, lonely? Love is the answer to all your problems! Just step right up and get yourself a dose of good old love! Each and every batch personally mixed by Dr. Cupid! The answer to every woman's dream . . . the answer to every man's prayer . . . just one to a customer! Get yours now!"

And like most medicines, love is used to treat the symptoms rather than the disease. Why bother finding out why we repress emotions, why we are dishonest, why we don't like ourselves? Just take a generous helping of LOVE, and you can keep on doing all the same wrong things, only you'll feel good doing them.

That would be fine, if it worked. But love has an unusual quality: When used properly it is practically indestructible; when misused it quickly falls apart.

Needs or Goals?

When we examine our priorities, and what we feel about them now, we often find that we are seeking goals rather than fulfilling needs. Are you goal-oriented?

Michael and Sylvia and Stan

Michael was an alcoholic and wife-beater. Sylvia finally couldn't stand it any more, and when he refused to go along she joined an encounter group on her own. She was immediately attracted to Stan, a single man in the group. She had pretty well decided to leave Michael, but the knowledge that someone else found her attractive made it a lot easier. She told Michael she wanted a divorce. She also told him she had gone to bed with Stan. Michael called Stan, after coaxing the number out of Sylvia, and said, "Do you realize you're breaking up a family? You are destroying a happy home! How can you live with yourself after doing that?"

Not a word about loving Sylvia, or about being hurt. Stan was stealing something that belonged to Michael, his home. His top priority was being taken from him. Sylvia began to realize that she had just been a thing to Michael all along. He had been the first to suggest marriage, and the first to suggest having a child. It was his second marriage, and his second child, and they had all been things. Goals. Achievements. Points on society's scoreboard.

Sex as a Goal

One of the areas in which people are most goal-oriented is in the sexual part of a relationship. Some of our sexual role-conditioning is responsible. Men are taught that sexual conquest is a monument to their masculinity. Women are taught that sex can be a medium of exchange, and used to gain popularity or security.

Thus, sex is isolated from love. It is a thing unto itself. The physical can be separated from the emotional, so the myth goes, and sex can be enjoyed for pure pleasure, with no emotional commitment on either side. Well, there's no arguing that sex can be a lot of fun, so why not? There's a very good reason why not, however. When sex becomes just a thing, used to manipulate, to score points, to merely gain pleasure, it becomes very difficult to once again tie it to an emotional situation. If you have intercourse with a dozen partners for whom you had no emotional feeling at all, it's going to be that much harder to feel when you want to. Some of your emotional responses are going to be dulled and repressed.

In truth, it is practically impossible to have sexual relations with someone without having some kind of feeling. So, if you think you are doing it just for the fun of it, you are probably kidding yourself, or possibly fulfilling some hidden and unhealthy need. The feeling may be anger, sadness, or hate, but there has to be a feeling. You can shut it off only by shutting yourself off, and like a big heater after a long summer, it may take a bit of doing to get turned on again.

Copulation can be very mechanical, unpleasant, and disappointing. It can also be magnificent, fulfilling, invigorating, and intoxicating. The difference is the feeling. You can have nonpermanent, nonexclusive sexual relationships but still share feelings. It takes a high degree of trust to really let yourself go and have a truly transcending sexual experience. This can come only with a sense of commitment. A commitment to be real and honest. A commitment to share what is there to share. At best the sexual act is an expression of real feeling, not a trophy to be won or a medium of exchange.

It can be useful to examine your attitudes about sex. Is it a goal or an expression of feeling in your relationship?

The Life Script

Having sex as a focal point in your relationship can be a form of goal orientation, but so can having marriage as a goal in the early stages of a relationship. The danger in having these goals is that we write a life script around them. Many people write their entire script, just leaving out the name of their co-star. Then, as soon as someone who isn't too repulsive comes along, he or she is signed for the role. The co-star usually isn't even aware of the script, and so it's no wonder these preplanned scripts seldom work out. It isn't just a case of MY NEEDS becoming more important than YOUR NEEDS or OUR NEEDS, but usually this early script planning involves MY IMAGINED NEEDS, and they quite often turn out to be very unrealistic needs.

Thoughts of sexual relations and/or marriage should come naturally because of the warm feelings flowing between two people. The relationship can then develop freely, without being molded and manipulated toward either the bedroom or the altar.

Your Love Script

Is your relationship script already written? Does your partner know about it? Can you write a synopsis of the script? Here's what one woman of twenty-nine wrote:

"We'll meet and have lots of fun right away. He'll just look at me and want to rip my clothes off, and I'll feel the same, but I won't let him know it. He won't be able to think or function, and I'll feel the same. We'll make love and it will be beautiful and right. He'll ask me to marry him, and after stalling him a bit, I'll accept. We'll honeymoon on an island and start making babies right away. He'll be in some profession that will have a lot of opportunities. I'll encourage him and support him on his way to the top. He'll really appreciate this and call me 'boss' when we're among friends. We'll have lots of friends, and go everywhere together, and everyone will say, 'That's what I call a perfect match!'"

Do you have a script this specific, or did you ever have one? If so, try to write it down, either in the first person, as above, or in a third-person account, as if you were merely an outside observer.

If you have a script, examine it for any unrealistic expectations, fantasies, manipulative factors, and goal orientation. Few prewritten scripts can be given a clean bill of health in these areas. Only one that is written as it is lived can really deal with honest feelings.

Often we pick priorities that have little to do with the life-style that would best suit us. A rigid list of priorties, and a rigid life and love script, can force us into narrow, constricted lives. If your script doesn't change as your life does, the resulting confusion can create a highly effective barrier to any free expression of feelings.

Relationship Fantasies

A fantasy can be a highly useful or a highly destructive force. If used to bury and avoid real feelings, it can prevent a relationship from going anywhere. But fantasies can also provide much insight if used creatively. They give us new views of ourselves and allow us to enter into new roles, trying them on for size. They can also bring reality into clearer focus. Positive fantasy can thus conquer negative fantasy material. If you are with your love-partner right now, you may be looking forward to the weekend, or remembering last night, rather than focusing on the here and now. Imagining, for instance, that both of you will be dead in one hour can bring you back to the present and make you acutely aware of what is really happening.

Fantasy Changes

Imagine what it would be like to be able to spend only one day a year with your love-partner. What would you want to do on that day? Share your feelings, and discuss how this might change your relationship.

The two of you are on a desert island. Discuss your relative roles. Who will do the various things that have to be done?

You inherit a million dollars on the condition that you live alone until the day you die. How would this affect your relationship? Would the advantages of wealth offset the negative factors involved?

You both suddenly have your sex changed. How would this new man and new woman relate to each other? What would you like and what wouldn't you like about your new role?

You have just been given immortality, and you will both live forever. Do you really want to spend the rest of forever together? Discuss how this might change your perspectives.

You each will be part of a new experiment, and will be required to cohabit with a member of the opposite sex on a desert island. Your desert partner will be a complete stranger, but attractive. You will be required to stay together for one year. At the end of that time would you want to return to this relationship? Would it change your feelings for each other? Would you want some kind of a commitment from each other, or would you rather wait and see how you feel at the end of this experiment?

Acting Out New Roles

One way to change perspective is to role-play. Become someone totally different, but with the same set of emotions. React from a new perspective. It can bring you a tremendous amount of new information, not the least of which will be how important your current role is to you and how many of your feelings are really no more than props that go along with your role.

In therapy this can sometimes be a rather intensive experience. Here it's suggested that you stay in each role only briefly, and only as long as it feels comfortable.

In this exercise each partner will get to try each role. For example, you might become Master and Slave. Each partner, in turn, say a sentence that seems to fit this role. It becomes a dialogue, and the more feeling you put into it, the better. You can choose a situation, or just wing it, but see if it can have some relevance to something that happens in your relationship. For instance:

MASTER: "Pop a grape into my mouth!"

SLAVE: "Yes, master, please don't beat me!"

Now discuss your feelings. Did you enjoy your role? Is there any other way you could have played it? Does it in any way resemble the way you act in your relationship? Now reverse roles:

SLAVE: "May I have some extra bread for my children?"

MASTER: "How dare you even ask! For that you'll get twenty lashes!"

Discuss and share again.

You can try longer exchanges. See if you can really get into it at an emotional level. Be aware of what you are feeling as you play the role. Be aware of which role you prefer.

Other roles you might try:

TEACHER and STUDENT
PROSTITUTE and CUSTOMER
PARENT and CHILD
PATIENT and THERAPIST
BIGOT and BLACK MILITANT
COWBOY and HORSE
FIREPLUG and DOG
JOHNNY CARSON and CELEBRITY GUEST

Don't hesitate to try creating your own.

Erasing the Blackboard

The most realistic priority is the one we feel at the moment. Preconceived notions of what we need often get in the way. If you can spend each moment with your partner as a totally "now" moment, erasing the emotional blackboard so to speak, then the priorities will come naturally, and be fulfilled naturally.

Robots

Dr. Dan Malamud, a psychologist responsible for many innovations in group techniques, leads large groups in an exercise called The Robot. Over about a forty-minute period the participants become simulated robots, with no control over their movements, and then slowly begin to become human again, learning to appreciate the freedom of choice we all have. Let's try a variation of Dr. Malamud's exercise:

You are both robots. No feelings. No creative ability. You must follow your strict programming. You each stand at opposite ends of the room. Taking one mechanical step at a time, walk toward each other. When you are several feet away, place a mechanical smile on your face. Keep walking, and when you make contact coldly embrace with precise robotlike movements. Disengage, walk ten steps backward. Close your eyes. Imagine that you are now becoming human again. Be aware of your breathing, and that your body is looser. Open your eyes. Now walk toward each other and embrace as humans. Hold each other for as long as it feels good. Share and discuss your feelings. Did you notice a difference between being a robot and being human? If not, you have serious problems, and should walk or run to your nearest therapist.

Another variation might be to walk toward each other as robots, and each time you make initial contact you have to walk backward five steps. Do this several times and see how frustrating it might be.

Another way to explore this is to do it with your eyes closed. Walk forward in a straight line. Each time you bump into something or someone, you have to slowly walk backward until you hit something else, then you go forward again. Back and forth. Then experience being human with your eyes still closed, walking around the room in any direction you like.

To a Feeling Level

If you haven't been dealing fully with your feelings, and you start to do so, your priorities may drastically change. You might examine how intellectual those priorities are. Are you filling intellectual needs, physical needs, emotional needs?

Do you know the difference? Can you sit opposite your partner, look into each other's eyes and say the following sentences, filling in the blanks?

"I am intellectually aware of you as ———."

"I am physically aware of you as ———."

"I am emotionally aware of you as ———."

Of course, sometimes we are aware of all three. You may be intellectually aware of your partner as attractive, physically aware of your partner as sexually desirable, and emotionally aware of the good feeling you have when looking at your partner.

It might be easier to embrace and try the three sentences again, especially for the physical awareness part.

Trade Space

Here is a new way to become physically aware of yourself and your love-partner. Sit across the room from one another. Get into a comfortable position. Close your eyes. Be aware of your breathing. Be aware of what kind of contact you are making with the chair or floor. Be aware of how tense or relaxed your body is. Change position if it doesn't feel right. Start to be aware of the space around you. Feel the space around you with your arms and hands. Move them all around. Up. Down. Front. Back. Left. Right. Let your arms come back to a relaxed position. Can you now be more aware of this space around you? Build an imaginary plastic bubble to enclose this space and you. As you breath out, imagine you are permeating the space with your life-force, your energy. You are flowing into and taking charge of this space of yours. Breath in to build your energy, breath out to fill your space with you. Keep doing this for a few minutes. Then stop and be aware of how your space feels. Slowly open your eyes. Look at your love-partner and see if this affects your space. Slowly walk toward each other and take each other's space. You are now in your love-partner's space. Try to assume, as nearly as possible, the position your love-partner was in. Close your eyes and be aware of this space so recently permeated by your love-partner. Can you sense his or her presence? Open your eyes and look at each other. Move closer together and share the experience. How did you feel about trading spaces? Were you more or less comfortable in your new space? What else did you notice?

Checking Your Experience

Have you learned anything from these exercises? You may have learned a number of things. You may have learned some new things about your love-partner. You may have learned some new things about the way you relate. You may have brought a new sense of joy and adventure into your life. You may even have found out that you don't want to share and grow and explore.

You may have changed your perspective.

Check it out.

Examine once again the list you made at the beginning of the chapter.

1. MY NEEDS.
2. YOUR NEEDS.
3. OUR NEEDS.

Have you learned anything that might cause you to want to change anything on either of your lists? As you go through this book it might be useful to check this list periodically, and modify it when you feel it necessary to do so.

ME

*You asked me
so I told you.
I think
Jane Fonda's happier than me.*
                    Judy Altura

Know thyself. Most psychologists agree that the most essential factor in determining one's ability to enter into a fulfilling love relationship is the presence of a healthy self-concept. Self-esteem and self-awareness are the two pillars on which the most satisfying relationships are built.

There is a single question that, if honestly answered, can provide an important indication of your love ability:

Do you really believe you are a worthwhile person, capable and deserving of a loving relationship with another person?

Let's face it, can you really expect someone else to love you, or even like you, if you do not love and like yourself? If you did have this expectation, couldn't you be saying, in effect, "I don't really think very much of myself, but I'm assuming that you are not going to be as perceptive or demanding of me as I am of myself. In other words, I expect you to accept this second-rate package I am offering you and love and cherish it, even though I expect a much better package from you."

Many men and women enter into love relationships to escape from an unsatisfactory self-relationship. It often seems easier to find someone else to focus on rather than engage in the sometimes painful process of self-examination and focusing within.

Obviously, the healthiest relationships are those involving two whole people who were happy and fulfilled without the relationship, and can bring these factors into the relationship in a full sharing process.

You are giving a love-partner an almost impossible burden to bear when you say, "I've been unhappy up until now, but I expect you to make me happy."

But isn't this what so many of us do so terribly often? How many people do you know who got married because they were unhappy in their single state? How many who got married to escape their parents?

What often develops is a frustrating vicious circle. The married couple then go on and have children because they are not happy in the relationship. Then they blame the children for preventing further escape, this time from the marriage itself. When will we learn that there is no escape from ourselves? Love is not a cure for an unhealthy self-image. The whole thing can become a dreary treadmill, which is why so many people who get divorced tend to marry the same type person all over again. We try to cure the symptom rather than the disease.

Liking Yourself

A good self-concept is vitally important for success in almost any endeavor, but never more so than in the development of happy interpersonal relations.

Modern psychology has shown that all emotional problems can usually be defined by one common denominator, and most people, no matter what their symptoms of emotional disturbance, are usually saying, "I don't like myself."

And there is so much to like! Do you realize that you are the most complex and sophisticated mechanism ever designed? That most human beings only use 5 to 10 per cent of their total brain power, and how much you use of what you have is really very much up to you? That the only restrictions we have on how far we can go, on how much we can make of ourselves, are those we place on ourselves?

Does the preceding paragraph seem overoptimistic to you? Corny claptrap, perhaps? If it did turn you off, examine why for a moment. Is there a possibility that you really don't want to believe you have a lot of untapped potential? Maybe the knowledge that you have capabilities as yet unused implies to you that you have fallen down on the job. That you haven't "made the most of yourself." This is often the kind of negative programming trip we put ourselves into. It may not be true for you in this instance, but has it ever been? Have you ever listened to someone or read something that told you you were better than you thought you were, and immediately dismissed it without even investigating the possibility that it might be true?

Our Own Programming

Science has proven beyond any doubt that our brains are more capable than any multimillion-dollar computer ever built. In some ways they operate much like computers, except for one important difference. Whereas both our brains and computers depend on programming, only man selects his own programming. Think a moment about the implications of this difference. WE SELECT OUR OWN PROGRAMMING!

During our early years we really don't have much choice over the programming that pours into our heads. But even this, if it proves to be counter-productive programming, can be changed. We can reprogram ourselves!

Let's examine an example of counter-productive programming. Look at the youth of today. Those United States citizens under twenty-five. What seems to be one of their major problems? The drug explosion usually heads the list. What do all these youngsters have in common? They were the first to grow up in the television generation. They were the first children who were practically raised in front of the TV set. There they were exposed to some of the most insidious programming ever devised. Day after day they were programmed by endless commercials. If you grew up in that generation, try to think back (though it's still happening today) to how many times you saw someone who was unhappy, or in pain, quickly end the pain and unhappiness by taking a pill. Is it any wonder that so many started reaching for pills, and worse, as soon as they felt the urge to explore themselves, as soon as they felt the need to escape, as soon as they felt unloved or unwanted? Actually, the amazing thing is how many have resisted that early programming.

We select our own programming starting at an early age, perhaps six or seven. Maybe, however, it would be better to say we *can* select our own programming if we choose to do so. Because we often make our selections in a completely passive manner, allowing things to come in without really thinking about it. We allow bad programming in. But we cannot blame the bad programming itself, we must take full responsibility for "allowing" it to enter our brains.

Scientists have discovered that the brain cannot really discern between actual events and vividly imagined events. There's a famous experiment that showed a basketball team practicing fifteen minutes a day and another team that *imagined* practicing fifteen minutes a day. Both increased their skills at about the same rate.

This finding validates a lot of ancient beliefs, and some more recent doctrines, such as positive thinking and Dr. Maxwell Maltz's PsychoCybernetics.

What it all means for you is simple. If you choose to believe almost anything about yourself, it will come true for you. If you say to yourself each and every day, "I am a delightful person. I am warm and affectionate and would make a wonderful friend and exciting lover. I deserve to be loved and appreciated. I am a giving person, and anyone who really gets to know me will like me," chances are you will enhance your self-image. We're not talking about acting conceited and telling the world how great you are. But tell yourself! Start feeling good about yourself.

All the negative concepts we have built up about ourselves can be removed. It may be a simple task for you, or a most difficult one. You may even need professional help. Psychiatrists, psychologists, social workers, and counselors are really teachers, and they are teaching us how to reprogram ourselves. We are not suggesting that you have an unhealthy self-concept, or that you need professional help. But if you have had a problem in love relationships, this might be the first place to look. We can all improve our self-concepts. There are a number of techniques being used today to examine how and what we think and feel about ourselves, and how to improve these factors.

Who Are You?

This is the basic question. Let's try to examine some of the answers.

The Introduction

Imagine you are being invited to address a large group of important people. The program chairman asks you to write your own introduction. Don't be shy or modest, write what you honestly feel about yourself. Write as long an introduction as you want. Write what you would like the world to know about you.

Now examine your introduction as objectively as possible. Is this someone worth knowing? Decide for yourself if there is anything you would really like to change or work on.

You might even write another introduction. In this one say the things you would like to be able to say about yourself, even if they aren't now true. Say the things you hope will be true, if you grow in the directions you would like to grow over the next few years.

Examine this introduction and compare it to the first. Is there a lot of difference?

The Daily Journal

This can be a beautiful way to monitor your own feelings about yourself. You can keep an extensive diary if you wish, but this might take more time than you are willing to consistently spend. Are you now willing to commit just a few moments a day to this project? It can be this simple: Each night, just before going to bed, write down one sentence that you think describes the way you felt during the day. The only stipulation is that it has to be an honest feeling. You might say things like:

"Today I really liked the way I communicated with a stranger."
"I was sad that I wasn't able to help my love-partner understand himself more."
"A happy, happy day of exploring nature!"
"A dull time, and I guess I really don't like them very much."
"I was frustrated that I can't let myself go like she can.
"I really got in touch with some things in myself after seeing the movie."

If you want to go into more detail, feel free to do so. But minimal commitment may make it easier to keep up the practice. Too often we jump into new projects with a lot of initial energy that is overambitious and destined to quickly disappear.

The Blind Date

Your best friend is going to fix you up with an attractive blind date. You're asked to provide your own description so your blind date will know what to expect. In just one sentence describe yourself as you would like a blind date to know you.

Examine your description. Is it honest? Did you err on either the optimistic or pessimistic side? How do you think a member of the opposite sex would react to the sentence?

What kind of sentence would you like to hear about a blind date you were about to meet?

Assets and Liabilities

List your assets and liabilities. The good things about you, and the things that aren't so good or need correcting. Try to write what you believe, not what you think other people expect.

After listing both sets of qualities, put them in order, numbering them from one on down the list, as you think they may affect you. Which are the good qualities that most people notice, or that really make you the person you are? Which are the bad qualities that get in the way of your becoming what you would like to become?

Starting at the top of your list of assets, cross one out at a time, and then imagine what kind of a person you would be without that quality. Then start crossing out your liabilities and imagining what you would be like without those. Try to decide which assets you'd really miss. Which liabilities you'd really like to get rid of.

Self-awareness

How aware are you? Not only of what's happening around you, but of what is happening inside. Finish this sentence for yourself: "Now I am aware of ——?"

What did you fill the blank with? Was it something inside yourself, such as, "Now I am aware of my breathing," or was it something outside yourself, such as, "Now I am aware of a smell from the kitchen."

There are really three areas of awareness. Inside Awareness; Outside Awareness; and Fantasy Awareness. This last would include a sentence like, "Now I am aware of the argument I had this afternoon," or, "Now I am aware of looking forward to tomorrow's party." It's focusing on something not happening right here and now, and so it isn't real awareness in the true sense of the word.

In and Out

Let's try an awareness exercise. First, focus on something you are aware of inside yourself. Then focus on something outside your body, something you feel or hear or smell in the room around you. Do the exercise with your eyes closed. Now try focusing back inside yourself, and switch to the outside awareness. Switch back and forth between these two focal points. Go IN then OUT at whatever pace you'd like to try. When you stop, try to be aware of what that feels like, too.

Now, with your eyes still closed, try to see how many things you can be aware of inside yourself, and then how many you can be aware of outside yourself. Don't forget to use all your senses.

How aware are you of your body? You might try focusing on various parts of your body during the day. All of a sudden, at odd moments during your everyday activities, take a few seconds and focus on your foot or your neck. See how aware you can become of the many parts of your body you don't normally feel or think about.

Self-touching

Lie down in the nude. Start gently touching your body. As you do, be aware of what your hands feel like to your body, and what your body feels like to your hands. Enjoy the experience! Feel your heart. Can you follow the beat by placing your hand over your heart? Can you take your hand away and still be aware of your heart?

Put your hands on your cheeks and get in touch with the temperature of your hands. Can you think about warmth and actually make your hands warmer? Try it.

Take your two index fingers and place them at the bottom of your nose at the sides. Breathe in and out. Can you feel the nostrils moving in and out?

Can you tell which parts of your body are relaxed and which parts tense?

Which parts do you feel most comfortable touching?

Do you have trouble touching any particular part?

Place your two hands softly over your genitals. Just rest them there, feeling the warmth from your hands. Can you feel good about your masculinity or femininity?

Can you come up with some new ways to touch yourself and new things to become aware of in and on your body?

Now, once again finish the sentence, "Now I am aware of ——."

Notice any difference?

Be aware of any discomfort you might have had doing these exercises. We have a lot to learn about awareness, each and every one of us. Our modern stress-filled society has done much to desensitize and dehumanize us. If you would like to see what total body awareness looks like, watch small children playing or watch an animal. Can you see where it may be useful and desirable to get back some of this awareness?

Breathing Energy

This is an experience that is part fantasy, part reality. Don't try to analyze it, just experience it. Lie down with your arms straight at your sides. Be aware of your breathing, but don't force it. Imagine a source of energy right in the middle of your body. You can picture it as the sun, or a roaring furnace, or anything else that means energy for you. See how vividly you can feel and be aware of this energy source. Now, as you inhale, imagine that you are pulling this energy up your body, up into your head. And as you exhale, it is returning to the center. Again, see how vividly you can feel this, how real it can become. You inhale and the energy flows up, exhale and it returns to the center. Keep doing this for a few minutes. When you stop, try to put into words for yourself what the experience was like. Did you feel anything happening? Did it make you more aware of your breathing? Was it a relaxing experience?

Music Induction

This can be a very powerful experience. The exciting thing about it is how simple it is to do, and how little you need to do it. A phonograph or tape player is all. And you.

What we're going to do is try to place the music in your body. This may seem like a fantasy, but it isn't entirely one. Music, like any sound, is merely vibrations. We normally pick these up only with our ears. But you can sensitize other parts of your body. At first it may be more imagination than reality. But if you practice this a few times, it can produce some amazing sensations.

Play whatever kind of music you'd like to hear. Start by being aware of your breathing, and what your body feels like. As the music starts, try to imagine it flowing into your body through the soles of your feet. At a pace of about twenty seconds for each change, slowly move it up your body in the following progression:

Feel the music in your lower legs.

In your upper legs and thighs.

In your genitals.

In your stomach.

In your chest.

In your shoulders.

In your upper arms.

In your lower arms.

Just in your hands and fingers.

Flowing back up your arms and into your neck.

In your mouth.

In your nose.

In your eyes.

In the center of your forehead.

In your ears.

Then, as slow or fast as you like, allow the music to flow back down your body and out through the bottoms of your feet.

Be quiet for as long as you like after the music flows out.

Then examine for yourself what the experience was like.

Did it feel good? Were you actually able to feel the music in various parts of your body? Were some parts harder than others?

This can be an energizing or relaxing experience, depending on the kind of music you play. It is also a good way to practice awareness almost anywhere, in any position, as you listen to any music. Even while riding an elevator listening to rather boring piped-in music, you might try to feel it in your feet and discover a new way of adding some new sensations to your life!

Aloneness

One of the signs of a weak self-concept is a fear of being alone. Are you afraid of being alone? Are you afraid you won't enjoy your own company? Are you afraid people will think less of you if you aren't always in the company of an attractive member of the opposite sex? Would you think less of yourself if you went out one evening without having a date? If you are involved in a relationship right now, would your love-partner have strong objections if you just said you wanted to spend an evening alone?

Building up your self-image can prove invaluable in giving you insight into why and how you communicate the way you do.

Plan an evening alone. Completely alone. Make it a project. Do something you really enjoy doing. Even if you've never done it alone before. Throughout the experience notice how uncomfortable you might feel not having a companion. And is it because you really need a companion in everything you do, or because you feel other people expect you to have one?

Can you really enjoy you? Being alone can give you an answer to this question. Aloneness is a primary need we all have from time to time, even in a strong, fulfilling love relationship. Try to understand your need for privacy and aloneness, and take pleasure from it. It is a healthy part of you. It can be a beautiful learning and reflective experience.

Do you see the difference between being alone and being lonely? A lot of it has to do with negative programming. If we are alone, and not by choice, we expect to be lonely and often are. If, instead, you can look at each period of time that you happen to find yourself alone as an opportunity for self-exploration, meditation, and increasing self-awareness, you'll be able to make constructive use of what often has been a lot of wasted energy.

Self-programming

It's now an established fact, backed by empirical evidence from leading researchers, that you can program yourself. What can you now do with that fact? Well, you can start trying it. For the next few days, for instance, how about waking up and saying to yourself "I'm really a fantastic person!" Don't elaborate, just say the one sentence, though you can put it in your own words.

It may seem silly to try this, but try it anyway. Don't judge it while you're doing it. Give it a few days, try to really feel it, and then examine what, if anything, has happened.

You just may have a surprise waiting for you at the end of this self-experiment!

Then again, it may not work at all. Your negative conditioning may get in the way. Or you may be unable to circumvent your analytical inclinations and intellectualize yourself right out of any positive results.

For the best possibility of this working, you have to not only say the words, but try to feel them as well. Feel good about yourself, be aware of your whole body. You might try taking a deep breath and then saying the sentence as you exhale, stretching afterward.

Create a Special Place

We all have special places. For some, it's the beach. For others, a spot in the mountains, or sailing the ocean. It may be a place we have been, or a place we have dreamed about. Can you imagine such a place for yourself, right now? Lie down and let your mind take you to this special place. Notice not only what it looks like, but what it sounds and smells like, and what you feel like being there.

This is an excellent way to get into a deep state of relaxation at almost any given moment. The more you focus on this special place, the more easily you will be able to go there.

Create a Special Person

Another useful fantasy technique is the creation of an adviser or counselor or wise friend in your imagination. This could be someone you have a lot of respect for, or you can manufacture someone to your own specifications. Try it. Again, with your eyes closed, conjure up a man or woman who will be able to advise you on just about any subject, from psychology to carpentry. Write a description of this wise friend, leaving out nothing. What does this person look like? Sound like? What kind of clothes is your adviser wearing?

You can create this special person and constantly go into conferences whenever you feel the need. Children often have imaginary friends, and this performs a valuable function. It allows you to have a conversation with another aspect of your consciousness. Yes, you are talking to yourself, but you are also experiencing yourself at a new dimension that may have remained untapped.

If you can really get into this, you'll find this special person in your own mind can often find solutions you couldn't seem to find for yourself. Again, this may sound silly to you, but don't dismiss it without at least giving it a chance to work for you.

Change in Perspective

We are too often locked into seeing ourselves from only our own viewpoint. It can be amazingly beneficial to try to see ourselves as others see us. Can you escape from yourself and take a more objective look at you? Try it. Close your eyes once again, and imagine yourself up on top of a fluffy white cloud. It is very comfortable and you have a floating sensation. Looking down, you can see yourself as others see you. What kind of person do you see? Can you re-create something you have done recently, and look at your actions as a stranger might?

It may be difficult to completely detach yourself, but even a partial success can produce useful information. Experiment from time to time with looking at various aspects of yourself from this cloud.

Self-conversation

Look into a mirror and have a conversation with yourself. Talk about anything you might find interesting. No one is looking at you except you, so feel free to let your hair down.

Now tell your mirror image what you see. What kind of a person is this? Is this a likable human being? Someone worth knowing? Is there anything you would like to say to this person you may never have said before?

Self-definition

Who are you? Again, we come back to the basic question. One way to find out your own feelings on this is to ask yourself the question, filling in the first blank with your first name: "―― is ――."

See if you can repeat this question over and over again, coming up with a completely different answer each time. How many different things are you?

A Sense of Self

All of the experiences in this chapter are aimed at giving you more of a sense of self. Letting you know who you are, making you more aware of what you feel. Self-sufficiency can make you a better, more desirable love-partner. It also can prevent your entering into love relationships for the wrong reason.

Too many people become too dependent on another person because they don't feel they can depend on themselves. Say to yourself:

I am a valuable human being. As valuable as I want to be. I can be more valuable than I am now, especially to myself. Only I can believe this and make it so.

If I love me, and understand me, and am really honest with myself, then full sharing relationships will come naturally.

I am the most important factor in any relationship I am involved in. Acknowledging this fact may be an important first step on my journey to a happy love relationship.

YOU

You . . .
are all the changing colors to me,
all the definites and maybes,
the reasons why.

Judy Altura

After increasing self-awareness, the next logical step is to increase our awareness of our love-partner, the "you" in "you and me." The best way to find out more about your love-partner is to ask. In this chapter you'll find one hundred questions to ask your love-partner. Before you get to those, however, it might be highly productive for you to examine how you go about selecting your partners in love relationships. Your selection process could be preventing you from fulfilling your needs.

It sometimes seems as if we spend a lifetime narrowing our choices, alternatives, and possibilities. We are conditioned and programmed from infancy, and foolishly go on assuming we have freely chosen what and whom we like. Think back to your childhood. To the first time you had a glimmering of an idea of what an attractive member of the opposite sex was supposed to look and be like. Can you remember? Where did that first impression come from? Long before you were ready to join the battle of the sexes, you had a pretty good idea of what you thought you wanted. Your present criteria may well stem from that early initial impression.

To allow ourselves the best opportunity for a fulfilling

love relationship, we must eliminate those restrictions and limitations that get in the way of our meeting our needs.

We all maintain images of what we would like in a member of the opposite sex. The more specific these images, the less chance we have of enjoying a successful relationship.

Jeff

Jeff is an attractive young man of thirty, earning a good salary as an electrical engineer, with a substantial amount of money invested in stocks. He would appear to be a highly eligible young man on the surface. Two factors make him unhappy and unique. Jeff lives with his parents, and hasn't had any sexual relations since a fleeting episode as a teenager. He lives with his parents primarily to save money, and has a grand plan to retire at thirty-five and become a sort of playboy and stock market wizard. His specific demands and many rejection factors have very successfully prevented him from having even the most casual of involvements with women.

Jeff would like to find a Jewish girl who doesn't smoke or drink, lives in her own apartment, is very attractive, and isn't promiscuous but is willing to go to bed with him early in their relationship.

After many years of trying to find the girl of his dreams, Jeff is just about ready to give up. He doesn't expect really to find anyone. This becomes a self-fulfilling prophecy, even further limiting his chances.

Of course, rejection factors are harmful only when they prevent us from finding what we need and want.

Even if you are now in a deep love relationship, it might be useful to examine your rejection factors. Can you describe the type of man or woman you would choose if you had the ability to set all the standards and have them met? Try it.

You can now further examine whether your standards have changed. Have you learned from experience? What particular characteristics would you have rejected a few years ago that you would be willing to accept now? Perhaps you learned that people who wear glasses can be as fun-loving and exciting as those who don't. Perhaps you learned that *brunettes* really have more fun.

Henry and Betty

Henry hadn't really been involved with a woman before meeting Betty. She seemed rather limited in scope, but he fell in love with her all the same, and she with him. She had gone to business school for a year after high school, and had no desire to further her education. She had a lot of common sense, and could hold her own conversationally. But Henry was going for his master's degree and hoped to eventually earn a doctorate, and he said to himself "She's fun and cute and I care for her a lot, but she just won't be able to keep up with me, and I'll end up being embarrassed and she'll feel inadequate, and it just won't work."

Henry ended it. He had projected the relationship into the future and didn't like what he fantasized. He never shared with Betty his fears, or his reasons for ending the relationship.

Henry moved to another town shortly thereafter, and lost track of Betty. Some eight years later he ran into a mutual friend, and was flabbergasted to learn what had happened. Betty met a young lawyer about six months after the breakup with Henry. They fell in love, and he turned her on to his love of politics. She went back to school and eventually got a master's degree in political science. Meanwhile, she married her young lawyer and he got active in local politics and was elected a state senator. At the time Henry ran into the old friend, Betty's husband had won his party's nomination for a seat in Congress. Betty's charm and knowledge of the intricacies of statewide politics were given much of the credit for her husband's accomplishments.

Henry often thinks about Betty. He is happy she has done so well, and realizes she has found probably just the right love-partner. If they had stayed together even for a while longer, she might never had had the same opportunity. But Henry does have regrets. He regrets not waiting to find out what the real potential of their relationship would have been. He regrets putting limitations on Betty, but even more on himself. He now has his doctorate, and has had several good relationships with women. But nothing really fulfilling. Henry has missed something he didn't have to miss.

Have you ever limited yourself in this way? Have you ever automatically eliminated the possibility of getting to know someone better, only to find out later you would have been very compatible?

When you were in high school, did you limit yourself? If you were one of the girls who wanted to date only football players, or one of the boys who wanted to date only cheerleaders, think how mathematically limiting your standards were.

Most of our early standards are the result of programming. If, as a teen-ager, you went for blatantly physical specimens, chances are you allowed movies to influence you. If you vowed never to go out with anyone who didn't meet very high physical standards, you may have missed out on getting to know a very sensual flat-chested woman, or a very masculine and loving man with a skinny frame and receding hairline. Do you automatically reject these as possibilities? Can you examine why?

Many happy couples report in encounter groups that their love-partner turned them completely off at their first meeting. Physically. Even their personality traits. But, for one reason or another, they continued to see each other and started to see beyond the superficial. Loving someone makes them very attractive to you. You don't have to go out and look for someone unattractive, but you may find it very helpful to examine your list of specifications, and see which ones are really realistic.

Try to imagine what kind of a man or woman would fit all of your qualifications. What would this person be like. Have you ever known anyone like this? Would such a person be likely to find you attractive?

The main question is a simple one: Do you, in any way, feel that you are limiting your relationship possibilities?

If you can honestly answer with a resounding NO, then you probably have avoided or eliminated many negative obstacles.

Tell Me This

This is not one of those quizzes so often found in magazines and designed to give you the definitive word on your ability as a lover. It isn't really a quiz at all, though it does consist of a series of questions. There are no answers at the back of the book. And no so-called expert is providing you with an instant analysis of your answers to help you decide whether you need immediate psychotherapy.

Many of the problems in a relationship are due to the simple lack of information. When you don't know something about someone, you tend to fill in the vacuum with assumptions, fantasies, and unrealistic expectations. During the beginning of a relationship, we often are so wrapped up in the initial excitement that we fail to ask some very basic questions. These can be very simple "who" and "why" and "what" questions, or they can cover much broader areas of emotional response.

The one hundred questions in this chapter are designed to provide you with useful information about yourself, the other person in the relationship, and the relationship itself.

There are no hard and fast rules, only recommended guidelines. It is suggested that you share this experience with a member of the opposite sex, preferably your partner in a relationship. You may also find the pace has something to do with how effective the experience will be. Instead of zipping

rapidly through all of the questions, you might try taking ten
at a time.

An effective format:

1. You ask the question, your partner answers.
2. Your partner asks the question, and you answer.
3. You both discuss the experience, and share feelings.

You can share feelings in many ways. You can tell each
other how you felt answering the question, what your feelings were on hearing your partner's answer, whether you felt
it was a worthwhile experience, and whether you now know
something you didn't know before. You can do the sharing
in any way you like and both agree to.

There are no right or wrong answers. You may very well
find some questions difficult or impossible to answer at this
point in your relationship. If so, just avoid them. Avoid also
the temptation to push for an answer if your partner is having trouble coming up with one. You can always try the difficult ones at a later date, when you are further along in the
relationship. One thing the questions may accomplish is to
let you know exactly what information you don't have about
each other, and what may be worth exploring now or in the
future.

These questions could be used as manipulative tools, even
unintentionally. Be aware of this, and share your feelings if
you feel manipulation is becoming a factor. This is not a competitive contest and there are no winners or losers. Try to
avoid passing judgment on your partner as you learn new
things about him or her. Try to avoid telling your partner
what you think his or her answer "should" have been.

The questions concern facts and feelings. Facts you know
about yourself. Facts you know about your love-partner.
Feelings you have about yourself. Feelings you have about
your love-partner. Feelings your love-partner has about you.
Feelings you both have about your relationship.

The questions progressively get more into the "feeling"

levels of the relationship. Thus, it would probably be best to start at the beginning of the list.

You might try different physical formats. For some questions, you can sit facing each other, making eye-contact. For others, you might physically make contact, such as holding hands. You might even try lying down together. Try to find something that you both find comfortable and relaxing. Now the questions:

1. What kind of a child were you?
2. Describe yourself as you think an adult stranger would have after spending an hour with you at the age of seven or eight.
3. How would your parents have described you as a child?
4. What characteristics did you have as a child that have remained?
5. What characteristics have you lost or changed on reaching adulthood?
6. What was your favorite toy as a child?
7. What is your favorite toy now?
8. What were you most proud of as a child?
9. What event or circumstance of your childhood do you think had the most impact on who you are right now?
10. What was your childhood nickname and how did you feel about it?
11. Do you like your first name now? If not, what would you like instead?
12. What is your favorite color? Can you think of a favorite object that color?
13. What is your favorite possession?
14. Can you name a favorite possession that you no longer possess, and describe your feelings at no longer having it?
15. What is the funniest thing you have ever done as measured by the reaction of your audience at the time?
16. What is the funniest thing that ever happened to you?
17. What is the silliest thing you have ever done?
18. What is the stupidest thing you have ever done?
19. What is your all-time favorite movie? Why does it have special meaning?
20. What is your favorite book? What in it has personal meaning for you?

21. What product, entertainment, or activity that hasn't been available in recent years do you miss most?

22. What fictional hero do you most closely identify with?

23. If you had a choice, would you rather vacation at the seashore, camp in the mountains, or take a luxury cruise? Why?

24. How loving a person are you? If you find it easier, rate yourself on a scale of 1 to 10, with 10 as the most loving. Give an example of something that you think shows how loving you are.

25. Are you a generous person? Give an example. (You may also choose a 1 to 10 rating scale for this and the following eight questions.)

26. How creative are you? Give an example of your creativity.

27. How honest are you? Give an example.

28. How good a friend are you? Give an example.

29. How sensual are you? Give an example.

30. How attractive do you think you are?

31. How well do you react to emergencies? Give an example.

32. How much fun are you to be with? Why?

33. How ambitious are you? Give an example.

34. If you had just one year to live, and no financial restrictions, how would you like to spend the year?

35. If you had just one hour to live, starting right now, what would you want to do?

36. If you had just one minute to live, what would you like to say to me?

37. What member of your family do you most closely identify with?

38. What member of my family do you most closely identify with? Why?

39. If you had to be someone else instead of yourself, whom would you choose? Why?

40. Who is your best friend of the same sex?

41. Not counting me, who is your best friend of the opposite sex?

42. What do you look for most in a friend?

43. Name something you hate to do? Why?

44. Name something you think I hate to do.

45. If you had just one word to describe me, what would it be?
46. What about me do you like the most?
47. What about me do you like the least?
48. What do I add to your life?
49. What have you learned, if anything, from our relationship?
50. Where do you think our relationship will be in a year?
51. Where would you like our relationship to be in a year?
52. What in life is most important to you?
53. What do you think is most important for us to share?
54. What would you like to change, if anything, in the way I act toward you?
55. What would you like to change, if anything, in the way you act toward me?
56. Close your eyes and picture me. What sort of expression do I have on my face?
57. What do you feel when I look at you?
58. What do you feel when I touch you?
59. What do you feel when I tell you I care?
60. Is there anything you would like to tell me that you haven't told me yet?
61. Is there anything you would like me to tell you that you haven't asked me yet?
62. What do you feel when you're alone and think about me?
63. Do I ever make you feel sad?
64. If we were to part, what feeling have we shared that you would most like to recapture with your next love-partner?
65. What first attracted you to me?
66. What activity that we haven't shared together would you most like to try?
67. If you could go anywhere in the world with me, where would you choose?
68. Do you think we see each other too much, not enough, or just the right amount of time?
69. What physical feature of mine do you like the most?
70. What physical feature of mine do you like the least?
71. What habit of mine do you like the least?
72. When I'm not with you, what do you miss the most?
73. What do I sound like? Do you like my voice?

74. What do I smell like?
75. What do I feel like?
76. What do I taste like?
77. Do you like the way I move?
78. What do you need most?
79. What do you lack most?
80. What are you most intellectual about?
81. What are you most emotional about?
82. Is there anything you sometimes pretend to be that you're not?
83. Do you ever dream about me? Can you describe such a dream?
84. Do you ever try to control or manipulate me?
85. Do you ever feel controlled or manipulated by me?
86. When I came into your life, were you a happy person?
87. How has your emotional outlook changed since we met?
88. What do you think you mean to me?
89. How much can you remember of the last time we made love?
90. How much can you remember of the first time we made love?
91. Do you ever have sexual fantasies about me?
92. What is the closest you have ever felt toward me?
93. What do I say to you that makes you feel good?
94. What do I do for you that makes you feel good?
95. What do I do for myself that makes you feel good?
96. When do you enjoy me most, when we're alone together or in a social group?
97. How well do you think we have communicated while answering these questions?
98. Is there any way in which you'd like to change the way in which you answered them?
99. What one word would you use to describe this question and answer experience?
100. Do you feel different in any way about me or our relationship since sharing this experience together?

Hopefully you have learned something from these questions, even if it's only that you don't like asking each other questions.

What next? Well, you might try inventing your own questions. Can you each think of five more questions that might provide you with more useful information about each other?

You might also try these same questions at some later date, particularly if the two of you had difficulty answering a number of the questions.

A further sharing of the experience could involve discussing it with another couple after they have also answered the questions for each other.

Try to be aware not only of the information brought forth by the answers but the feelings generated by answering and being answered, and what it felt like to share and discuss what happened.

US . . . THE JOY OF SHARING

*We've known
the flavor of forgiveness
the struggle-needs of growing
the satisfaction of surrender.*
                    Judy Altura

There is one thing we cannot do alone. We can comfort ourselves. We can amuse ourselves. We can sexually satisfy ourselves. We can love ourselves. We can do all of these things,
and doing them can enrich our lives. There remains, however, one vital need that must be accomplished with the
help of at least one other person. The need to share ourselves.
We cannot share ourselves *with* ourselves.

There are a number of levels at which we can share ourselves with another person. We can share our thoughts. Our
feelings. Our bodies. And perhaps something that transcends
all of these, which could be called our spirituality. This may
not be the best word to describe it, but there is some special
something that flows between two people who have opened
themselves up to each other. It can't be defined as something
mental, emotional, or physical, but it certainly exists. If you
have ever been in a full, sharing love relationship, you know
the feeling.

There is nothing mystical about this feeling, and it may
well automatically happen when there's a natural blending
of a number of positive factors in a relationship. We cannot
order it to appear, or force it to happen as an act of will. We
just have to allow it to happen, helping the process by removing as many obstacles as possible.

This special flow between two people may be a manifestation of the process described as synergy. George and Nena O'Neill describe synergy as it relates to couples in their book *Open Marriage*. In a personal interview with the author, Dr. O'Neill defined the term:

> Synergy occurs when two organisms work together to achieve more than either of them could alone, but in the process still retain their identity. Thus you have an equation of $1+1=2$, or $2+$, rather than $1+1=1$, or maybe -1 or 0, as in the case of closed or traditional marriages.

In *Open Marriage* the O'Neills also describe the benefits of synergy:

> It is this special effect, this enhancement, that makes it possible in open marriage for husband and wife to exist and grow as two separate individuals, yet at the same time to transcend their duality and achieve a unity on another level, beyond themselves, a unity that develops out of the love for each other and each other's growth.

This kind of unity can never be an overnight achievement, and may well be a lifelong process. The important thing to remember is that it's the working toward it, rather than the accomplishment of any particular goal, that can bring you fulfillment.

The Need to Share

The need to share may be the strongest human need of all, surpassing even the need to love and be loved, though it's doubtful these three needs could ever be completely separated. Certainly the need to be loved by itself is not as strong as the need to share, and not as fulfilling when it is met. We can often find someone who is loved but isn't happy or content at all, usually because he or she still hasn't been able to open up to whoever is offering love, or doesn't feel this is the person he or she can love or share themselves with.

To really share, we have to make ourselves vulnerable, and we've spent a lot of years building up defenses against just that.

Does sharing in a love relationship mean a 50–50 split down the middle? Does it mean that you have to share everything you do and feel with your partner? Absolutely not!

Nena and Dr. George O'Neill note in *Open Marriage* that total sharing of all activities is not desirable, and in fact can be counterproductive by creating a stagnating effect. The O'Neills state that there is a very healthy advantage to maintaining a high degree of individuality in the relationship, and *not* trying to share all your friends and all your interests. Certainly there will be needs you'll want fulfilled that your partner wouldn't want to share at all. If you, for instance, are a great football fan, and your love-partner enjoys puttering around in the garden. These are obvious separate needs or wants that there'd be no reason to share if the other person didn't enjoy these activities.

There are also other, more subtle needs that won't be shared.

What can happen, in a sharing relationship, is that you and your partner will share the pleasure you take in pursuing some of your individual needs. Just as a parent can have a soaring sense of joy watching a child play, or just feeling the child's sense of excitement coming in from play or a special adventure.

Of course, our old enemy, fear, can prevent this. If we are afraid that our partner will not want us any more if he or she enjoys doing something alone or with someone else, then it is almost impossible to have this kind of sharing.

Sharing may be the one factor that pulls it all together. The one measurable item that can determine for us what constitutes a real loving relationship. It is sometimes too easy to say, "I love you," but it is never easy to honestly share yourself with another human being. And it seems that this difficulty is good in many respects. To share ourselves, if we really care for ourselves, cannot be made too easy. But hopefully we will be able to do it when we feel the right person has come along.

We are conditioned against sharing. This not only protects us from being hurt, but it prevents us from being fulfilled. So, we have to find a happy medium. We've had plenty of experience protecting ourselves, but little or none in letting ourselves go. Thanks to humanistic psychology and the human potential movement, we now know we can decondition and reprogram, and remove some of these destructive roadblocks. All it really takes is some sample sharing. If we try out some sharing situations and find they are not harmful, that they don't damage us in any way, that the person we are sharing ourselves with isn't going to take advantage of us, then we will open up a bit. Enough of this sample sharing and we can begin to clear the emotional channels of the garbage of conditioned responses. And it will feel good doing it! So, we have a very good system of behavior modification:

1. We find out our fear is unfounded.
2. We receive a reward by venturing forth.

Many humanistic psychologists warn against the type of behavior modification advocated by B. F. Skinner. While it's true that Skinnerism is a dehumanizing philosophy, there are certainly a wide realm of things we can learn and adapt from traditional behavior modification. In fact, many of its principles are inherent in the way we think and feel and react to each other. Just because it's misused and carried to outlandish extremes by many behaviorists doesn't invalidate some of the basic concepts and truths. Just as the widely publicized incompetence of some encounter group leaders doesn't invalidate the basic worth of encounter techniques as practiced by trained, competent therapists.

Sample Sharing

Let's try some easy sharing experiences together. What would be the easiest thing to start with? Perhaps an object, something that may have great material worth, or something that means a lot to you.

Share an Object

Find something your love-partner hasn't seen before, and share it. This is sort of an adult "show-and-tell." Take the object and hand it to your partner. Tell the story of how you obtained the object, and why it has meant so much to you. Talk about your feelings concerning this object. Have your love-partner describe the feelings generated by your sharing of the object and its history. Then your love-partner shares something with you.

Share an Idea

Can you invent a credo for yourself and share it with your partner? Some sentence that describes your beliefs and philosophy in general, or a principle you live by. Some sample answers:

Steve believes in looking after himself.
Judy loves the whole wide world.
Howard is a great businessman and a nice guy.
Arleen is a lover of animals, children, and warm men.
Jackie is beautiful, inside and out.

Start your credo-sentence with your first name. After you have both said your sentences, repeat them to each other several times with dramatic emphasis and conviction. Now react. Answer the following questions for each other:

Do you think my sentence really described me?
If I were someone you didn't know, would you want to know me after hearing my sentence?
How did hearing my sentence make you feel?
How did saying your sentence make you feel?

You might try a variation on this theme by creating your love-partner's sentence rather than your own.

Share Your Childhood

Couples can spend most of a lifetime together with neither being aware of even the simplest facts of each other's early existence.

Can you share some of your childhood with your love-partner? Let's start with the home or apartment in which you lived. Can you describe it? If you like, you can draw a diagram of the rooms your family occupied. Describe what happened in each one, and which were your favorite, and which you spent the most time in. Describe the people who shared this home with you, and their relationship to the various rooms. Can you describe a day you spent alone at home, and what you felt and did?

In our mobile society, you may have had several homes. Describe the one you remember best, or the one you miss most. If you did move around as a child, try to describe what that felt like.

After you have both shared some of your early environment, share the experience. Can you finish this sentence for each other: "I think that, as a child, you must have been ———."

Can you see anything in this person now that reflects some of what the child experienced?

Most of what we are today had its roots in our childhood, but we rarely share this facet of ourselves, unless we are seeing a psychoanalyst. There is much to learn and share from those early years, beyond any traumas that occurred.

Next, describe and share an early childhood adventure. It can be something you are proud of, or something that upset your parents at the time, or it can be something you never told your parents because you were afraid of the consequences.

Finally, share a childhood game you remember as enjoyable. Describe the game in as much detail as possible, and when and how you learned to play it, and who you played it with. It can be a word game, a physical game, or even a card game or board game. After you have both shared your games, try actually to play them together. And try to let yourself go, so you can almost play them as a child would play them. If you feel silly, share this, too.

After these childhood sharing experiences, compare notes. Do you think you learned anything about yourself? Did you learn anything new about your love-partner? Do you think you would have gotten along well as children?

Share a Song

In the so-called good old days, before radio and TV and stereo, a common activity for a couple was the singing of favorite songs together. You both may have lousy voices, but try it anyway. Find a songbook, pick out one you both know, and start singing!

You can even make it into a game. Picking at random, select songs you think your love-partner will know. Each time you pick one your partner doesn't know, you lose a point. Take turns, and the first one to lose five points has to buy the other an old-fashioned ice-cream sundae.

Share a Book

Find a book you both would like to read, and get two copies of it. This can be done anywhere, but may be highly potent if you do it in bed. Read the book together. Each at your own pace. You can share comments as you go along, but save any deep discussion for the end. Share your feelings about the book. And your feelings at sharing this together. Were you able to feel comfortable reading so close to your love-partner? Did you feel you were wasting your time, that you could have been doing something more productive together?

If you felt nervous or uncomfortable, share this feeling. Don't do anything about it, but just be aware of the nervousness or discomfort. Don't start analyzing each other's reactions.

It may take a great sense of unity before a couple can feel comfortable relaxing and reading in each other's company.

Many love-partner's may have the attitude "How dare he find printed pages more interesting than me!" or "If she really loved me, she couldn't concentrate on that book!"

An eventual variation on this can be reading out loud to your love-partner. Possibly taking turns with the reading.

Share a Drawing

Even if you both have a total lack of artistic talent, it can be fun and very much a way to communicate if you draw a picture together. It can be abstract or something real. Take a box of crayons and divide up the colors. Use a fairly large sheet of paper or cardboard. You can start together or take turns. Without talking, draw something. After it is finished, you can discuss a possible title for the work. Also share your feelings and what you might have been aware of during the drawing. Did one of you dominate the other? Did the act of drawing or the finished product provide any insights into the way you relate to each other?

Share a Fantasy

Lie down together. Close your eyes. Imagine you are in a very beautiful place, walking down a path. You are alone. You may meet some people and/or adventures on this path. At the end of the path is something you always have wanted. You might want to hold hands during this exercise, but don't talk. Just take a trip with your imagination. Allow your mind to wander free. Don't analyze the fantasy during or after the experience.

At the end of your fantasy trip, keep your eyes closed for a couple of minutes. Then sit up, but try not to disturb your partner if he or she hasn't finished yet. To assure that you both finished at the same time, you might set a time limit, say fifteen minutes, and set some kind of an alarm. Otherwise, just let it take as long as you like.

Share your fantasies. Who did you meet along the path? Were you feeling happy, sad, or afraid while walking along? Did the things that happened to you feel good? Did you easily get whatever was waiting for you at the end of the path? Was it an easy or difficult path? If it was a difficult one, realize that you created it and could have made it as easy or pleasant as you wanted. Again, don't try to analyze any symbols you think you see appearing in your respective fantasies. This is an experience, not a psychological test.

Share ESP

Lovers are supposedly psychically sensitive to each other. It might be fun to explore your capabilities in this area. Take a deck of cards, and take turns going through the deck, with one love-partner trying to pick up the card the other is concentrating on. You can make it simpler by concentrating instead on simple symbols, perhaps a triangle, cross, circle, or square. Try to relax as much as possible before doing this exercise.

There are a number of books and games designed to test and develop your ESP potential. If you find this a worthwhile experience, there is plenty of opportunity to explore it further.

The Blind Walk

A beautiful experience employed by many group leaders is the blind walk. It is perhaps the most demanding and revealing trust exercise of all.

The instructions are simple. You decide who will go first. One partner leads the other on a walk, during which the partner being led must keep his or her eyes closed. As the partner doing the leading, you must take full responsibility for your partner's safety, and what environment he or she has an opportunity to experience, and the pace of the walk. It is particularly effective to have at least part of the walk outdoors. Give your partner time to fully experience contact with the environment, to feel and touch at will. Before sharing the experience in any depth, change places. *No talking during the entire walk!*

After you have both been led on the blind walk, share your feelings. What did it feel like? How did it feel giving up responsibility and trusting another person with your body? How did it feel to be responsible for another person? How sharply did you sense your environment, and what parts of your path do you think you recognized? What did it feel like finally to open your eyes? Was the walk too long, or too short, or just right?

After your first blind walk together, you might try some variations. One possibility is to allow each other two or three short one- or two-second snapshot-like peeks during the walk. These can provide additional sensory input without harming the total effect. Another variation can be to allow one or two comments or questions during the walk itself.

The Blind Feed

This experience can be a very strong one alone, or directly following a blind walk. You are going to have a very unusual meal together. You can choose the type of food, but salads may be best, as hot foods can get cold before the second partner gets to them.

You can vary the rules on this one to suit your own needs. The idea is to have the partner who will go first close his or her eyes. There will be no talking during the exercise. The second partner then starts to feed the first. You can decide whether the first partner fills up a plate before the exercise starts, or whether the second partner will choose all the food.

This is another exercise in trust and responsibility.

If you are the first to be fed, simply close your eyes, and be ready to open your mouth. If you get too much food in one spoon or forkful, let your partner know without using words. The same procedure applies if you receive something you don't like. You can try to signal when you might like something to drink, or just leave it up to your partner. Signal when you are finished.

When you are doing the feeding, try to pick a comfortable pace. Try to vary the foods, and not stick to a simple pattern. Let each mouthful be a surprise!

After you both have been fed, share the experience. Did the food taste any different? Which did you prefer, being fed or feeding? Did any of it remind you of early childhood? Did you feel comfortable letting someone else pick out the pace and pattern of your eating? Was the exercise fun? Did you learn anything from it? Would you ever like to repeat it, or tell your friends about it?

After the initial experience, you might try varying the blind feed by doing it with different emotional themes. One time you might feed each other with tenderness. Another time with lust and passion. Another with anger. Another with fun and zest.

Rolfing

Imagine a highly romantic scene. The young lovers are tenderly embracing. One of them pulls back and with some nervous hesitation says, "I've finally made up my mind, I want to be rolfed with you!"

Rolfing, or Structural Integration, to give the proper title, is sweeping the nation. It is one of many body therapies developed and publicized in recent years. These include Reichian therapy, Bioenergetics, the Alexander technique, and various physical forms of yoga. They are designed either to help us use our bodies more efficiently or to release certain emotional blocks in our bodies. Wilhelm Reich is usually given the prime credit for coming up with the concept that a lot of the emotional things that happen to us are manifested by a tightening or constriction of various physical areas.

No doubt you have felt a tightening in your chest, or throat, or stomach during some emotional crisis. Can you remember a specific incident?

Some of these body therapies are aimed at releasing all the built-up tension and constriction that Dr. Reich called body armoring. When this happens, quite often a torrent of emotional material pours forth and can be worked on for the first time. Naturally, for a couple this can be a powerful sharing experience.

Rolfing was developed as a purely physical technique by Ida Rolf, a biochemist with a great deal of medical training. Over a period of some fifty years, Dr. Rolf evolved a system to stretch, loosen, and release the connective tissue called fascia, which forms an envelope surrounding the muscles, bones, and organs. She saw that the fascia became distorted by accidents and emotional stresses over a period of years. This causes a breakdown in other systems, and forces people to compensate by putting more dependence on parts of the body relatively unaffected. This is said to result in a much less stable structure, with a great deal of loss of energy and highly impaired function.

The way rolfers treat this problem is by a series of ten one-hour sessions in which deep systematic manipulation is used to put the body back into alignment. Tendons and ligaments are thus repositioned, and the body is released so that its natural line of gravity runs through the ear, shoulder joint, hip joint, knee, and ankle. At the end of your tenth session, although the full effects may take a year or longer to be felt, you'll have what your grandmother called "good posture," but also a lot more. Chances are some emotional material will have come out. You may have more energy. Your breathing will be fuller and feel more natural. Your walk will probably change, and you'll feel more balanced and centered. Scientists have measured some of these changes, including some that occur in the biochemistry of the body. A lot more research will go on, but no one seems to have uncovered any harmful effects, and people continue to line up for treatment by the relatively small number of certified rolfers. Some have waiting lists that stretch out for eighteen months.

The actual manipulation of the connective tissue is accomplished with the rolfer's fingers, knuckles, and elbows. A lot of force has to be exerted to correct years of misalignment. This is a painful experience for most people, but apparently not unbearable, since few ever refuse to go on through the full ten sessions. Perhaps the most remarkable thing that happens to a person when he is having his first session is to see the before and after Polaroid pictures taken by the rolfer. There are visible changes in the body after just one hour. The subject may notice a fuller chest, more balanced stance, and other actual changes in his newly rolfed body.

Marc Shane is a certified practitioner of Structural Integration trained by Ida Rolf, as are all certified rolfers. Rachel Shane is a dance therapist, body awareness group leader, and former resident fellow at Esalen Institute. She is a teacher of Structural Awareness, a system of body education based on the Rolf lines. They have been experimenting with the possibility of rolfing a couple together. A process in which both partners are present, as are Marc and Rachel, and Marc rolfs one at a time while Rachel teaches the other partner how best to share the experience, including when it might be useful to hold hands and how to receive any energy released by the partner being rolfed.

Most rolfers work individually, but Marc and Rachel see a potentially powerful sharing experience in doing couples. They were rolfed together, and Rachel described the feelings shared: "A sense that together we were doing something that was critically important for each of us individually. It was an affirmation of our relationship, that in our relationship there's room for each of us to grow."

Marc agrees: "For me, I get a feeling that it's probably the most uniform kind of an experience that a couple can have. We certainly didn't start in the same place, and we didn't end up in the same place, but at least we went through ten developmental stages, and the growth process seemed to be taking place in a harmonious way for us. Somehow our changes were sort of shared, and reciprocated between us."

These changes are emotional as well as physical, and there is the danger that, if only one partner in a relationship is being rolfed and the other isn't, a wide gap will be formed. Marc Shane sees this as just as significant as if one person is in therapy and the other person isn't, whether he or she simply refuses to go along, or just doesn't see a need for it.

Marc and Rachel also see many couples as not ready or willing to experience this type of deep sharing. Marc says, "I've seen people sitting as far away as they could from their partner—across the room, and saying, 'I've never felt as close to you as I am at this moment.'"

Rachel adds, "I see competition as probably the critical

thing with couples, the critical wrong way to go. It's like: 'Oh well, that hour didn't hurt me,' so the partner will have to lie through his teeth and say, 'It didn't hurt me either.'"

Marc doesn't see this as a totally negative factor: "This is what people can get out of rolfing, that they realize their competitiveness. What comes out of the beginning feeling of competitiveness is that 'We don't really need to be competitive, because we're different.' And, if anything, the rolfing makes it clear that one individual is different from another. There's no way that you can really compare and therefore compete on an hour-to-hour basis as if they were innings. There's no score."

So, you might try being rolfed together. A list of certified practitioners is available from the Guild for Structural Integration, Box 1868, Boulder, Colorado 80302.

Sharing or Competing?

The competitiveness noted by the Shanes can be manifested in many ways in many types of sharing experiences. You may have learned from some of the preceding exercises that you or your love-partner can easily become competitors. This, in itself, can be valuable information. If it doesn't get in the way of your relationship, you may choose to ignore it or minimize it. If it does interfere, you may choose to work on it.

As a couple, you should be able to find many things you can share. Making a list of these can be useful.

After a number of sharing experiences, you may want to evaluate your ability to share. Do you feel you demonstrated you were really a sharing person? Do you feel your partner is really a sharing person?

Sharing is measured in depth and intensity, not in years. Many a couple has spent a lifetime together without ever sharing a moment with each other. The act of sharing transcends what is being shared.

SAYING THE HARDEST THINGS

Figurines of stone
remade apart.
Locking doors in
never countable directions.
                    Judy Altura

Your love relationship is often more affected by what is left unsaid than by what you actually communicate. There are always some things that we are afraid to tell our love-partner.

Some of the things most difficult to say are:

"I know you want my love right now, but I am not feeling loving right now."
"There's something you do that really irritates me."
"You do not always sexually satisfy me."
"You don't fulfill all my needs."
"I want to be alone right now."
"I'm having an affair."
"I'd like you to try some new sexual techniques."
"You're getting too fat."
"I'm getting bored and restless."
"I'm sexually attracted to your best friend."

Why are we afraid to say these things? There are several fears involved. We are afraid we'll hurt our love-partners. We are afraid we'll lose our love-partners' love or respect. We are afraid we'll make ourselves too vulnerable.

Fear as Motivation

Fear is a prime motivator in much of what we do and don't do in a love relationship. But fear doesn't always have to be a negative factor. You could say, for instance:

"I'm afraid that we aren't going to make it together if we don't establish a better way of handling things."

Or, as Dr. Bart Knapp suggests:

"I am afraid that if I don't let you know what's happening to me now, this is going to snowball."

Dr. Knapp says, "I see the fear itself being a motivator to establish communication."

What are you afraid of in your love relationship?

Can you finish the sentence "I am afraid that ———."

Can you see yourself sharing this sentence with your love-partner?

Make a list of anything you haven't said or haven't done in your love relationship that you really felt like saying or doing.

Examine the list, and for each item, say:

"If I had said that, my love-partner would have ———." or "If I had done that, my love-partner would have ———."

To check it out further, answer the following questions:

1. Is there any sexual pleasure you have enjoyed in the past that you have not enjoyed yet with your love-partner?
2. Have you ever been physically attracted to someone else with your love-partner present?
3. Have you ever pretended to enjoy sex with your love-partner?
4. Have you ever been with your love-partner when you would much rather have been alone?
5. Does your love-partner have any habits or characteristics that annoy you?
6. Do you feel the amount of sexual relations you enjoy with your love-partner is too much, too little, or just right?

7. Do you like your love-partner's friends and relatives?
8. Are there any friends or relatives you particularly dislike?

Often the failure to disclose some specific need or some major resentment is due to the assumption that this path is the lesser of two evils. That holding back will be less damaging and less painful than letting go. This is usually pure fantasy, and ignores the very real damage done by refusing to acknowledge or share a real feeling.

Why Let Go?

One very good reason for plowing right through the fear, and opening up, is the interconnective makeup of mind and body. Each part of our organism is so intertwined with all the other parts, each nerve is tied to other nerves in intricate patterns, each muscle affects those muscles around it. All thoughts affect our bodies in some way. All physical activities affect our emotions in some way. Hardly anyone has the complete control over mind and body that would be needed to hold back something in one area without affecting another. So, when we restrict or repress a thought or feeling, or decide we are going to avoid a certain subject, we can't help but influence other things. You can't repress in one area, and then be totally open and honest in all others.

The man or woman who has an unvoiced sexual desire, or unvoiced resentment, just can't help affecting mind and body during sexual activity. Being on guard and holding back in this one area has to inhibit freedom in the others. This partner has forced a curtailment of freedom of movement and emotional expression, creating a personal "iron curtain." Because of the fears and repressions in sexual areas, almost everyone has a degree of muscular rigidity and constriction around the pelvis. This can be measured by electronic instruments, and such therapies as bioenergetics and rolfing are aimed at releasing these tensions and constrictions physically and emotionally. Being aware of when you are holding back and trying to open up to your love-partner not only feels good and enhances the love feelings, it actually does you physical good.

The next time you hold back an honest feeling, you might repeat to yourself:

> "HOLDING BACK MAY BE HAZARDOUS
> TO MY HEALTH."

When and How to Be Honest

It seems useful here to repeat a comment made by Nena O'Neill in the first chapter of this book:

". . . You have to do it with . . . tenderness, and with care and concern for the level at which the other person is, and also with an awareness of how you are using the honesty and for what purpose."

Many a love-partner comes home from the strictly controlled environment of an encounter group expecting his or her partner immediately to be as open and honest as the group members were after an intensive weekend of trust building.

We asked Dr. O'Neill what he thought the most important prerequisite was for getting into openness in a relationship:

"Feedback. You have to get to a level of trust where, when you tell your gut feelings and your real desires and needs and fantasies and dreams and whatever to your partner, they are going to accept this, and they're going to respect it, and they're going to return in kind what *they* feel, so that you can come to some consensus about what you both want. And if what you both want is not compatible, or equitable, then you have to start thinking of modification, which may ultimately lead to separation."

If one partner is going to share a real feeling or unvoiced request or resentment, does the other have to always reciprocate? Of course not! The ideal situation may be complete reciprocity, but that isn't always realistic. We do grow at different rates. One partner opening up, in an honest sharing relationship, will always affect the other partner. As Dr. O'Neill puts it, "They'll become aware that there is change taking place, and they either have to accept it and go along with it, or re-examine themselves, but they're not going to be able to manipulate. It's only in a closed relationship that you can manipulate. Even in a half-open relationship you can't manipulate."

Demanding that your partner be willing to share a repressed feeling, without building the trust necessary for such a revelation, is manipulation of the highest order.

Blunt honesty is sometimes the cruelest manipulative tool. How can you complain when your partner is merely being honest?

Blunt honesty, or perhaps more accurately pseudohonesty, is often evident during initial contact between a man and a woman, and especially during initial sexual contact, when it is used to cover up fear and to hide vulnerability. The following are actual sentences said during bedroom encounters:

1. Woman to man: "I hope you're not one of those one-time lovers who want to go to sleep right afterwards. When I get going, I like to keep going, sometimes all night."

This rigid prestructuring put the man in a highly untenable defensive position. With just a few words, the woman removed the spontaneity, challenged his virility, made it an athletic contest, and put the burden of performance totally on him.

2. Man to woman: "Are you sure you really want to go through with this? You don't have to feel you owe me anything. If you'd really rather, I can just as easily take you home."

This made the woman, who was in a warm, giving mood, feel suddenly cheap and brazen. It can often be the response an unsure male will give a sexually aggressive woman so that he can keep control. Often the man in this situation just doesn't know how to cope with anything but a passive woman, and he may not want to be in a position of being unable to satisfy a sexually mature female.

3. Woman to man: "I'd really like to make love, but I don't want you to feel you have to prove anything to me. I'll understand if you're nervous and just can't make it."

This particular statement, couched in terms of caring concern, actually gave the man his first impotent episode in his entire sexual history.

All of these statements were used to gain an advantage and to avoid sharing the real feelings.

Good Emotional Timing

Most of the things we find hardest to say have to do with the sexual aspect of our relationship. This is only natural, since this is the area in which we feel most vulnerable. If our love-partner trusts us enough to become vulnerable and share a feeling, then in order to enhance that trust we must protect that vulnerability. One of the ways we can do this is through an awareness of good emotional timing.

Telling your partner during foreplay that you don't enjoy one of his or her sexual habits is just stupid timing.

Using the good feelings and pleasant relaxation that follows orgasm is manipulative timing. Whatever you have to say can't take away from the fact that you've interrupted a good feeling to say it. Of course, at some point following intercourse you might ask, "There's something I want to talk to you about, do you feel like talking right now?"

Again, it's not a terribly complex problem in logistics, but merely knowing what feelings are happening, and when your love-partner might be most receptive.

One of the best ways of achieving a good sense of timing, in the beginning at least, is simply to choose a time when you will each share something it is hard for you to say. It may seem contrived and overstructured, but it provides an easy way to get in the habit of opening up. If you know that every Sunday morning is set aside for whatever you want to share, it removes a lot of the anxiety of wondering when you are going to get it out.

It Gets Better

Saying the hardest things is like making love—it gets easier and better with practice.

Telling your love-partner you'd like to explore some new sexual forms of expression isn't likely to burst your relationship apart at the seams. The only real way to find this out is to say it. Once you say it, and see that it doesn't do any damage, you'll find you aren't as anxious the next time you have something difficult to share.

With Love

It's important that you know what you are feeling before sharing something you find hard to share. This is also a good way to check your motivation in wanting to say it here and now.

The most ideal feeling to have is one of calm and closeness to your love-partner. Unless, of course, you're going to tell your love-partner he or she makes you nervous and you don't feel as close any more.

Look again at the sentences that led off this chapter.

Preface each one with: "I love you, but . . ." Doesn't that make a big difference? But don't say it if you don't mean it.

Stay with the Real Feeling

One of the big mistakes that people make when setting up a situation in which they feel safe opening up is to extract a promise from their partner that he or she won't react to the new information being received. Asking your love-partner to say, "I promise not to get angry or be upset if you tell me," is really saying, "I want to be honest with you, but I don't want you to be honest with me, and if my being honest doesn't make you feel good, I don't want to hear about it."

Consider the following dialogue:

SHE: "I really enjoy our sex life together, but I think I would enjoy it a lot more if you would touch my clitoris more during foreplay, and caress my breasts sometimes while we are making love. How does my saying this and asking for this make you feel?"

HE: "Well, intellectually I think it's a reasonable request, and I want to say that I appreciate your telling me, but I don't really know how much I appreciate it. I love you and I want to please you, but somehow your telling me this now makes me feel as if I haven't been pleasing or satisfying you up to now, and I suppose I want reassurance that I have."

SHE: (Embraces him.) "Of course you've pleased me and satisfied me! I've only hesitated telling you this because it's been so good otherwise, and it's sort of been a why-mess-with-a-good-thing attitude. I think that, as good as it's been, it can get better. I want it better for both of us, and I want you to tell me what you'd like me to do for you that I haven't been doing."

HE: "Well, now that you mention it . . ."

The man in this dialogue could have repressed his feeling

of hurt and pain and sexual rejection, and what would that have done except make the sharing a farce? In honest communication there's a very simple truth: Pain and sadness are diminished by sharing and expressing them; they grow only when left unexpressed and unshared.

So, it's important not only to check our feelings before saying the hardest things but to check our partner's feelings after hearing them.

Preparing to Share

Where you share can be important. As you probably are well aware, most intimate sharing is done in the bedroom. We assume, sometimes incorrectly, that merely being together in a bed constitutes intimacy. Psychologists know that often physical intimacy isn't intimacy at all, but an effort to avoid it. This doesn't negate the fact that, in a love relationship, the bedroom may be the best place to have your heart-to-heart talks. As we said, the timing has to be determined by what is happening. Naturally, immediately before, during, or immediately after intercourse aren't examples of sensible timing. And demanding that your partner hear a revelation or confession when he or she is almost asleep can also be a form of manipulation.

Making some kind of physical contact with your partner can create a better mood for the sharing of important feelings.

Making eye contact may not be easy in this situation, but it does enhance the experience.

If the thing you find it most difficult to talk about is sex, it may prove valuable for the two of you deliberately to talk about all your sexual experiences, sexual attitudes, and sexual hang-ups. Dr. Herbert and Roberta Otto's *Total Sex* is an excellent and fascinating book on the subject.

If there is something you absolutely cannot bring yourself to share, and it's really a critical area of the relationship, you might seriously consider seeking outside help. This could be in the form of growth therapy, communications or encounter workshops, or merely sharing your feelings and fears with a close friend.

Balanced Sharing

Always remember that, in a healthy love relationship, we are making ourselves vulnerable. That vulnerability is a priceless and beautiful quality. Being honest doesn't mean just sharing the things we think might hurt our love-partner or the relationship; we also have to be able to share the good things that are happening. A balanced sharing of feelings produces a very balanced partnership.

Group leaders often use an exercise called "Resentments and Appreciations." Each member is to tell every other member of the group the things they appreciate about this other person, and the things they resent. In one such group a very pretty young woman told a young man that she resented his coming on so strong sexually, and she wasn't at all sexually attracted to him, but she appreciated his charm and wit, and really thought she'd like to have him as a friend if he could only relax and stop trying to seduce her. They hugged and held each other for a few minutes after this. The young man, for the first time, felt comfortable enough to tell the group about some of his fears of rejection and of being considered unmanly. After the group session ended, the two of them became friends. Several months later they became lovers, and are still together.

If someone tells you honestly that there is something about you that they don't like, it is easy to accept the fact that they are also being honest when they tell you something they *do* like.

It's also important to let a person know how difficult it might be for you to share something, and that it's only because you really trust them that you are willing to do so. As long as you don't use this declaration of trust to extract that promise that they won't become sad or angry if that's their honest reaction.

Emily Coleman is one of the nation's most highly respected and sought-after group leaders. In an encounter weekend, she suggested that each member of the group find the person they'd least enjoy being with, and go to lunch with that person. It produced some amazing results. It takes a lot of nerve to walk up to someone and, in effect, say "I don't like you." Once you've made that statement, what's left? Well, what was left was below-the-surface good feelings. Also the fact that if someone doesn't like you anyway, you can tell them all the things you'd be afraid would make someone dislike you. Several of these luncheon dates turned into real friendships, and almost all the members said they found some things to like about the person they'd chosen.

Emily Coleman also runs many groups for singles, and is famous for making men and women feel comfortable while making initial contact. Her book *Making Friends with the Opposite Sex* is a wealth of information on this subject. One way that Ms. Coleman suggests breaking the ice is merely to tell the other person how nervous and uncomfortable you are feeling in this situation. You'll usually find they are just as nervous. Saying, "I find you very attractive, but I really felt nervous about walking over here and saying hello to you," can be a totally irresistible introduction.

Is there ever any time your love-partner makes you nervous, and can you share that when it happens?

New Information

One of the hardest things to deal with in a relationship is change. But, if you accept the premise that we are all growing and learning all the time, you have to also accept that we are changing all the time. Having rigid concepts, unrealistic expectations, and a sense of possessiveness can make it very difficult to accept change. Assuming that your love-partner is always going to feel the same toward you is child-ish and idiotic. If you can't face the fact that he or she will always be changing, and may feel differently toward you to-day than yesterday, then you are not ready for an open and honest relationship.

It can become another vicious circle. If partner A doesn't expect partner B ever to change, then partner B is going to feel compelled to hide any changes. Eventually these cumu-lative changes will become evident, and partner A will prob-ably exclaim "How could this happen overnight?"

John and Pat

John and Pat decided to live together. Actually, it was John's idea. Pat was recently divorced and was enjoying liv-ing alone, though she did love John very much. They moved into a new apartment, and from the very first day Pat seemed somehow not quite herself. John kept asking her if anything was wrong, but she kept assuring him that nothing was. Ac-tually, Pat was going through a lot of emotional pressures. As much as she cared for John, she still resented giving up her freedom and the privacy she had been beginning to enjoy for the first time in her life. She realized that she never really wanted to live with John, in fact she just wasn't ready to live with anyone yet. She was afraid to tell him, because she knew how much it had meant to him. John had never been married, and had never lived with a woman before. Pat also felt guilty for encouraging rather than discouraging John when he first brought it up. But at the time she really didn't know how much she enjoyed living alone, and how much she would resent giving it up. This was new information for Pat, but she just couldn't see sharing it with John. So, they went on for several months. John not feeling good, but not know-ing exactly why since Pat was denying anything was wrong. Pat not feeling good, but trying to hide it. In trying to avoid destroying John's expectations, she managed very effectively to destroy the relationship. If she had been able to say at the very beginning, "I love you, but I realize I just don't want to live with someone right now," it might have hurt John's feelings a bit, but chances are they'd still have been able to have a love relationship. But too many resentments built up, and by the time Pat finally shared her feelings with John, three months after they moved in and she first felt them, hardly any of the good feelings remained.

Can you think of any unsaid sentences that could have avoided a lot of pain and hurt had they been said at the beginning of your relationship?

It isn't easy to take that first step. But it is important that you take it, if only to discover that the more you say the hardest things the easier they become to say.

SAYING THE SIMPLE THINGS RIGHT

I can tell you
all you want to know,
if you will hear me.
Judy Altura

The title for this chapter could well have been the title for the entire book.

Most of the concepts and techniques and methods described on these pages are aimed primarily at helping you learn to say the simple things right. No single technique is going to help you reach a state of fulfillment in a love relationship. We are all terribly complex creatures, with many factors dictating the way we react and what we contribute toward communication with another person. In many ways this is a reference work, offering you a selection of many approaches, all with a similar theme of open sharing and dealing with feelings in the here and now.

Honestly trying out those techniques and ideas that seem right for you can do a lot to uncomplicate your approach to life and love. In this context simple doesn't mean easy, but unadorned, and not artificial.

Part of the excess adornment consists of negative information, superfluous responses, and destructive conditioning. When you start operating at a feeling level, dealing with what is happening right now rather than analyzing and intellectualizing, you'll automatically start simplifying your mode of communication.

To start off, ask yourself this question, and answer it:

WHAT IS LOVE?

Can you put your answer in one sentence?

Did you describe LOVE as a feeling, as in: "Love is caring for someone else and wanting to share yourself with them."

Or did you see it as a word composed of four letters that describes a feeling, as in: "Love is a word that refers to an emotion between two people."

This last sentence may seem rather extreme and stilted, but you'd be surprised how many answers are in this category.

Or perhaps you found the question too complicated even to begin to think about or answer before you got this far down the page.

Words Versus Feelings

Words *are* symbols, and they really can never adequately describe or define emotions. Sadly enough, many fall victim to the practice of considering the words more important than the feelings. Have you ever ached to hear the words, "I love you," when the feeling may have been expressed quite clearly if you had only been aware of it?

Have you ever allowed the words to get in the way of the feelings? Do you need to be constantly reassured verbally?

Do the words make the feeling real? Or do they really dilute the feeling by obscuring it? If a love-partner is sending out the message loud and clear and you aren't getting it, the emotional generator is liable to run down and the message may get fainter and fainter, until you couldn't hear it if you tried.

Words can be strong tools in the sharing of feelings, but only if they represent real feelings, not as words alone.

What do the words I LOVE YOU mean to you if they're said to you softly by a love-partner? Do they mean that you possess this person, that he or she is promising to honor and obey you forever and ever, that you are the most wonderful person in the world, or do they simply convey the fact that there is an overabundance of good feelings felt toward you at this moment by this person? Which sounds more realistic to you?

Many people are afraid to say, "I love you" with or without words, for fear they will give the impression that they are making a commitment they have no intention of making. How much simpler things would be if we could say, "At this moment I have strong feelings of love I want to share with you," or, "Right now, you mean more to me than I can possibly tell you."

Honestly now, would that satisfy you?

Love is a feeling. Not a promise. Not a word. Not any sort of material object.

Love is a simple thing, and as such can be conveyed simply.

If you feel love toward someone right now, try to convey it without saying it. With a touch of just one hand. With a smile. With your eyes. With a sigh.

If you've got the feeling, you can put it into any form, and even into any word. Can you look at your love-partner and say the following words, and convey love just by the way you say them?

You
Nice
Soft
Kitten
Rain

Let's make it a little more difficult, and try it with these words:

Trash
Lust
Bang
Shut up
Athletic supporter

Did any of these make you laugh? Good. Laughter and love are old friends.

Love Chant

One way to assure yourself that the word LOVE is just a word is to chant it repeatedly. Say it over and over again, in a monotone, until it loses all meaning. Then examine it.

A Simple Thing

People have died in the name of LOVE, but it was always the word they were focusing on, or a distortion of the feeling, never the real feeling. The real feeling doesn't hurt. It doesn't demand. It just is. Love is. A simple thing.

The things we really want to know and hear are always simple things. Can you say some of these simple things to your love-partner?

I enjoy being with you.
I feel good sharing myself with you.
My life means more with you in it.
This moment is yours and mine to share.
I trust you.
I care about you.
I like knowing you care for me.

Can you put the essence of all of these words into just one word? Your love-partner's name? Try it.

Words seem more important than feelings only when they are more visible than the feelings.

You might make a pact with your love-partner. Decide on a length of time during which you will not use the word LOVE.

No restriction on the feeling, just the word will be forbidden.

An Abused Phrase

"I love you." How very abused that simple phrase has become. Abused, overused, and confused. Bruised and perused.

The movie gangster has just shot his sweetheart with a machine gun. He looks at her and says, "I love you."

The teen-age girl has just painfully lost her virginity. She looks at the pimply faced sex fiend lying on top of her and says, "I love you."

The depressed poetess slashes her wrists and leaves a note that says, "I love you."

It's a wonder we can even read the phrase any more without throwing up!

But it still can be precious. Because the feeling it refers to, even if it is often said to mean other things, is the most precious one of all.

To take it all a step further, why is it so important that *you* have to be part of the stated feeling? Can we let go of ego long enough to enjoy hearing our love-partners say simply, "I feel good." Isn't the fact that someone feels good when they are with you good enough, without the words "with you" having to be uttered?

Perhaps we can start saying simply, "I love."

Or better still, simply, "love."

Can you say this to your love-partner and convey all that you want to share in the way of feelings?

LOVE

Let's take it gradually. At a moment when you are feeling like saying it, and meaning it, say to your love-partner:

"I love you."

Then, with the same feeling, say:

"I love."

Then:

"Love."

Finally, just look at your love-partner, saying nothing, at least not with words.

Share with each other how you felt about these exercises. Do you resent having to let go of words? Do you see any value in doing so?

Can you think of a very simple way to express how you feel about this experience?

Simple, wasn't it?

Love Seeds

This part of the chapter evolved from workshops and conversations with Daniel Malamud, Ph.D. Dr. Malamud is a noted psychotherapist, and has innovated a number of group techniques in self-confrontation at New York University's School of Continuing Education.

At the very beginning of any relationship we are planting emotional seeds. Some of these are positive, healthy seeds that will grow into a rich harvest of communication and love. Others are negative seeds, which can eventually bring conflict, confusion, and crisis.

These seeds can be planted by our love-partners in many ways. By their attitude toward us, by their reaction to us, and by saying to us what Dr. Malamud calls "seed sentences."

While, in the first part of this chapter, we saw that words are not sufficient to convey most feelings, "seed sentences"

are examples of how words can drastically influence our behavior, giving out a much more negative message than any
feeling behind them. Faced with the results of these "seed
sentences," you almost always have to turn to new words to
wipe out the bad effects of the old words.

Cindy and Frank and Peter

After a six-year marriage, Cindy divorced Frank. She
started dating, fell in love with Peter, and began to have
sexual relations with him. But these were far from satisfying,
and Cindy decided to seek professional help. She couldn't
understand why she froze up every time she and Peter
started to make love. Working with her therapist, Cindy began to discover the reason. During their years together,
Frank had planted a number of seeds that told Cindy
she was sexually incompetent. Frank had done this unconsciously, to protect his own vulnerability in this area. He
never came out and said, "You're bad in bed," but he would
say seed sentences to her and their friends, often disguised
as slightly sarcastic humor. These included:

"Cindy was really excited during the earthquake, she thought
it was an orgasm."
"If you ever become a prostitute, you'd have to declare bank-
ruptcy."
"You remind me of your mother, except she's a bit sexier."
"She's so exciting in bed, I sometimes manage to stay up."
"I taught her everything she knows about sex, it's a shame she
became a dropout."
"Put on the sexy dress, you know, the one that covers your
body from head to toe"

These, of course, were only some of the things Frank said
and did that planted seeds of doubt in Cindy. She was a
naturally sensual person, but this programming from her
long-time love-partner did its damage. Luckily, with a good

therapist, and Peter's understanding, she was able to overcome these destructive seeds.

Words can have a very potent effect on us, especially when they reinforce our own doubts, or evolve into negative concepts. The seed sentences that can have the most damaging effect on our love relationships are those planted during childhood. These have a lot to do with our psychological makeup. Dr. Malamud describes these as "various suggestions, warnings, injunctions, guidances that we got from our parents, or other very significant people in our lives. The whole idea is to get in touch with some commands or advice that you really have taken very seriously in your life, sometimes developing a whole life script around some particular seed sentence."

For example, many people often had a parent give them the seed sentence, "Children should be seen and not heard." Really taking this to heart, an individual could become very reticient, and feel he or she had nothing worthwhile to say or contribute.

Our national obesity problem may be blamed, in part, on the seed sentences, "Clean your plate! Remember the starving children in Europe!"

A lot of sexual repression is based on such seed sentences as, "Playing with yourself can make you go blind!" "Nice girls don't do such things!"

Howard and Judith

Howard and Judith had been married for three years. Though each had had successful sexual relations with other partners in the past, they couldn't seem to have satisfactory relations with each other. They searched through books, tried new techniques, even went to a few encounter groups, but nothing seemed to work. Finally, working with a good therapist, Howard discovered the problem was primarily his.

Howard's father had planted a number of seed sentences, all on the same theme:

> "If you want to get married, find a nice Jewish girl, if you want to get laid, find a *shiksa* (gentile girl)."
> "When it comes to sex, *shiksas* hunger for it, Jewish girls are from hunger."
> "Have fun while you can, pretty soon you'll be married."

All of these sentences reinforced the basic idea that sex wasn't very good with Jewish women, and that sexual pleasure ended with marriage, particularly marriage to a Jewish partner. Needless to say, Judith was the first Jewish sexual partner Howard had ever experienced. She was also one of the most sexually aggressive women he had encountered. He couldn't equate this with his image of a "nice Jewish girl," and thus couldn't feel comfortable in a sexual situation with Judith. She, on the other hand, had been told that "Nice girls don't," and began to relate back to this because of Howard's reaction.

Dr. Malamud suggests that the best way to change these negative factors is to realize that "new self-guiding sentences can be created and can replace what we learned at the hands of our parents . . . and that these new guiding principles can be a basis for developing new scripts for our lives."

Once Howard and Judith were able to recognize and examine their seed sentences, they were able to come up with new ones. Each invented their own new seed sentence, and had their partner repeatedly say it to them.

Howard told Judith her new seed: "It's all right to be sexually aggressive with me. I appreciate it and love it."

Judith told Howard his new seed: "Jewish girls are terribly sexy and more fun in bed than anyone else."

In short order their sex life was fulfilling and fun.

Your Seed Sentences

Try to make a list of the seed sentences that influenced you as a child. Cover all subjects.

Next, focus on sentences that had to do with sex and love. Things your parents might have said to you about members of the opposite sex, either directly or indirectly. Dr. Malamud says he would also ask couples to focus on specific don'ts the parents might have expressed, again either directly and explicitly or by example, perhaps even by facial expressions.

Each partner list these seed sentences. Try to pick out the most important one, or the most influential. Discuss how it might be affecting your reactions and responses in this relationship. If it is having a strong effect, create a new seed sentence aimed at undoing the negative programming. For example, if you're a woman who can't or doesn't want to have children, and your mother always told you to look forward to "growing up and raising a family" as the true measure of happiness, your husband might say to you "You don't have to have children for me to love you."

It's useful to start each seed sentence with the recipient's name. For instance: "Michael, you don't have to make love to me three times a night to prove you're a man."

Remember, you make up the seed sentences you want your partner to say to you. Say the sentence your partner selects almost as a chant, repeating it until he or she asks you to stop.

While receiving the seed sentence keep your eyes closed.

After the experience, share your feelings. Did the new seed take hold?

Dr. Malamud notes, "The exercise doesn't perform miracles. What it does do is sensitize a person to some basic issue in his life, which, if he really gets involved in the exercise, will keep him thinking about it for several days thereafter."

In his group exercises Dr. Malamud usually has the group chant the seed sentence repeatedly to the recipient, and for the second part each member of the group says it and touches the person receiving it in whatever way feels comfortable. He suggests a variation of this for couples: "I think it might be interesting to adapt it by having the second part involve one lover saying the sentence repeatedly to the other, but each time you say it you touch your lover in a new way. Each time in a new way which will emphasize your real caring and wish to plant the seed, while the person receiving simply takes it in with his eyes closed."

Not only is planting new seeds useful for removing negative programming, but Dr. Malamud also sees it as a way to open yourself up to being helped by your love-partner, and letting someone else in on what is a central difficulty in your life, even if only in a ritualistic way. It's a way to communicate to your love-partner that you want to help, and that you care.

You can help each other plant new seeds, even if they have nothing to do with your relationship.

You might also look into the possibility that you have planted some negative seeds in your love-partner. Discuss this, and see if you can find any. The same replacing process should work as well on these seed sentences.

You can constantly repeat the seed-planting exercise until the partner receiving the new seed feels it has become firmly rooted, and has thoroughly replaced the bad seed.

Relying solely on words to convey feelings could conceivably produce bad seed sentences, while communicating at a feeling level can help to eliminate both dilution and distortion of those feelings. In a healthy love relationship, each partner will be automatically planting good love seeds all the time.

"I love you" may be the most powerful seed of all, but not if it only consists of three little words, and it is most powerful of all when it can be shared without having to be said.

When you're saying the simple things right, you probably

are planting good seed sentences. Your awareness of how important the things you say really are can lead you toward communicating your real feelings in very real words, and avoiding saying things you really don't mean. When a love-partner complains that, "He doesn't talk to me!" what is really being said is "He doesn't let me know how he feels!"

Simplicity may be the single most important factor in communication, and as you realize how powerful your words can be, how verbal seeds can grow into strong emotional entities, you'll begin to appreciate the fact that verbal complexity is an extravagance you can't afford in a love relationship.

Saying things indirectly, or in a complicated manner, or oversaying them, can lead to a sort of verbal overkill. This, in turn, can lead to a situation in which we automatically bury our feelings under protective shielding as soon as our love-partner starts talking to us.

Look back at the simple things you have said to one another as you experienced the exercises in this chapter. Didn't they feel good? Enough said.

SAYING IT WITH TOUCH

Now we have touched.
I am prepared to
brave the day.
                    Judy Altura

Touch can communicate feelings more honestly and more easily than any words or deeds. There are many reasons why we are not touching as much as we need and want to. For one thing, touching requires more of a commitment than words. Words can much more readily be recalled, or we can say, "I didn't really mean that!" Touch is less subject to misinterpretation.

By far the most saddening factor in our reluctance to touch is that we have relegated the act of touching a member of the opposite sex to the narrow context of a purely sexual act. To touch someone has to mean we sexually desire them.

As Dr. Bart Knapp explains it, "Our culture attributes sexuality to touch and to the mere sharing of touch, and whereas the infant gets a great deal of nonsexual touching, caring touching, as he gets older (and this doesn't take very long), by the time he's three or four or five, touching becomes less acceptable, more of a taboo. To leave touching as solely a sexual thing means that there's a whole range of experiences that are not open to the couple."

Psychotherapist Marta Vago agrees: "Touch is a way of caring and pleasuring each other that really takes the physical contact out of the bedroom and expands it to the rest of the house. Somehow, once a couple gets comfortable massaging and touching, they find that they touch each other much more frequently in the course of their daily lives. Touching becomes a very natural and accepted part of the relationship, and not just limited to the number of times a week that they decide to make love. So, it really enriches and enhances the entire relationship. Not only the physical aspect of the relationship, but the whole emotional tone, the ambiance of the relationship changes."

Bart Knapp and Marta Vago, in addition to their work with couples in private and group therapy sessions, have also developed a system of tender and loving massage they call "Affective Massage." They've led workshops for groups all over the country demonstrating and teaching this new art of communication. This is not the type of massage you'd receive at the "Y" or the local massage parlor. It is most closely related to the famous Esalen massage, and, in fact, Bart Knapp was first trained in massage at the famed growth center, further developing it on his own and evolving it still further as it became a joint effort with Ms. Vago. Participants in these massage workshops quickly learn that there is a difference between sensual caring touch and sexual touch. Knowing this difference adds a new dimension to the relationship, more fully incorporating touch as a means of expressing nonsexual affection and thus widening the horizons of the relationship. This also has the paradoxical effect of enhancing the sexual aspect of the relationship.

If the only use we have for touch is for sexual expression, then we may well sometimes indulge in the sex act, not from any physical desire, but merely to fulfill our need to touch.

Psychologists have noted that many men and women engage in sexual relations for the cuddling closeness that follows orgasm rather than the act of intercourse itself.

Marta Vago says, "Some of the couples we've worked with really don't know how to care for each other and how to express tenderness to one another, except by fucking. And it's pathetic. If they're horny, they fuck. If they're lonely, they fuck. If they want to be held, they fuck. If they want to be cared for, they fuck. What they've done is they've limited all these diverse needs, and pushed them into one bag. They really don't have a range of expression for all these feelings. They know they want to do something physical, but they don't know what."

Dr. Knapp adds, "If you don't have a rubric of touch in your relationship, so that touch is acceptable and touch outside of sex is acceptable and almost expected as a way of living, you're limited in what you can do when the other person needs caring. If I have a headache, Marta can give me an aspirin, or she can massage my head and my back. And very often the latter is more effective than the former."

A Touching Laboratory

The encounter and sensitivity facets of the Human Potential Movement have provided people a needed opportunity to find out their own needs and capacities for touch. Sensitivity groups, employing a number of nonverbal communication exercises, have acted as a human laboratory. Though no one has catalogued and quantified all the findings, they do provide powerful support for the concept that touch can help us reach more of our potential, and teach us how to more effectively communicate.

It is all well and good for someone to lecture on the merits of touch, or write a book about our need to touch, but that doesn't give us the incentive or permission to act. It is a sad fact, but a fact nonetheless, that what the sensitivity groups have provided more than anything else is a permissible place for us to be ourselves and express our real desires, and act on them.

Why Touch a Stranger?

Many people ask the question, "Why should I go to one of those groups and touch a bunch of strangers, and let them touch me? I don't want to touch strangers, I just want to touch the people I love, and I already am doing that."

Many have described these sensitivity and encounter techniques as a means of creating instant intimacy. That may be missing the point. It isn't important that you touch a stranger, but it *is* important that you learn how to touch freely to communicate nonsexual feelings. It *is* important that you are able to touch when and whom you choose. Practicing on strangers is a lot less risky for most people, especially since all the members of the group are equally nervous and you're all trying this new experience together. We need to touch. Having a group of forty strangers close their eyes and all mill about, then all crowd toward the center of the room, provides a new sensory experience and demonstrates some of the beauty of human contact. Fear prevents many of us from trying this, but, almost without exception, those who do try it report good feelings, new awareness, and a new sense of joy at being alive and a part of the world community.

It's not learning to touch a stranger, it's learning that *you* can safely touch, and be touched, without being taken advantage of or ending up in bed.

You don't have to join a sensitivity group to explore touch. But, because of our restrictive conditioning, you do have to have permission. So, see if you can't give yourself permission. Say to yourself, "I can touch my love-partner in many ways that will express my feelings without necessarily leading to sexual activity."

One further point on this: If you are sexually frustrated, it will of course be most difficult to engage in nonsexual touching. In fact, one of the rewards of a sexually fulfilling love relationship is that it gives you the freedom to explore nonsexual intimacy.

Massage

Learning how to give your love-partner a loving massage can add greatly to your mutual pleasure and communication. You can experiment on your own, giving each other firm but

gentle strokes, and tender kneading, all in flowing movements. You can add to the experience by using baby oil or
some other body oil.

If possible, attend a massage workshop. If you're on the
East Coast, contact Bart Knapp and Marta Vago at Laurel
Institute, 2010 Pine Street, Philadelphia, Pennsylvania 19103.
They do their massage workshops in many major cities, but
primarily in New York, Philadelphia, and Miami. If you're on
the West Coast, contact Esalen Institute at Big Sur, California, or in San Francisco. You might also check any local
growth centers.

The Massage Book, by George Downing, with fine draw-
ings by Anne Kent Rush, can give you a lot of good information on massage, and while it's not nearly as good as a live
demonstration, it does as good a job as any book can in in-
structing the novice.

First Touch

Can you remember the first time you and your love-partner touched? Can you try to relive that moment? Discuss
how you felt the first time, and how you feel doing it now.

Hand Talk

This is a popular method many group leaders use to in-
troduce people to the possibilities of touch. Sit facing your
partner and close your eyes. Take each other's hands. Now
start to explore the hands. Notice what you're physically feeling. How these hands feel to your hands. Can you feel a difference between your partner's left and right hand? Notice
the weight of the hands, and the temperature. Start slowly
to get acquainted, and begin to express affection through
your hands. Become children and play with your hands. Become competitive and have some kind of a contest with your
hands. Get angry. Be sad and hurt. Make up and start to like

each other again. Become passionate with your hands. And, finally, say a temporary good-bye to each other's hands. Keep your eyes closed. Just stay with what you're feeling, without trying to think about it. Stay this way as long as you like. Open your eyes, and if your partner's eyes are open start to share your feelings about the experience.

Face Feel

Sit facing each other and close your eyes. With your hands each begin to explore the other's face, as if you are both blind and wanted to know what this person looked like. Do this until you really feel you know this face. Note the textures, the temperatures, the sizes of the various facial features.

Facial Follow the Leader

With one hand on each other's face, and eyes closed, one partner starts slowly moving over the face. The second partner has to mirror these movements. It can become a sort of dance of fingers. Let it take you wherever it feels right to go.

Body Exploration and Nudity

When exploring each other's body in a nonsexual manner, don't feel you've failed if one or both of you become sexually aroused. Nonsexual touching is meant to enlarge your touching experience, not replace sexual touching. It has to be learned, and it's quite naturally going to slip into the area of erotic activity from time to time.

If you are already on intimate physical terms with your love-partner, then being nude during these body exploration exercises will present no problem. If not, then you might discuss your feelings about nudity. Another valuable awakening

couples can have is the discovery that nudity doesn't have to
be purely a sexual experience either. A lot of how you react
to nudity in a nonsexual context is related to your feelings of
body shame. Dr. Herbert and Roberta Otto have helped a lot
of couples work this out, and much of their work is outlined
in *Total Sex*. This feeling that the body is shameful and in-
decent also strongly inhibits a couple's sexual potential.

The Finger Trip

One partner lies down and the other travels lightly over
the body with a single fingertip. As you do this to your partner be aware of the contours and textures of the body. As
it is being done keep your eyes closed and try to keep in
touch with your feelings as various parts of your body are
touched.

The experience can be continued by traveling over the
body a second time with two fingers, then three, then four,
then five, then the flat of the hand, etc.

Weights and Looseness

Get in touch with some parts of your partner's body by
lifting them gently. Start with the head. Your partner should
be lying flat on his or her back. Lift the head and feel its
weight, and whether it feels tight and hard to move or loose
and relaxed. Do the same for each arm and each leg. Lift
just the lower half of each limb, then the full arm and leg.
Feel how loose or tight these are.

A Body Check

Find the warmest part of your partner's body. The smooth-
est part. The roughest textured part. The softest place. The

hardest place. You can help keep it a nonsexual experience
by avoiding any prolonged touching of the genitals. You can
decide beforehand whether you want to avoid these alto-
gether. It might prove a highly worthwhile part of the exercise, however, to include genital touching in the context
of a total body trip. You may find this gives you a sensual
awareness without becoming sexual or erotic, or needing
orgasm as a completion.

Guessing Game

Your partner should be lying down, with eyes closed.
You're going to touch various parts of your partner's body
with different parts of yours. See how sensitive you each are.
Start by touching some fingers to your partner's body. See if
your partner can guess how many fingertips are actually
touching. Then touch your partner's body with other parts,
including the heel or your hand, your chin, your nose, an
elbow, a toe. You may be surprised to find how hard it is to
tell exactly what is touching your body.

Body Music

This is a variation on a group experience developed by
Paul Silbey, who put his classical musical training to good
use when he started leading groups.

Body music could almost be called a dance massage, and
can be as pleasurable to give as to receive. It can act as a
transcending experience, and heighten consciousness if you
allow yourself to flow with the feelings.

Your partner should lie on the floor, with a blanket for
comfort if there is no rug. Put a sheet under the body. You
are going to perform a ritualistic dance on your partner's
body. Select music for the massage, and let your partner help
pick it out. Strong rhythms are suggested for the first time.

The exercise should last from thirty to forty minutes. You'll need baby oil, or some other suitable body oil, rubbing alcohol, and some type of powder, possibly baby powder. Also a towel. Decide whether you will start on the top or bottom, with your partner starting out by lying face down. Start the music. Warm the oil in your hands, and start moving your hands over your partner's body in rhythm to the music. Use smooth strokes, patting, kneading, and piano-like tapping with the fingers. All in rhythm to the music. Let yourself go with the music, as if you were dancing. You probably will be able to find a comfortable sitting position, and let the upper half of your body move along with your hands. After you have covered the back with a light coating of oil, and rubbed it in, use the towel to dry your partner, moving it in rhythm to the music. Then take some rubbing alcohol and sprinkle it over the body. Be careful to protect the anal area with the towel. Rub in the alcohol. Keep up the rhythm, and follow its changes. Before the alcohol dries, lean over and blow a smooth current of air over your partner's body. Massage some more, and then dry with the towel again. Now liberally pour the powder over your partner's body. Rub this in in rhythm to the music. When you are finished, signal your partner to turn over, and repeat the entire process on the front of his or her body. Avoid genital contact, and be sure to protect the genitals from the alcohol with a towel.

It will take a while, but you will start to let go and flow with the music, not focusing on the massage as a task, but just letting it happen. You will decide when it is time for the next move, and what kind of touching to use at each change in the rhythm of the music.

It is probably best to use different rhythms and different artists. You may start out with rock, and end up with a waltz.

After you have done your partner, let the music fade out, and neither of you move for a few minutes. Close your eyes and get in touch with what you are feeling. Don't speak or interrupt what your partner is experiencing. When he or she is ready to open their eyes, you may choose to touch each other in some affectionate way. Don't talk too much or share too much until you, too, have been done. After you have both experienced doing and being done, caring and being cared for, share your feelings and your physical sensations. This can be a beautiful way to share something new and special.

The Crawl

This can also be a new way to understand and know one another. Each of you sit on the floor at opposite ends of the room, with the lights out and your eyes closed. Start slowly to crawl toward each other. Make no sound. Be aware of the first instant of contact and what it feels like. Hold each other closely without talking. Share your feelings.

You can vary this experience by adding fantasy. Imagine you are crawling through desert or jungle. Imagine you have been lost to each other for years, and are just coming together. What are your feelings as you first touch? How do you first touch?

Touch Experimentation

There are many things you can discover and explore together through touch.

Touch your partner in a way that she or he has never been touched before.

Touch your partner to express playfulness in a childish, silly way.

Can you reduce your fear of appearing foolish enough to try talking to various parts of your partner's body? As you touch your partner's knee, can you tell it when it feels like, and how you feel touching it?

Can you make up your own ways to explore and experiment and share this wonderful form of expression?

As in all your experiences together, it is important that you take your emotional temperature before starting any touching. What are you feeling, and especially what are your feelings toward your love-partner?

If the touching makes you feel uncomfortable, say so, and be able to withdraw.

Be aware that it is hard for many to accept pleasure. We often feel we don't deserve it, or that it will obligate us in some way. At the end of each experience, be aware of whether you try to end it quickly, and start talking right away, or are able to let it still be a part of you, and end the mood only when you have taken your fill of it.

Be aware of whether you feel a need to laugh and joke rather than flow with the experience, and whether this isn't a sign of discomfort or anxiety.

Touch when you want to touch, and be able to refrain from touching when you don't want to, and be able to tell your partner, "Not now."

Only when you learn to touch freely can you truly be free in a relationship, and within yourself.

Touching can become a whole new language for you, and one you can keep studying for the rest of your life. As in all growth, the learning is much more important than any goal or graduation present. If love is the most precious feeling, then touch is the art that can most clearly express it.

MUTUAL MASSAGE

To touch;
to memorize by skin.
Judy Altura

In the preceding chapter we explored touch; in this one we explore a specific touching experience. As developed by the author, Mutual Massage can provide you with a unique adventure in simultaneous touching. While there is much to be said for being able to relax and fully enjoy the passive experience of being touched by your love-partner, this new set of exercises can provide yet another dimension to your relationship, and provide you with a rich meditative experience. It can also be a beautiful sexual/sensual form of expression. It all depends on your needs and moods at the time.

At this point you should be quite accomplished at using touch in a nonsexual way. From now on let's not concern ourselves with categorizing touch. These Mutual Massage exercises may turn you or your love-partner on sexually, or they may merely communicate tenderness and caring, or they may even turn into a transcending spiritual experience. You can be aware of which is true for you by keeping fully aware of what is happening as it happens, without talking or analyzing. If, however, you feel you do not yet understand the value and beauty of nonsexual touching, you may choose to go back to the exercises in the preceeding chapter, trying these again before going on to Mutual Massage.

Guidelines

This form of massage can be most thoroughly appreciated when both partners are nude. If this presents a problem, you may try them with clothes, though a bathing suit might be a good compromise.

We only briefly mentioned body oils in the preceding chapter, so let's elaborate a bit. Rachel Shane, a former Esalen masseuse who has developed her own form of massage, suggests a peanut oil base. She advises against baby oil, saying that it robs the body of vitamins, and also rules out mineral oil of any kind for the same reason. She usually adds a few drops each of wintergreen, lemon oil, and eucalyptus oil, but suggests you can experiment with a wide variety of scents. Always warm the oil between your hands before applying it to your partner's body.

The best massage stroke is a smooth gliding action, using the hand with palm down, and with gentle firmness rather than a feathery touch or health-club-type rubbing. You are going to be learning as you go along, so try not to worry about technique. Just flow instead with an easy rhythm.

It would probably be best to start out with eyes closed as you actually massage. Later on you might want to experiment with making eye contact in those exercises that have you facing each other.

Take responsibility for yourself in determining what feels right and pleasurable. Don't do anything that strains your muscles or puts you in an uncomfortable posture.

Mutual Massage ✗1 (Standing)

Stand facing each other, at arm's length. Place your hands on each other's shoulders and start massaging. You don't have to mirror exactly each other's movements, but it would probably feel better if you kept your movements in the same rhythm and speed. This is true for all of the mutual massages. You can experiment with duplicating your partner's exact movements, but you might find this too structured and restrictive.

Mutual Massage ⚹2 (Standing)

This can be a follow-up to ⚹1. Massage the back of each other's neck, using fingertips curved slightly inward. Move up the back of the head, ending by slowly sliding off the forehead.

Mutual Massage ⚹3 (Standing)

Move closer together, still standing up. Place your hands on each other's heads. Slowly slide your hands back, with palms down and fingertips touching, and going all the way down the back as far as you can comfortably reach. Then pull the hands smoothly toward you, pulling them off at your partner's side. Repeat this several times.

Mutual Massage ⚹4 (Standing)

You can move from ⚹3 right into this one, or do it separately. Start with fingertips touching, palms down, at your partner's small of back. Pull the hands around to the front and lightly massage the stomach with your fingertips.

Mutual Massage ⚹5 (Standing)

Massage the top of each other's head with your fingertips while resting the heels of your hands on the temple.

Mutual Massage ✕6 (Standing)

Gently massage each other's ears, ending with palms against the ears to shut off outside sounds. Stay at this last position for about a minute, preferably keeping eyes closed.

Mutual Massage ✕7 (Standing)

Stand at arm's length, clasping your hands around the tops of each other's upper arms. Move slowly backward, pulling the hands down the arms in a smooth but firm gliding action, and stopping at the wrists. In a much lighter pressured grip, slide your hands back up each other's arms. Repeat several times. This may take some practice before you can easily co-ordinate your hand and foot movements.

Mutual Massage ✕8 (Sitting)

Sit on floor with legs crossed and knees almost touching. Place hands on each other's knees. Bending at waist, slide your hands to the upper legs while simultaneously bending head forward. Let your faces touch at the sides, and if your relative height allows it, you can rest your heads on each other's shoulder. Massage each other's back from this position.

You can also choose to skip the back at this point, but merely repeat the glide up the leg several times. This also may take some practice, since you want a smooth flow as your body bends and your head moves forward in unison with the hands going up the legs.

Mutual Massage ✳9 (Sitting)

Facing each other, stretch your legs out, with man's legs resting over the woman's thighs and curving around her back. Woman's legs can curve around man's back or stay straight out, whichever is most comfortable. Your genitals should be about a foot apart. Lean forward, almost in the same bend as in ✳8, and rest your heads on each other's shoulder if possible. From this position you should be able to massage more thoroughly each other's back.

Mutual Massage ✳10 (Sitting)

Sit side to side facing in opposite directions. Tilt toward each other and embrace, massaging each other's back.

Mutual Massage ✳11 (Sitting)

Sit facing and alongside each other, with feet slightly above partner's knees, flat on floor, legs close together. Lean forward and massage one of each other's legs at a time.

Mutual Massage ✳12 (Sitting)

Sit facing each other, with legs stretched out and bottoms of feet touching. Massage each other's feet, with your feet, using your hands to brace yourselves. Bend your knees and test the pulling and pushing power you each have.

Mutual Massage ⚹13 (Sitting)

Partner A sits in front of partner B, both facing forward. Partner A is enclosed between partner B's legs, and can rest his or her head against partner B's chest. Partner A massages partner B's legs around the knees while partner B is massaging partner A's chest and stomach, letting the hands come around to the front under partner A's arms. This may sound confusing, but it's well worth trying. Switch places and repeat.

Mutual Massage ⚹14 (Sitting/Lying)

Both partners face in same direction side by side sitting up. Partner A lie back. Partner B massages partner A's stomach and upper legs while partner A is massaging B's lower back. Switch places and repeat.

Mutual Massage ⚹15 (Sitting/Lying)

Partner A is sitting up, with partner B lying on side. Partner B's chest is approximately at A's waist so that B can reach around and massage A's lower back. A leans forward and massages B's buttocks and the backs of B's legs. You'll have to experiment with this one to find comfortable positions, and may want to rest B's topmost leg over one of A's legs. It should be fun figuring out. Repeat after switching places.

Mutual Massage ※16 (Lying)

This is a variation of ※12. Again, the bottoms of your feet are touching and are going to massage each other, but this time you are lying down. You may find this a better way to do it than ※12.

Mutual Massage ※17 (Lying)

Lie side to side on your backs, facing opposite directions. One of each partner's legs are touching, with the foot of that leg approximately at the partner's armpit level. Massage the inside of the leg nearest you.

Mutual Massage ※18 (Lying)

Same basic position as ※17, except you've each moved back so your feet are at your partner's chest level. Massage the feet. If it feels uncomfortable to massage both feet from this position, just do the one closest to you.

Mutual Massage ※19 (Lying)

Both partners on backs lying in same direction, but with partner A's head at about partner B's waist level. B raises leg closest to A, with foot flat on floor and knee bent. A massages this leg while B massages A's chest. Switch places and repeat.

Mutual Massage ⚡20 to ?

The rest is up to you. Perhaps as you tried these you were able to think up your own variations. If not, try now. Each partner has to come up with a new way to massage the other.

Whether these mutual massages lead you to greater touch-ability, a sense of peace and calm, or the bedroom, you'll find they've added yet another facet to your relationship.

As you decide to try the various mutual massages, make certain you are both ready to enjoy them and share your feelings as you go along.

Be able to suggest "You massage mine and I'll massage yours," but also be able to say "Let's stop, I'm tired and uncomfortable."

THE BIOFEEDBACK COUPLE

I saw deep into you last night,
and there was love there
everywhere I looked.
                    Judy Altura

The poet of the future may think of love and say, "My alpha soars at thoughts of you." Biofeedback is an exciting new science, with a bright and promising future in medicine, psychology, education, and possibly even philosophy and religion. Much of the basic research remains to be done, but the initial indications are most encouraging, and this science may have the most fringe benefits in human terms of any yet examined.

The concept of biofeedback is a simple one. Electronic measuring instruments are used as mirrors, to show us how various physiological functions are doing. We can take this immediate feedback of information and use it to become more aware of these bodily functions, and to learn, through trial and error, how to begin to control these functions. If, for example, you were hooked up to an electromyograph, which measures individual muscle firings, and you could see that you had a lot of tension in your frontalis or forehead muscle, and could see that tension level rise or lower as you made various mental/emotional efforts to relax or tense, then you would soon learn how to relax that muscle at will.

We use feedback for most of our learning. If you are learning to play tennis, you are using visual feedback. If you see the ball hit the net, you start automatically to correct your swing. Seeing the results of a good swing keeps you on the right path, and reinforces your correct action. Blind-folded, you would have a pretty difficult time learning to play tennis, though it is possible you could make progress by more keenly developing another sense. You would have to know, however, where the ball was going. Until biofeedback came along, we were basically blindfolded in regard to a number of so-called autonomic or involuntary functions. Scientists have now learned that these functions weren't in-voluntary at all, but we just had no way of tuning into them to start to exercise choice over their operation. These func-tions include heart rate, blood pressure, muscle tension, brainwave activity, skin temperature, gastrointestinal secre-tions, and, in fact, any bodily function that can be measured.

For every change in your body, there is a corresponding change in your mind, and your body reacts to every feeling you have emotionally. You may not be aware of these things happening, but biofeedback can show you very quickly that they are happening.

Perhaps the most exciting single factor in the whole amaz-ing field of biofeedback is the fact that it offers us cold scientific proof that we are more capable than we have be-lieved. It is all well and good for someone to tell you that you have more potential than you think you have, but hear-ing it and believing it are often two entirely different en-tities. When you find you can start learning to control something you've never controlled before, and can see or hear it happening, then you have to begin to believe. This proof of our own capacity can have a potent effect on our lives and love relationships.

Many religions and philosophies have told us that many of these things are possible with faith. You don't need faith or any kind of doctrine with biofeedback, just the machine and the willingness to practice.

Biofeedback is no panacea. Many people won't be willling to take the self-responsibility to make it work for them. We are a pill and push-button society, wanting things done for us rather than doing for ourselves. Biofeedback is doing for yourself. The machine doesn't do anything *to* you, it merely records what you are doing for yourself, and feeds you back the information so that you know if you are doing it right and can make corrections. It is a teaching aid, but you are the teacher and student.

The primary effect on love relationships through biofeedback will probably be the psychological one. The sense of individual power that gaining internal control can provide will eliminate much of the power-struggling of man–woman relations. The learning to let go, to increase both awareness and the ability to take charge of oneself, will widen our perspectives.

But there will also be many other benefits. Most of the research in this area is in its infancy, but the future looks bright indeed.

Dr. George Whatmore, a Seattle physician specializing in internal medicine and functional disorders, has been a pioneer in electromyographic biofeedback, using an EMG to teach people more efficiently to use and relax their muscles. He sees the basic problem as one of errors we make in the expenditure of energy, errors that interfere with the function of our nervous system, and thus cause us to lose control of the functions of our organs. He has successfully treated impotence and frigidity with his "effort training," a combination of engineering, relaxation, and neurophysiology. If you'd like more details on this work, you might read an article in the journal *Behavioral Science* dated March 1968 and titled "Dysponesis: a Neurophysiologic Factor in Functional Disorders."

Various studies have shown that men can learn voluntarily to control penile erection, an autonomic response heretofore thought involuntary.

In the future it may be possible to have voluntary birth control. Preliminary studies have shown that the sperm count can be reduced to zero by teaching men voluntarily to raise the temperature of their scrotums. Don't, however, look for this as a contraceptive device before a lot more research is done, probably several years' worth.

Alpha and Love

Alpha brain waves occur at a frequency of eight to thirteen cycles per second, or eight to thirteen hertz as measured by an electroencephalograph, or EEG. They indicate a quieting down of the mind, which operates normally, or most often, at fourteen hertz and above, or beta. Below the alpha state, which is associated with meditation, lies theta, at four–seven cycles per second. Theta is a state that may be related to high creative activity, with a lot of visual images popping into the brain. Below theta is delta, or the sleep state.

Alpha is a very natural state, and you produce it at random moments throughout the day. Children are great alpha producers. This involves letting go of conscious thought, and letting your mind float into nothingness. The subjective experience is different for different people. You can learn to increase and maintain alpha by having a small EEG measure your brain waves and send you back a visual or audio signal when you produce alpha. By relaxing and letting go, you'll quickly find you can keep the signal going. Eventually, as in all biofeedback, the object is to be aware of what you are feeling subjectively during the alpha experience, and learn such total awareness and control that you will no longer need the machine to tell you when you're on the right track.

Psychotherapist Carole Altman, a founder of the Biofeedback Institute, says, "The ability to be fully aware of what your body is doing, and to let go of your defensive systems and let your body respond naturally, leads to a certain kind of personality and character. The biofeedback couple has a great deal of strength, they are more relaxed, calmer, less judgmental, less concerned with pettiness and 'ego trips.'"

Martha and Frank

Martha and Frank took an alpha biofeedback training course together. They reported not only a great deal of pleasure in sharing this new type of experience, but a more relaxed attitude toward one another, and more of a feeling of aliveness. The most dramatic change came in their sexual relations. They both described more of a feeling of "flowing" and body-awareness. Frank said, "After orgasm, on several occasions, I would go into this strange state, feeling very high and getting a lot of strong theta images: bright colors and flashing pictures. It felt great, though I don't fully understand it. I think the big change for me is in the greater pleasure I now take with Martha in my arms following our orgasms." Martha reported that she no longer felt concerned or anxious about achieving an orgasm, and seemed to achieve deeper ones. She didn't see any flashing pictures or bright colors, but did feel a pleasant floating sensation after intercourse.

These are, of course, subjective reports from just two subjects. You may have intensive alpha training with results that are entirely different. Like meditation, biofeedback training, and particularly brain-wave training, is a very personal and individualized experience.

GSR and the Love Relationship

Psychologists and physiologists have known about galvanic skin response for a long time. Adapted to biofeedback, the GSR measuring instrument is proving highly useful to therapists, It measures skin moisture by checking skin resistance to a tiny electric current. Part of the polygraph, or lie detector, consists of galvanic skin response, and it's a very acute barometer of the emotional state. With a small

GSR device, with two electrode bands that fit around two fingers, you can learn to lower your arousal level and deeply relax. The device emits a high-pitched tone. As you relax, the tone lowers. If you think of something exciting or something you feel anxious about, the tone rises again within one to three seconds.

You can find out your feelings about various love-partners by thinking of them and seeing how the machine indicates your response. If you deeply love someone, there is hardly any way you can visualize that person without the tone climbing up. Dr. Marjorie Toomim, a clinical psychologist in Los Angeles, uses the GSR in therapy to find out a patient's general level of arousal and activation, and to help him find out what he is actually feeling about certain things. She sees it as one of the few ways you can measure the sympathetic nervous system without the parasympathetic system becoming involved. You may feel all your anxiety is because of your feelings about your mother, but if the GSR is attached, and nothing happens when you talk about your mother, then this is not causing you anxiety, and you and a therapist can explore other possibilities.

Couples have used the small, portable GSR's, costing about $40–$50, to measure their erogenous zones. One partner touches the other, and if the tone jumps sharply, this may be an easily aroused area.

Two people lowering their tone as far as possible prior to intercourse may find their sexual experience heightened by starting out at a lower arousal level.

There are all kinds of possibilities, and the low price of the units makes this a popular form of biofeedback exploration. The alpha and muscle-measuring units range from $200 to $500 for accurate engineering and calibration.

Is biofeedback the only way to achieve these capabilities of heightened awareness and bodily control? Of course not! People have been doing some of these things with yoga and Zen for hundreds of years. Biofeedback is merely a Western-oriented approach, with direct scientific evidence being supplied as you begin to accomplish internal control.

It is a science that will soon be affecting all of our lives in many ways. A way to get away from 1984, and technology taking over. This is a situation involving the harnessing of technology to make ourselves more human and more aware of our humanness. Man using machine to be better able to use his own body.

The biofeedback couple can learn to share this increased awareness and enhance not only the biofeedback training but their relationship at the same time.

It may also give us a way to chart emotions by measuring the physiological correlates of those emotions. "I love you thirty microvolts of alpha at eleven hertz, with theta bursts, and a three-microvolt drop in my frontalis tension" may be a much better way of saying it, and the first real answer to the question, "How much do you love me?"

For more information on biofeedback you can contact the Biofeedback Institute, P. O. Box 1803, Miami, Florida 33143.

LOVE RELAXATION

And in the torrent
of a world gone mad,
this could be
everything.
        Judy Altura

"Relax and enjoy it." This old cliché is often given, only half humorously, as advice to women who may be confronted by a rapist. It can be funny because of the incongruity of anyone being able to relax under such a tense situation.

Love and sex, for many men and women, is also a tense situation. Unfortunate, but correctable.

Much of our inability to relax in a love relationship comes from the same old fear responsible for our repressing information and feelings. If we relax, we may be caught off-guard and found wanting. The honest sharing suggested throughout these chapters can eliminate a lot of the tension, and create a more relaxed and comfortable atmosphere. But more may be needed. Getting rid of the reasons for the tension doesn't mean your body is going to become immediately loose and relaxed. The symptoms have to be treated, as well as the underlying emotional causes. And often working on these symptoms can remove the emotional obstacles as well as the physical effects of the anxiety.

Psychologists and physiologists have done a lot of research on a fascinating human condition known as the "fight or flight response."

In prehistoric times, when man was confronted by a ferocious animal, he had two choices: He could either fight for his life or run for his life. In order to give him the energy to do either, his body would start an immediate reaction. Blood pressure might rise. Heart rate increase. Muscle tension rise. Adrenaline would be produced. Blood lactate manufactured. Skin resistance increased. And a number of other physiological changes might take place in the body all at once. Today we are not confronted by ferocious beasts in the everyday course of our lives, but we still have the fight or flight response handed down from generation to generation. Without having to run or fight for our lives when some anxiety-producing situation occurs, we don't really have any way to use up all this excess energy, and much of it is retained in the body as physical tension. This high arousal state eventually causes all the stress-related disorders, such as heart disease and high blood pressure.

It also gets in the way of communication in a love relationship. One of the qualities people cherish as most special in a good love relationship is being able to feel relaxed with another person, with a member of the opposite sex.

Relaxation can also help in the process of getting in touch with feelings. Throughout this book it's suggested you say to yourself, "What am I feeling right now?" You can make certain the answer to this question will be more real and honest if you preface the question with an awareness of your physical state, and give yourself instructions to relax.

How Relaxed Are You?

Using physiological measuring devices, the Biofeedback Institute found that many people don't know when they are relaxed. Some subjects actually increased tension when told to relax, others claimed they were tense when actually they were quite relaxed. Some people overestimate their anxiety, others overestimate their ability to relax.

Ask yourself the following questions:

"What feels different in my body when I am relaxed?"

"How relaxed is my body right now?"

"Can I stay relaxed and think about my love-partner?"

"Can I stay relaxed when I'm with my love-partner?"

"Am I relaxed prior to sexual activity?"

"Am I more or less relaxed during sexual activity?"

"Does my relaxation level go up or down following sexual activity?"

You might now share and discuss your answers with your love-partner.

Are you both at different levels of relaxation? If so, do you see where this might be getting in the way of the natural flow of feelings?

It's not only a question of relaxing, it's a matter of learning to more efficiently use your muscles. Dr. Edmund Jacobson, whose "Progressive Relaxation" techniques have been responsible for numerous heavily documented and highly successful treatments of organic disorders, teaches people to avoid making an effort to relax. His book *Progressive Relaxation*, originally published in 1938, is still in print and a firm mainstay of many medical libraries. The Jacobson techniques are being used with biofeedback training in a number of research projects, but few doctors have had the patience and dedication to teach these valuable methods to their patients. And many doctors and patients are just not willing to spend the year or two it takes to learn the skills. Dr. Jacobson might spend a month or two just training an individual how to properly relax his arm, and this indicates how very little we all really know about relaxation.

Making yourself aware of your state of relaxation can be the first step. Learning a simple technique for relaxing your body can be the next. Drs. Tom Budzynski and Johann Stoyva of the University of Colorado Medical Center have found that Progressive Relaxation, another older therapy called "Autogenic Training," and electromyographic biofeedback training, to teach people more muscle control and awareness, can be combined to provide a very effective means of getting people to learn to relax. They use this training to treat tension headaches, essential hypertension, and other stress-related disorders. You can use some similar techniques for basic relaxation.

Autogenic training is much more widely used in Europe than in the United States, and is often an important part of a psychiatrist's basic treatment procedures there. This training method was developed over half a century ago by Dr. Johannes Schultz, a German psychiatrist and neurologist. It involves a series of exercises that are self-suggested, and are more meditative in nature than hypnotic, though Dr. Schultz used a lot of the early hypnotic research into human suggestibility. A full autogenic training program can take someone several months to complete, with the end result being that the trainee will have developed the ability to achieve a low arousal level at will.

Drs. Budzynski and Stoyva have just adapted a very small part of Autogenic Training and Progressive Relaxation for their work but have found it can have some startling results in reducing adverse physiological reaction to stress.

Relax Together

Here, then, is a variation on the Budzynski–Stoyva technique, which can be an important prelude to any activity between two love-partners, as well as a beautiful sharing experience in itself.

Lie down, without making physical contact, and close your eyes. Be aware of what your body feels like. Are you in a comfortable position? If not, shift until you find one. Arms should be in a relaxed and comfortable position at your sides. Be aware of your breathing, but don't force it. Finish this sentence for yourself: "Right now, my body feels ——."

You're going progressively to relax the muscles in your body, tensing one muscle or muscle group, and then letting go of the tension. Try to do the relaxing or letting go in a passive way, without physical effort.

Start by making your feet as tense as possible. Then tighten them still further. And still further. And . . . let go.

Travel up the rest of your body, tightening the muscles in those three stages: Tight. Tighter. Tighter. And then letting it go. Do it in this order, after relaxing your feet:

> Lower legs and calves.
> Upper legs and thighs.
> Genitals.
> Abdomen.
> Chest.
> Shoulders.
> Upper arms.
> Lower Arms.
> Hands and fingers.
> Entire arm from fingers to shoulder.
> Neck.
> Face. (Scrunch it up in tight grimace.)
> Your entire body from head to toe.

Still lying down, take a deep breath and stretch. Again, finish the sentence "Right now my body feels———."

During this exercise you may have noticed that it was easier to tense some parts of your body than others, and this is normal. We do not have as much control over certain parts of our body. This might even indicate muscle constriction due to some emotional repression. It is worth being aware of, though you may find it easing through repetition of this exercise.

Keeping your eyes closed, you are going to go on to the autogenic phrases. These are simple phrases that you suggest to yourself. You may not actually feel the bodily changes that are suggested happening to you. Don't let this concern you. It would be unusual if you felt all the changes happening the first few times you tried it. Some of the changes may be so subtle you may never be fully aware of them. Don't expect anything in particular to happen, just allow whatever happens to happen, and be aware of it at the end of the series of phrases.

In your mind, say or feel the following:

My right arm is heavy.
My left arm is heavy.
My right leg is heavy.
My left leg is heavy.
My right arm is warm.
My left arm is warm.
My right leg is warm.
My left leg is warm.
My right arm is heavy and warm.
My left arm is heavy and warm.
My right leg is heavy and warm.
My left leg is heavy and warm
My heart is calm and relaxed.
My forehead is cool and calm.
My solar plexis is warm . . .
   it breathes me.

Be aware of what your body is feeling right now. Finish the sentence "Right now, my body feels ———."

You have to decide for yourself the pace at which you'll follow the relaxation instructions. You may choose to experiment with different speeds.

It may add to the experience if you take turns trying the exercise with your love-partner, each of you leading the other through the verbal instructions. Or you may choose to tape the instructions, playing them back as you listen and relax together. After a few times you should easily be able to commit them to memory.

The two parts of the exercise can be done separately. The progressive tensing and letting go of muscles is an excellent way to prepare yourself for a good night's sleep.

Trying the entire exercise prior to sexual relations has had a very positive effect for a number of couples.

Warm communication in a love relationship can enhance each individual's ability to relax, and, conversely, learning some relaxation skills can enhance the warm communication.

Making "love relaxation" a prelude to any important sharing you will do together can add to your awareness of the experience and of each other.

It's also another way of getting to know more about your body and how it reacts to various situations. Those situations that may cause it to tense up can begin to have less of an adverse effect if you can voluntarily learn to relax when you feel the tension starting.

It not only is healthier, and not only allows you to probe deeper emotional levels, but it feels good!

It's really a question of "Relax and enjoy it more."

MUTUAL MEDITATION

Half the day after our night
I hear you,
as though your voice
were but another level
of my consciousness.

                    Judy Altura

A flowing love relationship, with its suspension of sharp analytical focusing, and the absence of extraneous thought, is in itself an act of meditation. There is nothing mystical, anti-intellectual, or unrealistic about meditation. It is merely learning to more efficiently use your mind and body.

Meditation is the art of letting go. Letting go of conscious thought, letting go of self-imposed limitations, letting go of ego. In love relationships many people are afraid to let go, to give up the discipline. But Eastern meditative masters have known for centuries that giving up rigid willful control is the only way to achieve true control of mind and body. The scientists now call it passive volition, wanting to do something but allowing it to happen instead of striving, and not really caring if it doesn't happen.

The act of meditating has been as ill-used and misunderstood as the act of love. In recent years it has sometimes been compared to drug experiences, most often by drug users trying to rationalize their sad dependence. No comparison could be further off the mark. Taking drugs is giving up control, but only to replace it with an external control, allowing an external force to rule your mind and body. Meditation is enhancing awareness of your own capacities to rule your own organism.

We are used to dealing with the five senses, and they all have the capacity to be expanded in a hallucinatory manner. You may be able to imagine sights, smells, sounds, and other sensory experiences that aren't really there. Drugs conjure up or exaggerate such sensory impressions, which are really pseudoimpressions. Meditation does not. True meditation is letting go of sensory impressions, and going deep into your inner being. You may come out of a deep state of meditation with enhanced sensory perception, but this is really a happy fringe benefit. The main purpose is to be able to let go of that which is around you, so you can more clearly know yourself. On this adventure, sights, sounds, smells, taste, and touch can get in the way, but only if we focus on them. Meditation is the training of our focusing skills, so that we may choose what to focus on at any given time.

During sexual intercourse we may choose to focus on the tactile sensations, the sounds, the smells. Or we may choose to let go of all of these, and feel a deeper sense of oneness with our love-partner.

No one is suggesting that you give up sensory pleasures, in fact most of the exercises in this book are aimed at increasing sensory awareness. But you add another dimension to yourself to be able to go beyond the mere senses. And as you develop this ability, you find that you are not giving up or dulling your senses, but actually more fully sensitizing them by not making the effort to focus on them. And every sensory awareness exercise ever created can be a better experience for you if you can just let it happen, with passive volition, rather than try to make it happen.

Psychotherapist Carole Altman, a founder of the Biofeedback Institute and co-director of the Consultation Center for Women in New York, trains her therapy patients to meditate and highly recommends that couples meditate together. She says, "What happens is you get so quiet within yourself and so aware of your immediate surroundings that you're totally tuned into the person with you and his feelings. Whether it be joy or pleasure, pain or orgasm, whatever the feelings being felt by the person with you, you feel them, too. What you actually feel is no beginning or end of yourself. You become circular, one with the other. Your energies are merging, and actually being transmitted as messages to each other. So that it's almost a constant round robin, with your energies, feelings, sensitivities going into him and vice versa. Finally, it's just the two of you, in a floating spherical relationship of energy and love, joy and pleasure. Your empathy is increased so tremendously that you just understand each other. Not on an intellectual level, but on an emotional level."

This may sound rather complicated and difficult to you. It can be so if you make it so. Carole Altman was describing an ideal situation, and one that may come fairly far along in a mutual meditation effort. Though you can certainly start feeling some of these things almost immediately, it isn't the achieving of any final goal or merger with the universe that should motivate you but the actual experience of beginning to let go together. Ms. Altman goes on to say, "The mere experience of being quiet together, whether it be meditating by watching a candle, or by touching hands, or making eye contact, or meditating just lying in each other's arms, that experience alone brings two people closer together. Because it's just the two of them, with none of the outside stuff that we in our society are constantly using. There's no television on, there's no movies, there's no books. Just them. And they learn to enjoy each other."

Letting Go Together

Sit quietly, or lie down together, without making physical contact. Close your eyes and just let your mind go. To start, you might focus on just one thing, perhaps your breathing, or a part of your body. Choose the one thing to focus on, then use it to clear your mind of all other thoughts and impressions. It may take several days or weeks for you to develop the ability to give up conscious thought, but eventually you will be able to focus on the one point, and then you will be able to let go of that one focal point. You can enter deeper levels of consciousness only by emptying the conscious mind of thoughts. While you may choose to try this meditation exercise alone, you'll find that the support of another person adds to the experience, as does the sharing of it afterward.

The Candle

Light a candle between you. Have the room completely dark, except for this one candle. Stare at the candle. Feel your awareness increase as you begin to merge with the flame. As you begin to feel something happening, become aware of your love-partner, and what it feels like to be sharing this experience. After a ten- or fifteen-minute period of staring at the candle, take it in your hands. Be aware of the feel of it. And the smell of it. And whether it is making any sound. Feel the difference between the still hard parts and the soft melted wax. Give yourself a full sensory impression of the candle, and then hand it to your love-partner. When you have both taken this impression of the candle and feel you know it well, let go of the sensory awareness, put the candle back in the center, and stare at it a few minutes more. Discuss and share your experience.

Third Eye

Sit opposite one another. Imagine that there is a third eye located right in the middle of your love-partner's forehead, between the two other eyes. Spend at least ten minutes staring into this third eye. Don't be frightened if you begin to lose touch with reality, you are merely beginning to let go, and no harm can come to you since you are still in total control. This can be a powerful sharing experience.

A variation may be to have one partner at a time stare into the other's third eye, thus alternating roles.

Eye Contact

Just stare into each other's eyes. As simple as these instructions are, this can be a very fascinating experience, and different things may happen each time you do it.

Hand to Head

One partner places a hand, palm down, on top of the other's head. Let it stay there for a few minutes. Each of you be aware of the physical sensations. What a head feels like to a hand, and what a hand feels like to a head. Remove the hand, and try to remember and re-create those physical sensations. This is not an intellectual exercise; try to feel those actual sensations again. Then, switch roles.

This can be done with eyes open or closed, and you might try comparing the two. During the exercise both partners should move as little as possible. The hand is resting on the head, not caressing or massaging it.

Breathing Together

Breathing is a very important part of meditation. There are many good books on this subject, and an introductory yoga course can teach you to improve this vital function.

Don't, however, get hung up on breathing. Just by learning to become quiet you can be improving your breathing skills. Someone thirty-five years old who's been using poor breath-

ing habits for all those thirty-five years all of a sudden comes
to this realization and often panics, and begins a strenuous
program of trying to make up for lost time. The art of breathing is much more than a mechanical skill. It is best learned
at a leisurely pace, so that it can be integrated into our
every conscious moment.

Breathing together can be a way of heightening awareness, and sharing something in a new way.

Lie down side by side. Place your hand on each other's
stomach. Feel the stomach rise and fall with each of your
partner's breaths. Breathe naturally, without forcing it. See
if you can't start to breathe in unison.

After ten or fifteen minutes of this, without changing position, tell each other what you are feeling. Notice whether
you are breathing any differently than when you started the
exercise.

A similar exercise has one partner lying down, the other
resting his or her head on the first partner's stomach. Feel
the stomach rising, and start to blend in with it. Switch
places after about ten minutes.

You can also embrace, and feel the air coming from your
exhaled breaths. Try to remove the sensory impressions of
physical contact, and just focus on that air from your partner as it hits your face or neck. Another variation of this is
for one partner to rest his or her face on the other partner's
chest. This should be done so that one partner is breathing
out into the hair on top of the other's head while the other
partner is breathing into the chest. Focus on this awareness
and, when you feel ready, switch places.

Listening

Lie side by side. Have one of your ears pressed against
one of your partner's ears. Start to focus on what you
are hearing. You are listening to the sound of your partner.

Just flow with this for as long as you feel comfortable doing it.

You might try switching ears and positions. First your right ear might be listening to your partner's left ear, then your left ear might be against your partner's right ear. You also can lie stretched out in opposite directions, touching either left ears or right ears.

Bathtub Meditation

One partner sit between the other's legs, with the back of the head resting against the chest. Slowly slip down into the water, so that the back of the head goes under first, then try to have just the nose and mouth above water. Just become aware of what you are feeling. Your partner can add to the experience by slowly massaging your head. Then switch places.

You may, depending on your bathtub, both be able to lower your ears below the water simultaneously. You can have a lot of fun just trying to figure out how to do this.

Head to Head

Lie down with the tops of your heads meeting. Just let go and see what happens. No talking or other physical contact. What does this awareness of your partner's head feel like to you?

A variation on this would be to touch foreheads and meditate on this sensation, eventually flowing past the sensation itself.

Chanting

Chanting is one of the oldest forms of meditation. It can bring you a great sense of peace, of being alive, even of excitement.

The most universally chanted sound is OM. Ohh . . . mmmmmmm. Try chanting this together. Remove your restrictions and let your voice soar, but be aware of your partner's sound. It you find the experience worthwhile, it will get more so with practice. You might read up on some traditional chants, or invent your own. Any word or words can be chanted as long as they don't create an intellectual awareness that gets in the way of the experience. Constant repetition of the sounds can eliminate this. One group of businessmen got terribly high after a few minutes of chanting "money" as the word's meaning became meaningless.

You might try chanting each other's names.

Body Chanting

This involves one partner chanting OM, or some other simple chant, into the other's body, usually traveling up the back. If you want to learn the yogic chakras, or energy centers, you might read a good book on yoga, and then try chanting at these points. For a beginning experience, however, you can really chant anywhere on the body. Have your mouth an inch or two from your partner's body, and start chanting. Your partner will both hear and feel the sound. Do it for at least five minutes. Then switch roles, having your partner chant on your body.

If meditation turns you on, you may want to get more involved in it. There are a number of ways to do this, and it doesn't really matter how you get there. Yoga, transcen-

dental meditation, and alpha brain-wave biofeedback training are all proven techniques. But meditation is most of all
a personal experience, and individually, or as a couple, you
can find the best way by letting go and doing what feels
most natural and most comfortable. You can read about
the various methods, and then decide which ones to try.

Tantric sex is one form of meditation worth exploring.
There are several books on this subject. One way to start to
get into this is to pause together at times during intercourse,
just becoming quiet for a couple of minutes. This can
heighten the meditative aspects of a good sexual experience.
Try it.

Energy Flow

Many of the meditative methods deal with energy, with
the concept that we have energy centers in our bodies and
can learn to develop this energy and concentrate it on specific points in our body, and even transmit it to others.

Flap the fingers of both hands against your palms rapidly.
Keep it up for two minutes. Bring your fingertips on one
hand toward those on the other. As the fingertips approach,
be aware of when you can physically feel the presence of
the other hand. You may even feel a tingling flow of energy.
Try this with your partner, approaching each other's hands,
trying to feel the hands without touching them together.

Have your partner lie down, with eyes closed. Concentrate
on your hand, trying to imagine that all of your energy is
focused on that one hand. Slowly lower the hand toward
your partner's forehead. Touch the forehead and rest your
hand on it, palm down. Try to imagine that you are sending
energy into your partner. This can be a fascinating experience. You may even be able to become so attuned to the
energy flow that you can tell your partner what part of your
body his or her hand is approaching. This can be a healing
experience, and the laying on of hands has been an im-

portant means of caring for another person for thousands of years.

You might try doing the same lowering of your hand toward your partner's forehead without actually touching the forehead.

Still another variation on this is to lay one hand palm down on the forehead, and then place your other hand on top of it.

If you can't accept the concept of body energy as an actual force, just be aware of the thermal energy or body heat that is being transmitted.

Since meditation is a highly personal and individual experience, one important thing that mutual meditation accomplishes is to let you share something together while you are both becoming more aware of your own beings. It can help demonstrate that you don't have to give up self to share experiences and feelings with another person, to love another person.

It works toward a synergy of being. You are more aware of you when meditating alone. You are still aware of you when meditating with another person, but something new has been added. It doesn't detract from the self-awareness but transmutes it into something more, something fuller. You are aware of you, and you are simultaneously aware of this other person, and you are aware that this other person is aware of himself or herself, and is also aware of you. It becomes, as Carole Altman described it, "circular . . . a floating spherical relationship." And you become aware of a very basic truth: Love is meditation, meditation is love.

SAYING IT WITH POETRY

A man who's not unlike a poem,
possessive of a certain rhythm
a quiet style that's all his own
a warm and touching symbol
of my life.

Judy Altura

Real poetry consists of feelings honestly expressed, and all feelings can be transformed into poetry through honest expression. At one time poetry consisted mostly of fantasy and unrealistic expectations. You can examine much classical poetry and almost always see what kind of unrealistic and self-destructive expectations the poets had. Romantic love was most often depicted as a tale of unrequited desire for an unattainable object. Wallowing in tragedy and self-pity, these early poets were merely reacting to their conditioning, trying to create an illusion that could not be challenged by reality. It's the same motivation that puts most fish stories in the category of "the one that got away." Rather than focus on the reality of problems in a real relationship, it is much easier to imagine how much better things would have been if the one that got away hadn't gotten away. Of course, the one who got away never had to endure the real confrontations of a real relationship, and is thus always captured in that first sparkling excitement of first desire.

Today, poems are much more real, and more beautifully alive. Elaborate structure isn't necessary. Anything that flows out naturally can be good and right if it expresses what is really happening.

Poetry professors will probably gnash their teeth at this, but structure and technique often get in the way of honest expression. You can learn poetry technique and perhaps build better poems, but if you focus on the technique rather than your feelings you would probably be better off without the technique.

Many of the poets who are now striking the most responsive chords for the poetry-reading and poetry-buying public had little or no formal training.

The first task, then, is not to say, "But I don't know the first thing about writing poetry!" You and your feelings constitute that first thing.

Many therapists are starting to use poetry in their private and group sessions. They've discovered what poets have known for a long time: Repressed unconscious material can often flow forth as poetry.

Dr. Denis O'Donovan is a psychologist and poet and a former president of the Association for Humanistic Psychology. He conducts "Gestalt Poetry" workshops at his Maitreyan Foundation in Boca Raton, Florida, and at other centers around the country, and says, "One of the things that keeps happening is that when somebody who may seem to be quite inarticulate writes his or her first poem, it contains a lot of information to and for the lover. It contains a lot of beauty which I might feel about my loved one, but had never expressed. Poetry gives an opportunity to do that and sometimes makes a breakthrough."

Dr. O'Donovan tells of a man and a woman who made a breakthrough together: "I think of these two in a sort of rhythm. Here's a man who had always been considered crude and dull and without magnificence, and has all his life been chosen to play the role of the clod. And here's a woman sharp and brittle in body and words, always so very disciplined. In his case, the flow was so dammed up by all the people surrounding him casting him in this role, and his coming to live that way to fill other people's expectations, and eventually having the same expectations himself. The two of them shared a poetry experience, and each began to flow. She became less and less afraid of loosening her discipline. She had felt something terrible would happen if she let any undisciplined words come out of her, and that any words she uttered should be under her control at all times. He became less afraid that his poetry would be as clodlike as the rest of his life. Because this was a new experience for him, it sort of snuck up on him. No one had told him that he oughtn't to flow when he wrote poetry, so he did flow when he wrote poetry. They moved toward one another in a beautiful way."

As Denis O'Donovan puts it, "After I do something, it's hard for me to define myself ever again as a person who can't do that. And it spreads. If I define myself as incapable of doing X, and I do X, then it's a little harder for me to define myself as not being able to do Y, no matter what Y is."

There is nothing so precious as receiving a poem inspired by you, except perhaps writing a poem your love-partner has inspired.

By being aware of the poetry that is now in you, yes, this very moment, you can expand your awareness of life and love, and of yourself.

Like most good and real things, you cannot force it out, it must be given a breathing space, an opportunity to be allowed to happen. Dr. O'Donovan says, "Now I'm in the process of discovering some of the ground rules for poetry, but I wrote a thousand poems first."

Getting Started

When your senses are fully alive, and you are in touch with your feelings, all life can be a sensory poem. You and

your love-partner may go to a movie, and afterward you
might write something like:

> *I love you at the movies.*
> *The way your leg touched mine*
> *and our holding hands,*
> *and the tear in your eye*
> *at a screen love lost,*
> *and the sharing of popcorn,*
> *and the other things we*
> *do so well together.*
> *But especially, its*
> *not being over*
> *when the movie is.*

If you look at the above as a poetry critic, you can find
much fault in it. But look at it for a moment and imagine
that your love-partner has just handed it to you.

You are not writing poetry to create a literary sensation
but to let someone know how you feel at a certain moment,
and it can be a most mundane moment.

So, the way to start is merely to say some sentences to
yourself when you have a feeling that something is happening that is good. You don't have to share or even write down
the sentences. You might even try writing some of the
thoughts down, and sharing them at some later date with
your love-partner. Remember, he or she is not going to receive those words as a critic, and you don't even have to
call them "poetry" if you feel that definition will set up expectations.

You might perhaps go back over some of the answers to
some of the questions in preceding chapters. Look at the
ways you described your feelings, and chances are you'll find
at least one sentence that is poetry. That is all you need, for
no poem is ever incomplete if it describes a whole feeling.

Metaphors can also be useful as you first try to let poetry
happen. Just finishing the sentence "My love for you is like
———" can get you started. Try it.

Judy Altura is a mother of two, and most of the poems she writes are to and for her husband. Her poems, or parts of poems, head up these chapters. They were chosen to do so because they so vividly express real here-and-now feelings. She often uses metaphors, but in very simple and beautiful ways. For example, from an Altura poem:

> *My body feels disjointed.*
> *Puzzle pieces scattered*
> *by a careless child.*

And:

> *We are a gallery of light.*

Or:

> *Your laughter*
> *is a small café I never knew*
> *in Paris.*

One short sentence can say so much, and convey so well the depth of feeling, as in another line from Ms. Altura:

> *There is no carbon*
> *of the way you love.*

You can find so many examples of this art of brief but meaningful messages today. On posters. In sensitivity greeting cards. In the little books of poetry you can find at your bookstore or card shop. Even in some of the music of today.

Poetry written by others can also have meaning for you in your love relationship. To share together. For one love-partner to give to the other. Denis O'Donovan says, "The most beautiful gift one person can give to another is a gift that reflects a sensitive awareness of where the other person is at the moment. If I send someone that I love a poem written by Yevtushenko, the fact that I picked this particular poem from a whole variety of poems is a beautiful experience, if and when it hits the mark. It's an esthetic experience in itself to connect a piece of poetry written by somebody else with a person that you care very much about."

Share a Poem

Find a poem that has meaning for you, and share it with your love-partner. Discuss what feelings it touches off in you, and how you relate to these specific thoughts and words.

You might decide to share a number of poems back and forth, discussing and comparing feelings evoked by the poet's words.

What can you tell about the poet from the poem? Is this someone you could have an interesting conversation with? Someone who could be a friend? Someone who enjoys life?

Many poets are expressing their emotional views of everyday happenings. If we remove the poet from the literary pedestal, and see the poem as an expression of very human feelings, we can start to identify more closely with those feelings. And we can sometimes understand the poet's motivation in putting down the words. Judy Altura says she considers her poems, not only as something to share with her husband and friends, but also as a very selfish act. A release. A reinforcement of the feelings. "When I have a feeling that I like, a feeling of great love, I want to feel it twenty more minutes or twenty more times, so I write it down, and every time I read the poem or show it to Alan, I feel that feeling again. I don't want to forget any of the very deep feelings that I feel. So, like somebody will take a picture because they don't want to forget that beautiful ski slope they saw in Aspen, I write the poems, because I don't want to forget that feeling."

Ms. Altura also sees it as a way of checking out feelings. "Very often it's not so much that I can't say these things to

Alan, but I'm not sure about what I want to say, so then I write it down and it comes out as poetry. Then, if this is what I want to say, I show it to him. Very often if you see it in print, you know whether it's real, whether your feelings are honest."

And the putting down of the words on paper often allows us to crystallize our feelings. If we are angry or sad or confused or frustrated, we can put the feelings down and see them from some new perspectives. It can be a valuable prelude to the actual sharing of those feelings. Judy Altura describes a frustrating situation that led to a poem that can strike a responsive chord in many married couples:

"On a Saturday afternoon, maybe the kids will be napping and we'll have a few hours to ourselves. We'll have a glass of wine, we'll talk, we'll make love, and we'll really be totally into one another. I can't imagine two people loving each other any more, and then we go to a party, and after a couple of drinks sometimes I don't know him. We can pass and avoid each other's eyes. It's not the kind of thing where we look deep into each other's eyes questioningly, and say, 'Let's get out of here and discuss this.' It's nothing like two lovers who've had an argument. It's like strangers who don't even want to know each other."

And here's the poem this situation produced:

> *You have me tender wild.*
> *So close*
> *we nearly touch our blood*
> *in rhythm flowing,*
> *breathing time away*
> *in time together.*
>
> *And then at eight,*
> *a crowd is gathering for cocktails.*
> *You are turning on or tuning in*
> *or checking out*
> *another*
> *less familiar face,*

and I am chasing fantasies
into a double bourbon,
trying to recall
the reasons for my life,
or turning on or tuning in
or checking out. . . .

Can you remember how
we loved today,
and what it is
that makes us strangers
half a dozen hours later?

Can you share this poem with your love-partner, and the feelings it evokes? Has this kind of feeling ever happened to you? Do you see it as the removal of a mask or façade during intimacy, and the barrier being dropped again when other people are around? This kind of feeling is often felt by people who may share intimate feelings with each other in an encounter group, and then get together a week or two late to a poem can be a new way to facilitate communication from your love-partner when other people are present, or in specific kinds of circumstances? Discuss and share your feelings on this.

This kind of sharing of your own experiences as they relate to a poem can be a new way to facilitate communication and the opening-up process.

Give a Poem

Give your love-partner a poem, with a single sentence describing why you picked this particular poem out. It can be on a poster or greeting card, or copied from a book of poetry.

Write a Poem

Using a poem you identify with as a model, phrase the same thoughts in your own words. When you're ready, you can share this poem with your love-partner.

Back and Forth Poetry Reading

Each partner choose a poem. Read each poem out loud, with each partner reading alternate lines. Discuss and share your feelings. Which poem most accurately captures any feelings you've shared together in the past? Which did you most enjoy reading? You can then read the same poems again, this time with each partner reading a complete poem to the other. How was this experience different than the reading of alternate lines?

Write a Limerick

A good way to avoid taking yourselves too seriously as you explore poetry. You can start out simply by finishing the old standard:

> *Roses are red,*
> *Violets are blue.*

One group of couples came up with the following:

> *Roses are red,*
> *Violets are blue,*
> *I'm not getting younger,*
> *But I am getting you.*

Roses are red,
Violets are blue,
I'll go to bed
With no one but you.

Roses are red,
Violets are blue,
But diamonds are needed
For me to stay true.

Roses are red,
Violets are blue,
I'm color blind
So let's just screw.

No, they're not masterpieces, but they were a lot of fun to write and to share. See if you can't do better. You might try to twist around and improve other childhood rhymes. Work your way up to an original limerick. This can be a way to express tender feelings, as well as getting a laugh.

The Love-partner's Name Poem

You might try a more ambitious project, writing a poem with each line starting with the letters of your love-partner's name. This one was written to a woman named Stephanie, who lived in another town:

So many things come to mind
To say to you.
Each is important in its own way.
Put together, a symphony of feelings,
Happening even at this distance.
And most overwhelming of all:
Nicer ones are yet to come.
In our hearts, I think we know
Each of us helps the other grow.

Particularly when you are just starting to write poetry, this can be a way of personalizing your poem, and making it a very special gift for your love-partner.

Simple Name Rhyme

If you can find a word to rhyme with your love-partner's first name, here's another easy way to make a short rhyme a very personal thing. For instance:

> *I get so blue*
> *when away from Sue.*
>
> *There's a real beauty*
> *by the name of Judy.*

And no one is stopping you from taking poetic license if it's hard to find that rhyme:

> *I feel peanuty and pecany*
> *all because of Bonnie.*

Surely you can top these!

As Dr. Denis O'Donovan says, "Poetry is a thing for which many people seem to have some kind of inner yearning. One of the things about poetry is that it's so cheap and easy. I can be driving along in the car, and I make a poem, or a poem makes me. If I were into painting or writing music, or this, that, and the other thing, I would need equipment. One of the joys of poetry is that it's something that I believe potentially anyone can do anywhere."

It makes it all so much easier when you realize that all love feelings are a form of poetry, and when you're loving and being loved, you, too, are a poem.

Just by listing your sensations and feelings and appreciations, you could probably write a dozen poems a week, but quantity is not the point. When writing the poem becomes a chore, or a "should," it is no longer a creative act but a technical one. By all means try some poetry writing exercises, but once you get the hang of it, once you find you can do it, write when and what you feel when and how you feel it. You cannot ask your love-partner to write a poem for you, any more than you can ask, "Love me more than you're loving me." Do not give a poem merely to receive one in return. This is one love expression that almost has to be unilateral for it to be real. You may be inspired to write a poem to answer a poem you received, and a sort of rhythm can be built up this way. If that happens naturally, enjoy it, but you can't force it to happen. All you can do is try to set up an atmosphere where poetry becomes another way you both express yourselves.

It's very much related to meditation, in that it's a question of allowing it to happen rather than asking for it to happen. As Denis O'Donovan expresses it, "If I try to put down in words, if I try to keep something important in mind in order to put it down in words, something for my lover, that's a heavy weight. I've never said, 'Gee, I want to put something in words.' That's really a barrier between me and my own flow. Words have come to me, and I let them happen."

How you deliver your poem can have meaning, too. Said in a tender tone, "You're very special to me" can be a poem all by itself.

Poetry can indeed add a new dimension to your love relationship, and help you say things you haven't been able to say in other ways.

THE RELATIONSHIP CONTRACT

> As of this
> green-leaved
> mustard-bark day
> I resolve
> there will be more
> to seven years of marriage
> than an itch.
>
> Judy Altura

"Love, honor, and obey . . . till death do us part." This is an example of an unworkable contract. Few people entering into it give it much thought, or really check out how they feel about such an unrealistic commitment. When marriages work, it is *in spite* of this archaic contractual commitment rather than because of it. No one can honestly make a commitment to have a certain kind of feeling about someone else at any future date.

With so many couples entering into an agreement that they know, deep down, just isn't real, is it any wonder their mutual respect and communication begin to ebb almost immediately?

The marriage contract is thus a farce. It gets in the way of the real contract. For, married or single, in any relationship you have, there is a contract. It is probably an implicit contract, not explicit, and certainly not written down, or even negotiated out in the open. It is an understanding you each have, and includes your assumptions about each other and your expectations of each other.

The most destructive of all relationship conflicts are those that center around undeclared assumptions and expectations. A few months or a year after the relationship got started, you get a surprise from your love-partner, an assumption they had about you that just wasn't true. One that you didn't even know existed, usually with an expectation that you were never willing to meet, though your love-partner assumed you were willing to meet it even though you never heard it. A contract eliminates the sudden appearance of an unstated assumption or expectation.

The negotiating of a Relationship Contract is really the simple task of making the implicits explicit. It is defining the contract you now have, making it clear, checking out whether you are mutually agreeable to these terms, and re-negotiating where necessary. Few implicit contracts brought out in the open are totally agreeable to both parties.

Thus, the writing of a Relationship Contract is not adding additional structure to your relationship but a clarifying of the structure that already exists.

Edward L. Askren II, M.D., an Atlanta psychotherapist, has been a pioneer in working with couples and defining their relationships in terms of the contract. He says, "The explicit contract frees the relationship. When people know what the terms are, what the outer limits are, they paradoxically have a greater sense of freedom as to what they can do within that relationship. When the terms are not explicit, a sense of 'Am I doing it right?' exists on the part of both parties. Then you end up with what I call a manipulative contract, in which one person tries to coerce the other to do what he wants by adding an extraneous issue to the negotiation, like, 'If you don't do what I say, I'm going to do something bad to you,' 'If you do what I want, I'll do something good for you.' This last statement is like the giving of trading stamps, appearing to bribe someone to do what the salesman wants."

The first task, then, is to define your current implicit contract. Dr. Askren sees all relationships as being contracts that are either implicit or explicit. He says, "The problem arises in interpersonal relationships when one person's expectations implicitly do not meet those expectations of the other. A is disappointed by B, and a fight ensues in an attempt to coerce the other person to live up to the implicit contract. The contract has to be renegotiated. That's what a psychotherapist does in any kind of relationship, help the parties make explicit what the hidden terms were, so they can be agreed upon as terms, and then agree as to whether or not they will carry out those terms. That's how a contract is renegotiated. People have to know what it is that they have, and what it is that they don't have. What it is that they have that they are willing to part with, and what it is that they have that they are not willing to part with. Then, those things have to be communicated to the other person in specific terms. What I do in my practice is develop the understanding of a contract. We define it. We go over how to achieve one, and then we write out the contract that we want between the client and the therapist. Using that as a model, the couple then negotiates their own contract between each other, with the therapist as a guide, teaching them how to do it."

The first thing to learn is how to define your current contract. The best way to do this seems to be by answering the following questions:

1. What are my needs?
2. What are my expectations?
3. Which of these needs and expectations do I want fulfilled in a relationship?
4. Which of these needs and expectations do I think you will fulfill for me?
5. Which of these needs and expectations are you willing to fulfill for me?
6. Which of your needs and expectations am I willing to fulfill for you?

Items 4 and 5 are the critical areas, and can most easily lead to conflict. By clarifying for each other what you are willing to give to each other, you have an explicit contract.

The important thing in a growth-oriented relationship is to have a flexible and easily renegotiable contract. A major clause in your relationship contract can set up a means for you to communicate your feelings, and any changes in those feelings. It can be as simple as:

"Each Thursday we will meet after dinner to discuss our relationship and what's happening to us, and whether we like what's happening or not."

Though it doesn't have to be as structured as this, such a clear-cut avenue of communication removes a lot of the anxiety created by wondering "When can I talk to her about this?"

At Laurel Institute in Philadelphia, Dr. Bart Knapp and Marta Vago often have couples work out their contracts and renegotiate them in explicit terms. In one couples workshop, Debbie and David were a young couple trying to work out some of their conflicts. The Knapp–Vago therapist team helped them clarify the issues and come to a mutual agreement. Though actual, their situation is by no means typical.

David and Debbie

David and Debbie were living together. They had agreed to an open relationship, in which each partner had the freedom to date other people. David had assumed that Debbie would want to wait until their relationship was on firm ground before exercising her freedom. Debbie happened to meet Phil, liked him very much, and began to have an affair with him. While David intellectually granted Debbie her freedom, he did not like the way she seemed to focus more on Phil than on him. Because they were all in similar professions, he knew Phil, and at times all three of them were at the same gathering. David felt the main problem was that Debbie just couldn't seem to be involved in a casual relationship. Phil was a nice guy who wasn't in love with Debbie but was very attracted to her. Debbie claimed she enjoyed Phil's casual attitude but found herself becoming very excited whenever she thought about him, and resenting, for instance, his inability to plan ahead when they would get together. This put a burden on David, because on any given night Phil might call and Debbie might rush out to see him. David liked to make some plans ahead, and this angered and frustrated him. He felt Debbie was being manipulated by Phil, and that he was also being manipulated by Debbie and indirectly by Phil.

During the workshop, attended by four other couples, Debbie was able to tell David for the first time that she really didn't want to live with him any more, though she wanted to continue the relationship. David was able to tell Debbie how inconsiderate he thought she had been of his feelings. How unhappy he was that they didn't seem to be sharing anything any more. She told him that there were times when he physically turned her off, due to the weight he had recently been gaining.

They facilitated this sharing of information by each making three lists:

1. My needs in a relationship.
2. My expectations of you in our relationship.
3. The expectations you are not fulfilling for me.

They both said they wanted to resolve their conflicts and work toward a healthy but open relationship. Each decided what they were willing to give the other to help make it work and bring them back to some of the good feelings that had brought them together in the first place.

Their contract was a relatively simple one, with each

partner stating what he or she agreed to contribute. Word-for-word, it read:

David and Debbie's Contract

Agreed to by David:

1. I will stop telling you what you "should" do, and instead report my feelings about what you are doing, and any demands I want you to consider.
2. I will help maintain the apartment more, taking out the garbage and such.
3. I will move out within three months.
4. I will try to include you in any activities I know or think you will enjoy.
5. I will give you a massage anytime you ask for one, without demanding one in return.
6. I will start trimming down my weight.
7. I will give you at least one weekly unilateral report on my feelings about our relationship.
8. I will work toward giving you a sense of freedom in our relationship, and be as open and accepting of your friends as I can be.
9. I'll honestly try to keep our relationship in the here and now, leaving behind past experiences, past expectations, past hurts, and dealing with the entity of David and Debbie as if it were a totally new one, starting right now.

Agreed to by Debbie:

1. I will be more sensitive to your romantic nature.
2. I will not act in ways that make you think I am a callous person.
3. I will be more decisive in expressing my needs.
4. I will not embarrass you in my actions with other men.
5. I will make sure that you see when you have my attention.
6. I will go on a diet with you.

7. I will do yoga exercises with you.
8. I will go to the gym with you.
9. I will stop comparing my feelings about you to those I might have for someone else.
10. I will plan some special events for us.
11. I will share more of my decision-making process, so you can see how I consider you.
12. I will be more decisive about plans with you.
13. I will let you know how your moods affect my mood.
14. I will revive some plans we had together.

Agreed to by David and Debbie:

1. We will check out with each other our time schedules and major plans.
2. When either of us feels it is urgent that we discuss something, an emergency session will be scheduled within twenty-four hours.

This contract was written by David and Debbie a few days after the weekend workshop with Bart Knapp and Marta Vago. That workshop clarified the issues for them, showed them what their existent implicit contract looked like, and gave them a method of negotiating a new contract. The one they produced had some notable flaws in it, but could have worked if they had both been honestly committed to making it work. As it turned out, what the writing of the contract did more than anything was show David and Debbie that they just weren't going to be able to stay together in a love relationship. Debbie, particularly, with her strong infatuation for Phil, found she really wasn't willing to do all those things for David. She really hadn't checked out her feelings on each promise before making it. She was just listing a number of things she thought would make David happy rather than the things she was really willing to do. David's promise of a massage on demand could be considered an attempt at bribery, or what Dr. Askren called "bringing in an extraneous issue."

The contract David and Debbie wrote points out some of

the difficulties in writing an extended contract, one that involves other possible partners, before really defining the one-to-one contract, or without really being committed to the primary relationship. You'll find much more on opening up a contract to other partners in the panel discussion on "Opening Up the Man–Woman Relationship" at the end of this volume.

The first rule of any Relationship Contract is that you both have to agree openly to all the provisions, with no coercion or manipulation. You have to check out whether you are both really willing and able to meet all the terms of the contract. Saying something just because you know your love-partner wants to hear it isn't going to work.

You'll find no model of a good or perfect contract included in this chapter. There's no such thing. A good contract for you is one that honestly reflects the essence of your relationship and what you both want out of it.

Marta Vago sees a relationship contract as three contracts in one: the Relationship Contract; the Functional Contract; the Situational Contract. She says, "By the Relationship Contract we mean the 'what' of the relationship. It defines such things as the time and duration and the finality of the relationship. The 'until' or 'as long as' aspects of the relationship. For instance, the Relationship Contract Bart and I have is that we are not married, we are together by choice, and will be together as long as both of us wish to be together."

So, in a sense, this Relationship Contract is seen by Ms. Vago and Dr. Knapp as the equivalent of the formal marriage contract. Dr. Knapp says, in fact, that he sees it as the "till death do us part . . ." but hopefully with a much more realistic statement of commitment.

Ms. Vago sees the Relationship Contract as the umbrella under which the other two come, and an overview of the love partnership. She describes the Functional Contract as "part of the 'how' of a relationship. How you are going to stay together. How you are going to share and express feelings to one another. How are you going to fight, and how you are going to get back together. Issues of privacy and mutual respect. It's the affective component of the relationship, the emotional maintenance part of a contract."

Dr. Knapp sees it as related to the "love, honor, and obey . . ." statement in the marriage contract, dealing with individual integrity and autonomy.

As Marta Vago describes the Situational Contract, "It has to do with such things as task allocation. It's more evanescent. Like: 'You can take out the garbage today, and I can take it out tomorrow, and next week we might decide that nobody's going to take out the garbage.'"

Bart Knapp calls Situational Contracts those that are tailored to particular situations, and adds, "They come and go, they're maintained only as long as they're useful, as long as they're effective, and then they're modified."

While you may not care to divide your contract into its relationship, functional, and situational components, it can be useful at least to know the difference. Marta Vago notes that when you start changing the Functional Contract, or the over-all Relationship Contract, you are really changing the essence of your relationship, while the Situational Contract covers things that really aren't as essential. She also says, "Separating these three things might be a very nice way of looking at your relationship as if it were someone else's, and getting a perspective on your own relationship that can be shared with your partner, so that you're not assuming one thing, while the other person is assuming something else. It also gives you a way of checking, maybe six months from now, 'Are we still at the same point, or have we modified either our Situational or our Functional Contracts, or the over-all Relationship Contract?' I think it's a nice, neat way of keeping tabs on where you are with one another."

No matter what kind of contract you decide to negotiate, it will give you a good way to organize your feelings about the relationship, help you design some basic guidelines, and provide a way to change and modify the relationship, as you both feel a need to do so.

The prerequisite is, of course, a fully mutual agreement to define your current contract and work on an explicit version. The initial negotiation sessions can easily start a sharing and communication process that can become a permanent part of the final contract. You can find out a lot about each other just from the way you each negotiate.

For a successful and realistic contract, you have to avoid trying to second-guess the future. So, no long-term promises of devotion. Note that this is what you want and are willing to give today, but plan specific times to check out and re-negotiate.

Remember, you set the tone for your Relationship Contract. Some critics of a contract concept say it's too constrictive, kills spontaneity, takes the fun and excitement out of a relationship. Nonsense! It can be as loving and fun-filled a process as you want it to be, and as exciting. You use the negotiating periods to keep the growing aspects of what you have together on the path you both decide is most desirable. You are charting your own waters, and your latitude and longitude are beyond the horizon.

A Relationship Contract is not a series of promises but an affirmation of what is happening now, and a commitment to keep it happening as long as you both want it to.

One way you might decide on what to include in yours is to go over the chapters in this book and decide which principles you'd both like to see incorporated into your relationship. In the situational context, you might have a clause reading:

"We will try to share one growth exercise together each week."

or

"Every night we will try one nonverbal experience."

You can always make it more specific, to cover any reluctance you feel either partner might have. For instance:

"We will practice at least one awareness/trust/communication exercise each week, no matter how well our relationship is going, and no matter how unnecessary we may think it is."

The functional, or affective, component could include a clause like:

"I will respect your privacy in regard to your first marriage, and not ask you to share anything that happened then, unless you volunteer the information."

This can then become almost an implicit factor, once you've negotiated and agreed to include it. It can also be the most difficult kind of a thing to negotiate, and may involve a lot of sharing of feelings to reach agreement.

You may decide to include a statement that covers the over-all relationship, such as:

"We love each other, and as long as that continues we will work hard at trying to understand each other and communicating our honest feelings when we first feel them."

Whether your Relationship Contract covers one page or twenty, is very general, very specific, or both, it is uniquely yours. Cherish it as a process rather than a document, as a beginning dialogue rather than any final decision on your status.

Look at it as focusing on life rather than the relationship. The modifications or changes in the relationship will reflect what is happening in your life. Don't end up changing your life to fit the relationship. That's not a contract, it's a cage. And like "love, honor, and obey . . . till death do us part," you'll more than likely end up resenting each other instead of growing together.

You don't need a contract to communicate with your love-partner. But it can be a highly dependable vehicle to get you there with a minimum of fuss and stress, and a maximum of sharing. The more of yourself you each put into the effort, the more real and meaningful it can be.

Try to share, not only your feelings about the issues and the things you decide to include in your Relationship Contract, but your feelings about the contract itself. When one partner starts to feel trapped or resentful, it may be a strong sign that some major modifications are needed. Be able to finish the sentence "Our contract is a —— one, and makes me feel ——."

Remember, most of all, that this is a Relationship Contract, not a business agreement. Try to avoid a lot of "shoulds" and value judgments. It can be an accurate barometer of what's happening in your relationship, as well as a means for making new and good things happen. Invested with feeling and energy, it can't help but enhance, expand, and clarify your relationship.

Is a Good-bye Clause Necessary?

A good Relationship Contract can keep you informed as to when a love-partnership may be ending, eliminate a lot of the pain and bitterness associated with most such endings, and allow the dissolving of the partnership to become as much a learning experience as the beginning was. A well-written contract provides all the necessary tools, without your having to spell out when and how you are going to end it all.

A lot of what determines how easy or how difficult it is for you to say good-bye to a love-partner has to do with your early conditioning, and whether you've responded to such phrases as:

"Happily ever after."
"Till death do us part."
"A lasting relationship."
"A lifetime together."
"End up together."
"Mine forevermore."

If these words have struck a responsive chord, then you probably can't help considering the end of a relationship as a personal failure, your failure to live up to expectations. The fact is that most relationships do end, and quite often those that end are much less a failure than those that persist against all reality and good sense.

In an honest sharing relationship, good-byes are rarely tragic, and the end of love can usually provide insights for the future, while the parting can be amiable and doesn't have to be a total and final separation. The bitter endings usually occur because feelings have not been shared until the final painful moments, as they finally pass the bursting point. Expectations have not been declared, and thus failure to meet those expectations has produced more unnecessary pain. A relationship never ends overnight, and by sharing what's happening when it actually happens, you can avoid sudden surprises. This can lead either to ending a relationship sooner, and on a much more friendly basis, or solving problems by catching them early, when the relationship seems worth the mutual effort.

Think back to all the relationships you've had, and see if you can't focus on a moment when more communication would have lessened the pain, quickened the end, or eliminated the conflict before it reached the point of no return.

It can also be useful to examine other relationships around you, and how they ended.

A Possible Ideal Good-bye

In the best of all possible worlds, the splits would all be friendly ones. In any relationship involving deep feelings, you each have been meeting some of the other partner's needs. If you grow apart, or eventually come to the realization that this partner cannot meet enough of your needs, is there any real reason to end it completely? Can't you still fulfill some of each other's needs? In a break-up consisting of unshared feelings, bad communication, and unexpressed sadness and anger, this is probably impossible. But if you've shared the process of growing apart, there is no reason to completely destroy everything you've had together. Even more radical a proposal: Is there any reason, if you've had a good sexual relationship and have a good friendship, why you can't continue to meet each other's sexual needs? And even if you each enter into other primary relationships, can't you still share some of this sexual feeling and any other needs you may meet for each other? In a spirit of honest sharing, how can your new partner possibly resent someone he or she has already replaced as a primary partner? If there is a need for external relationships, this kind would be so much less threatening than one that could develop further. You've already charted the outer boundaries with a former love-partner, and have already made your decision. Of course, to an insecure new love-partner this wouldn't make any sense at all, and would be extremely frightening.

With the feeling that a love-partner is an object to be possessed, one can't help but feel a deep sense of loss when the relationship ends. When you focus all the responsibility for happiness on the relationship rather than each partner taking personal responsibility, then all seems miserable and empty when it's over. In fact, the burden of such expectations can't help but hasten the end of a relationship.

There is no need to bemoan the passing of love, because real love doesn't pass. It is self-nurturing, never-ending, always growing. You can lament the passing of the good feeling when a relationship is over, but realize that what you had together would still be there if it was still worth having.

Love is a "now" experience. Much of it has to come from within. You may feel sorry for yourself, lonely, and unappreciated. The sure cure, of course, is to find another love-partner. The lingering feelings of sadness, usually described as "carrying a torch," are due more to the lack of someone in your life here and now than to the loss of something precious.

Time is relative. If your relationship was a beautiful one, and lasted only three months, you can try to see it as a "three-month relationship" rather than feel bad because it didn't last longer. In those three months you may have shared more than many people share in a lifetime together. Dwelling on thoughts of rejection, building the end of a relationship into something lost that can never be replaced is silly and self-destructive. And it can negate whatever good and pleasurable experiences the two of you had together. You can come out of every relationship ahead, either in expanded awareness of your own feelings or insight into someone else's.

There are those who will tell you that love without pain isn't possible. Raised in an atmosphere of romantic fiction, it is hard not to overdramatize the good-bye. No one is suggesting you repress any painful feelings that actually exist, but you can more closely examine those feelings and determine how many have to do with reality and how many with fantasy projections.

The rigid lack of alternatives lessens the possibility of a painless ending. If the only choice you have is to stay together forever, fulfilling all of each other's needs, or to totally sever all contact, complete fulfillment or complete failure, then you have eliminated a lot of realistic alternatives.

Lack of a strong self-image brings forth the proposition: "All the good things in my life are due to this relationship, all the joy comes from what we have together, and without this, I would be a terribly sad and lonely person."

In a synergistic relationship, with two whole persons bringing their strength, vitality, and individuality together, the end of the relationship does not mean the end of this strength, vitality, and individuality. One facet of life ends, not life itself.

It is the person who can say, "I am happy in this relationship, but when it ends I will still be me and still find joy in life," who has the best chance to really grow in a relationship, and not be scarred if and when it ends.

Mary

Mary seemed unable to enter into any satisfactory relationships. She had had her first sexual fulfillment with Harold, whom she had married. He was killed in an automobile crash

two years later. Emotionally, Mary felt she would be betray-
ing Harold's memory by enjoying any other man. Sexually,
she felt she would never be able to duplicate or improve on
what she and Harold had shared. She was unhappy and depressed and very confused and lonely. A therapist suggested
to Mary that she might consider the possibility that, if she
really had loved Harold, then that capacity to love and be
loved that he brought out in her should still be there, and
would be, in fact, an everlasting memorial to the love they
had shared. That if she did love another man it was an affirmation of what she and Harold had known together rather
than a betrayal. Mary was able to take comfort in this advice, and soon began a good relationship with a warm and
loving man.

It's a matter of saying:
"If loving you was a growing experience, then I should
eventually be able to love even more, not in spite of what we
had together, but because of what we had together."
This can be true for you no matter how or why the relationship ended.
But what can you do to minimize the pain? It is easy to
talk about why it shouldn't hurt, but it so often does. It's not
even so much a question of pain-killing, but one of putting
things in proper perspective. Was your relationship a worthwhile one? Did it depend on some fantasy goal of permanence for all the good feelings that you had from it? So that,
when that chance of permanence was ended, all that was
worthwhile ended?
Is it rejection that hurts? One way to check this out is to
imagine that your love-partner died instead of it ending any
other way. Would this make a difference?
What if all the blame could be taken off your shoulders?
If a psychiatrist were to certify that your love-partner was
insane, and the whole world made aware that ending a
relationship with you is a completely irrational act? The
point is, are you mourning the public knowledge that one

person decided you couldn't meet all of his or her needs, or are you really missing the good things you had? Or, are you missing the good things you thought you still had coming?

What if you had documented evidence, for example in a relationship that lasted three months, that there were exactly three months of good feelings in this relationship? That's all there was for the two of you together, though you could each go on and find joy and fulfillment with other partners. What if you had had this information at the beginning? If there were a certifying board that informed you there would be three months of good times and loving feelings with this particular partner, and that's all, would you have gone ahead with it?

To take our fantasy exploration a bit further, what if you had been told that this partner had only three months to live?

This is a case of using fantasy constructively to examine what, if any, part fantasy expectations play in your feelings about a particular love relationship coming to an end.

There is an old Russian fable that says when two people fall in love they exchange souls. If they should amiably decide to end their relationship, they give these borrowed souls back to one another. But if the ending is a bitter one, the souls are not returned, and each lover must wander and struggle through life trying to recapture this lost soul. Does this fable have any meaning for you?

While there really is no such thing as unrequited love, there certainly is unrequited infatuation, unrequited respect, unrequited lust. These can be very deep feelings, and all have been mistaken for love. We often mistake loneliness and disillusionment for the loss of nonexistent love. There is also, of course, short-term love, consisting of very real feelings that may not be there as both partners grow in different directions. There is also the increased information we receive as we get to know someone very well. If initial feelings are good, we tend to ignore even highly specific information that tells us this is not a good love-partner for our needs.

It doesn't really matter if the love is real or not; at the end of the relationship it is no longer real. The romantically appealing picture of the man or woman withering away because of a great love lost is the great adult fairy tale.

It quite often happens that one partner wants to end the relationship and another doesn't. If you find it appealing to consider yourself a tragic figure, then living this myth may be a worthwhile effort. This situation is almost always a case of lack of communication. One love-partner has a fantasy about how much the other one cares, and an assumption as to the permanence of this caring. When confronted by the truth, disbelief is the first reaction. "How can he say he doesn't love me, when I know better?" Then comes self-blame: "What did I do wrong?"

It isn't the loss of something you have, but the loss of something you thought you were going to have. If your love-partner says, "I don't love you any more," that's the reality of the situation.

This doesn't mean it doesn't hurt, particularly if it's new news.

Sometimes the only honest sharing done throughout an entire love relationship is the saying of "Good-bye."

Modern psychologists don't say "Feeling hurt is silly, so stop it!" If you feel hurt, you feel hurt, and the healthiest thing to do is to focus on that hurt, really feeling it and experiencing it, and letting it out. It's all well and good intellectually to say to yourself that there's no reason to be sad or angry, but if you are, you are.

But at the same time you are feeling the hurt, you can examine the why of it, and the realization of how much of it was due to unfulfilled and possible unstated expectations.

There's no need for a good-bye clause in a good Relationship Contract, because open communication eliminates the surprise ending, and can often facilitate a most pleasant good-bye.

Looking at love as a learning experience can help you look at the end of a relationship as graduation, not flunking out.

THE LOVE JOURNAL

And now
a thousand Sundays later
you ask for an appraisal
of this show you're running.
Follows my review:
I think we're really quite a hit.
No, I'm never sorry.
Not only do I love you still,
but more.

                           Judy Altura

Documenting your love relationship as you live it can be a highly valuable experience in many ways. It can provide a means for checking out feelings, keeping track of the growth of the individuals and the couple, showing you what direction that growth is taking, and facilitating still another level of sharing.

There are several kinds of Love Journals, and both partners can discuss and share their feelings as to which type seems most desirable at this point in the relationship.

In Chapter Three we considered the keeping of a daily journal of feelings as a way to increase self-awareness. This format could easily be adapted to include both individuals in a love relationship.

A Short Entry Journal

You could start out simply by each writing one or two sentences about your feelings toward each other. Try this daily for a week or so, and see whether it provides you with any insights. One day's entry might read:

ALLAN: "I felt good about the way Alice looked tonight, and the looks of envy I got from other men at the party. I felt proud and pleased that she was there with me, and I must admit it was somewhat of a possessive feeling on my part."

ALICE: "Allan was so attentive tonight, I was feeling warm and wanted. I knew we would make love when we came home and that it would be good, and the looking forward to it was almost as good as the sex itself, but not really."

At the beginning, if you're feeling hesitant about the sharing part, you might just write your feelings down individually, and share them at some later date. You could, in fact, find out a lot about each other in the simple act of deciding whether you want to share these entries. One way to help yourself decide is to ask the question "What's the worst thing that will happen if my love-partner sees this entry and knows my feelings about this?"

What you'll usually find is that our conditioning has given us a habit of secrecy, even when totally unnecessary. It's almost like the fanatical TOP SECRET classifying the government has encouraged, even on such mundane items as paper-clip requisition forms. There are, naturally, some things you might not feel too comfortable immediately sharing with your love-partner. They may need further clarification in your own mind, and more discussion together than would be provided by merely writing them down in your journal entries. But you'll also probably find a lot of items that could have a positive and reinforcing effect on your relationship via the act of sharing them, with no chance of any negative effect.

Your Journal Format

Whatever kind of a Love Journal you decide on, it will be best contained in a loose-leaf format. This also will give you an opportunity to keep your own entries private until you feel ready to share them.

As you get into the pleasant habit of keeping a journal, you may want to expand it in many ways. You could subdivide it into separate sections. One section might include pictures. You could paste in articles or quotes that seem significant. It can become a sort of workbook on your growth process.

Each time you do an exercise together, such as those in this book, you might write down your answers or feelings, and thus have a permanent record charting your progress.

As you go along, you might want to enlarge the format and put more of your feelings down. Certainly, as you become more comfortable with the idea of a Love Journal, you'll find it easier and more rewarding to open up.

One interesting possibility is the sharing of your individual feelings about something that you did together.

ALLAN: "I really didn't want to go on the picnic, but just didn't have the nerve to tell Alice. Once I got there, I began to enjoy it, and was really sorry that it started raining."

ALICE: "I know Allan hated going to the picnic, and I couldn't enjoy it, knowing I had forced him to go. I suppose the rain was the best thing that could have happened, though I was ready to smack him if he had said anything like 'I told you so.'"

When Allan and Alice shared the above entries, they felt much closer together. Here was a situation with several unknown feelings that came out through simple sharing. Allan ordinarily wouldn't have told Alice that he began to regret the fuss he made about going and was actually starting to enjoy himself when it began to rain. When he saw how pleased Alice was to hear this, and how affectionately she began to treat him after seeing his entry, he learned a good lesson in the value of sharing even seemingly unimportant thoughts and feelings. Alice was feeling guilty and resentful, as she had no way of knowing that Allan had changed his original opposition to the picnic. His entry clarified the situation, and she was able to share her original anger feelings with him in a context of loving revelation. Both learned a lot about each other and, needless to say, decided to go on another picnic at the first opportunity.

Sex Feelings

A Love Journal can provide you with a good way to tell each other what is happening in your sexual feelings. One couple even decided to rate each time they had sexual relations, using the little stars pasted on school papers by teachers. Gold stars were for a spectacular transcending sexual experience. Silver stars were an indication of a very good and satisfying episode. Red stars were for a pleasant and comforting experience. Blue stars were for an unsatisfying sexual act. Green stars were for something wrong that couldn't quite be defined or pinpointed.

You might decide to use just gold, silver, and red stars. Anytime no stars are rewarded by either partner, you can discuss it further.

This, of course, takes a greater commitment to sharing and honesty than sharing feelings about everyday activities, like dinner or a movie you saw. It can be a way to open up an area you may find difficult to share. Whenever you each rate a particular sexual episode differently, you've brought out new material to work on. Be aware and able to share whether a particular rating upsets you, or makes you feel inadequate or rejected.

The Love Check-up

Your journal can help you examine specific growth trends. You might give each other ratings in nonsexual areas, too. This could be done on a weekly basis. You can catalogue:

An act of tenderness toward your love-partner that wasn't reciprocated.
An act of tenderness from your love-partner.
Something that made you angry.
Something that made you happy.
Something that frightened you.
Something that made you sad.
Something your love-partner misunderstood.
An act of thoughtlessness on the part of your love-partner.
Something that bored you.
Something that excited you.
A time your love-partner tried to make a value judgment, or tell you something you "should" do.

All of these should be confined to your love relationship, and something actually done or not done by your love-partner. You may be surprised how unaware you both are about the emotional affects of the things you do and don't do to and for your love-partner. Rather than just listing these items, you could write out your feelings about each.

Remember, your list should be as individualized as possible, and doesn't have to include any of the above items.

There are many other categories to choose from:

An unfulfilled expectation.
A touch you appreciated.

A sharing experience.
A facial expression you particularly remember.
A compliment that pleased you.
A dream you had about your love-partner.
Something you would have shared, but you didn't think it was important enough.
Something you would have asked your partner to share, but it didn't seem important enough.

As in all sharing, the Love Journal has to be a mutual effort, and one that you both agree is worthwhile. One partner should not be coerced into making entries. The loose-leaf format allows you to space your entries anyway you'd like. You might decide to make an entry only when you really have a strong urge to do so, and several days may go by between entries.

As your journal grows, it becomes something else to share. You can check out how your feelings have changed, and may find things that were hard to share at first come out much more easily now.

Honesty is relative, as is communication. You may have an honest relationship now, and one in which you communicate. Each of these factors can be enhanced, and practice is the only way to accomplish this. Your Love Journal gives you an easy way to practice. It is a continuing format for individual expression and mutual communication. It can be as creative an effort as you wish to make it. As in all new efforts, take it gradually at the beginning, and don't set such ambitious goals for yourself that you'll soon tire of the project.

It can be a multimedia experience, and a sort of scrapbook of your relationship, including pictures, poems, souvenirs, clippings, letters. But most of all, your feelings about each other.

It can be an exciting joint project, and provide you with many hours of new things to share, and many fond memories. You can go back over previous entries together, and share your feelings about those, even writing comments on the margins of the older entries. You may even decide to tear up and remove old entries when the feelings expressed no longer seem valid or completely honest.

There are no rules or regulations, and the only structure is the basic idea of a journal format. It can be as loose as you want it to be, as little or as much a part of your sharing activities as seems necessary and desirable, and any of these factors can change whenever you want them to.

Again, whatever you do should be done with mutual agreement, and care and concern on the part of each partner.

The Love Journal becomes a microcosm of your relationship, and gives you a chance to hold the relationship in your hand and examine it.

It can seem to have a life of its own, but in reality it has only the life you each give it, and expresses only the love you actually have for each other.

LOVE GAMES

Catch me if you can.
Tomorrow's game rehearsed
the night before.
                    Judy Altura

The word GAME has come into disrepute when used to describe some of the things that happen between people. "Playing games with each other" is one of the things we are told to avoid.

But we all play games of one kind or another. The man–woman relationship is taught to most of us as a game, with elaborate rules and penalties.

The Relationship Game

Men and women are given the rules, and their individual role-goals at an early age. For most women, the role-goal is to reach "Home and Family." Men are taught to stack up as many sexual conquests as possible on the way to "Bedroom," without being trapped into "Home and Family," and passing "Go" as many times as possible, collecting the $200 each time, and hopefully avoiding having to go to "Jail." If the man doesn't get to "Bedroom" before being tricked into "Home and Family" he may lose some of his "Masculinity" cards. The woman collects only $100 when she passes "Go," can lose many points if she's maneuvered into "Bedroom," and the whole game if she actually tries to end up there.

Since our society is just one big playing board, and it's pretty hard to leave the game, unless we want to become recluses and hermits, one way to get out of the role-dictating aspects of the Relationship Game is to replace it with a more acceptable game. If we play games to deceive and manipulate each other, why can't we learn new ones that will help us understand one another?

The most obvious objection to bringing a game format into the love relationship is that it's contrived and artificial, and takes the romance out of it. But, realistically speaking, isn't the love relationship itself already overly contrived and artificially structured? While each new lover likes to think he or she has created something beautifully original, they are usually falling into age-old patterns, rituals, habits, and roles.

While we now unconsciously may play games with one another, setting up many destructive situations, we can actually learn to use the art of game-playing to gain valuable insights.

One dictionary describes a game as a competitive activity, involving skill, chance, or endurance. Other definitions include: amusement, sport, trick, or strategy. Many of these are present in most relationships. How about yours? Let's start using them to advantage. Let's not say that games are bad and we should eliminate every one of them, but admit instead that most of us enjoy playing games. They can thus be made part of our educational process.

This is not to say we should keep the dishonest and manipulative games we play, but merely removing them isn't the whole answer. Games fulfill a strong human need. We all need to play. We all need to be competitive. We have distorted these needs and made them more harmful than useful in our adult lives. We have to revert to the childhood concept of a game as fun, and competition as fun.

The competition and game-playing itself isn't the harmful factor in relationships. It's the games we don't acknowledge, and the competition that is misdirected that gets in the way of honest sharing. If we mutually decide the games we're going to play, and have fun playing them, and check out our feelings while playing them, then they become constructive tools rather than destructive handicaps.

Even if you want to eliminate all game-playing, it may be best to do it gradually, first replacing the bad games with good games.

The games included here fulfill several functions. Some are like children's games, some are like gambling games, some are like sports, some are word games, some are physical movement and contact games. All are designed to be entertaining, amusing, and provide you with some insights and information about each other.

The Prizes

You may find it easier to play the games if there are prizes awarded, though eventually you'll probably find that the fun of playing is better than the winning. These prizes can be anything you want them to be, but should probably not be money or anything that costs very much. The loser may merely do something nice for the winner. A back rub or massage, perhaps. Or making dinner. Or the loser may have to be the aggressor the next time you have intercourse, with the winner just responding, relaxing, and enjoying.

The Ask Me Game

Ask your love-partner to do something for you. Then, your love-partner asks you to do something. The object of this game is to try to get your love-partner to do as many things for you as possible, without hitting something he or she has an honest and strong objection to doing. It might go like this:

A: Run your fingers through my hair.
B: Get me a cookie.
A: Tickle my ear.
B: Rub my shoulder.
A: Bark like a dog.
B: That's silly, I don't want to do it.

And so, A would lose that round.

The Ten Parts Game

There are ten parts of the human body that contain just three letters. Name them. Slang terms and contractions such as "lid" from "eyelid" don't count. Each partner writes down the parts that come to mind. The answers are at the end of this chapter. The winner is the one with the most correct parts.

The Kissing Game

The first partner has to start with the letter "A" and kiss a part of the second partner's anatomy starting with that letter. Anything goes here, including slang terms. The second partner then kisses a "B" part of the first partner's anatomy. You may have some trouble when you get near the end of the alphabet, but by then you probably won't care. As in all really good games, the loser has as much fun as the winner.

Switch Names Game

Switch names with each other for a specified period, perhaps twenty-four hours. Address each other by your new names. The first partner to address the other by the old name loses.

The First-name Game

Make a sentence that makes sense using the letters of your love-partner's name as the first letters of each word in the sentence. JERRY could be "Just everyone's rollicking raving yokel." Keep on forming new sentences until one partner runs out of words or ideas.

Movement Director Game

Pick a goal to achieve physically. For instance, sitting in a chair or getting to the other side of the room. Each partner guess how many movements it would take to reach that goal from your preselected starting point. You might, for example, select reaching the front door as your goal. You might say it would take eighteen movements to get there, and your partner might say it will take twelve. If you say eighteen, then your object is to direct your partner in movements that will reach the door as close to your guess of eighteen movements as possible. You can easily make up extra movements to reach your goal, but your partner can gain advantage by minimizing the size of the movements. Direct each step of the movement. Both start from the same point.

The value of this game goes beyond any points scored. Try to feel what it is like to direct another person's movements, and to be directed in turn. Do you like control? Or being controlled?

You can make this less structured and possibly more fun by simply practicing directing each other in movements. You could even try it to music, with such directions as:

Bounce three times.
Twirl and spin.
Move your hands.

A variation on this would be for one partner to make random movements while the other has to mirror or duplicate those movements as accurately as possible. This also can be done with or without music. Moving together can bring you new information about each other and a new fun experience to share.

The Betting Game

Some couples have found a good way to enjoy their competitive spirit by making silly little bets on almost anything that comes to mind. On whose mother will call first. On how many blue cars you will pass within the next hour. On who will be served first at a restaurant. On who will lose five pounds first. On who will get a letter from a friend first.

Just use your imagination. But remember to keep it in the context of playful fun, and not to work off anger or aggression.

Love Olympics

This can be a series of events, perhaps each taking a week. It can add a dash of excitement to your lives, and a lot of laughs if you don't take it too seriously. You can decide how many events there will be, and the prizes. It might be fun to have a trophy made for the winner, announcing the winner of this year's Love Olympics.

Some suggested competitive events:

Plant-growing. Buy equal small plants, and the winner is the partner whose plant grows most during the specified period.

Silliness. Winner is partner who can come up with the silliest thing, and actually do it.

Arousal. Winner is partner who can sexually arouse the other without touching.

Adjectives. The winner is the partner who can, without a

dictionary, come up with the most adjectives describing good qualities in the other partner.

Laughing. The winner is the first partner who can make the other laugh.

Learning. The winner is the partner who can learn the most new things. These are things, not facts. For instance, how to knit, or type, or do karate.

Places. The winner is the partner who can pick the most new places to go.

Friends. The winner is the partner who can meet the most new people.

Presents. The winner is the partner coming up with the most imaginative present to give to the other partner.

Whipped cream. Cover each other's body with whipped cream from aerosol can. Winner is first partner to run out of whipped cream.

Bathtub. Winner is partner coming up with most imaginative new thing to do while taking a bath together.

Minute Game

Take turns caressing each other for a minute, using kitchen timer. Winner is partner coming closest to a minute without timer going off.

Dialogue Description Game

The comedy group known as The Committee came up with an interesting premise that could be fun and informative to try as an interpersonal game. A man and woman talk to each other, but instead of using words they use a descriptive dialogue telling what kind of words they would have used.

For instance, Harvey and Ellen might have the following bedroom dialogue:

HARVEY: "Strong indication of desire for affection."
ELLEN: "Soothing words to misdirect his attention."
HARVEY: "Angry comment of sarcastic nature."
ELLEN: "Angry retort filled with insult."
HARVEY: "Attempt to make up and sexually arouse."
ELLEN: "Teasing promise of good time tomorrow night."
HARVEY: "Reluctant acceptance of offer."

You can try something like this cold, or actually transform one of your own conversations into these descriptive terms. You probably would find this much easier to do if you taped it.

This can be highly productive, and doesn't have a winner, unless you want to figure out a way to come up with one.

You can make games out of a number of the exercises throughout this book, or invent your own. Share your feelings about playing games together, and what, if any, benefit you think they are to your relationship.

If you don't feel comfortable playing games together, games that you've chosen to play, then you might discuss the feelings connected with this discomfort. As in all growth activities, if it doesn't feel right, just don't do it!

Games you choose to play can fill a lot of your competitive needs, and you should be aware of how it might affect any negative game-playing you've been practicing.

Note: The ten parts of the body that have only three letters are: Hip. Arm. Leg. Rib. Jaw. Lip. Gum. Eye. Ear. Toe.

SEXUAL FUN

You smiled at me
that day when love
was not enough.
Judy Altura

We take love and sex much too seriously, and thus deprive ourselves of a great deal of playful joy in the love relationship. Co-therapists Dr. Herbert Otto and Roberta Otto see this as a vital missing factor, and have taught many couples to experience this carefree, mutual pleasure-taking in their "More Joy in Your Marriage" workshops. They devote a major segment of their book *Total Sex* to this topic, and note, "To venture and explore playfully, openly, and joyously with another person requires caring, trust, and support."

The Ottos and other therapists have reported an interesting fact: Most couples find it difficult to experience sex as playful, fun-filled, and laugh-producing. When is the last time you laughed during sexual activity?

The sad fact is that much of the laughter evoked during sex is a nervous reaction. We overstructure with technique, anxiety, and competitiveness.

Watch children or animals playing. No need for structure, and a great sense of spontaneity and freedom. Most adults have lost that capacity to let go and just have fun. This childhood ability to playfully let go is of vital importance in personality development and emotional growth. For an adult it can provide a beautiful means of letting go of expectations, inhibitions, fears, and stereotyped roles.

The exercises included in this section are designed to provide you with an initial experience of letting go and having fun, with the hope that you will then go on and explore even more spontaneous sexual fun.

Being Silly

How uncomfortable are you with being silly? Can you sit across from your love-partner and make a silly face? Try it. Can you then make a silly sound? Can you combine an action and a sound? Be aware of any difficulty you may have with this form of expression. Discuss and examine that difficulty, and your feelings about it. If you can really let go in this experience, you'll find some new sensations emerging, and will want to share and explore these. If one or both partners just can't seem to do or say something silly, then you might try again at some later date. This can be a very difficult area for many people. It can teach you something about how much we've become restricted and uptight in this simple act of having fun. There are a number of reasons for this difficulty. Some people feel they just don't deserve that much pleasure. Others are afraid of appearing foolish, and afraid that letting down their guard this much will show the world that they are really not very worthwhile or desirable. Do either of these reasons ring any familiar bells with you?

Of course, some people use their ability to be playful and silly to escape emotional responsibility and dealing with issues. There is a difference between nervous laughter and the genuine expression of joy.

Your Fun History

Can you remember a time when you laughed because you were nervous or uncomfortable? Can you remember a time when you laughed because you were having a fun time? Can you compare the two and share the differences with your love-partner?

Can you remember a fun-filled sexual experience? One in which you weren't concerned about looking silly, but were able to let go and enjoy.

Ann and Terry

Ann and Terry were just starting to explore their sexual attraction to each other. They were in Terry's bedroom, and after several hours of highly arousing mutual exploration, they had undressed and were ready to have intercourse for the first time. Terry went over to a bureau drawer and took out a package of condoms. He started to put one on and it disintegrated. He was anxious about this, and tried another, and it too fell apart. The whole packageful crumbled at the slightest touch. He and Ann looked at each other, and smiled, and then laughed, and kept on laughing back and forth through the night. Terry told Ann how he had bought the condoms at an Army PX, more to show off than anything else, since he was a very shy person, and had limited sexual experience. They had been six years old when he tried to use them this very special night. They laughed and held each other all night long. Since Ann couldn't take birth control pills, Terry made a trip to the drugstore the next day, and they began a joyful long-term love affair.

This could have easily been a tragic episode. Terry could have withdrawn himself with total embarrassment, and never again been at ease with Ann. The spark of humor that ignited and saved the day also set a lovely tone for their entire relationship, one of good fun and mutual trust and understanding. What could have been a terribly anxious and frustrating moment actually turned into something that brought Ann and Terry closer together.

Sense of the Ridiculous

Perhaps unconsciously, we all realize that the sexual act puts us in rather a silly and ridiculous situation. Two figures straddling, huffing and puffing, building to a fever pitch, then letting go with exhaustion. If you can see the silly side of sex, you can begin to enjoy the beauty of it. Share this with your love-partner. Isn't the whole thing rather silly? Can you imagine a creature from Mars coming down to Earth and seeing the two of you locked in sexual embrace? How would you explain to him what you were doing? Try making such an explanation.

Renaming It

Can you come up with a new name for sexual intercourse? Some sample possibilities:

Forning (from fornication)
Dipitee Doing
The Bedroom Bounce
Humplethumping
Pushing-Pulling-Filling-Spilling

Can you come up with a new name for the male and female sex organs? Something much more playful than penis and vagina, and more fun than any of the slang terms now being used.

Can you give each of your sexual organs proper names? Susan and Larry named their organs Priscilla and Humphrey. Whenever either partner was in the mood for love-making, they would say something like, "Humphrey would like to get together with Priscilla." Silly? Of course! That's the whole point.

Relocation

If you had to move your sexual organs to some place else on your body, where would you like them to be relocated? Each partner can select his or her own preference, and then share the choices, and see if you can both agree on new locations.

Flavors

Pick a new flavor for your sex organs. What would you like? Cherry, chocolate, pizza, beef stroganoff? First pick a new flavor for your sex organ, then one for your partner. If you find it embarrassing to even discuss this, you might share your feelings and your discomfort. This, too, can be useful and revealing.

A Different Orgasm

Imagine that you have been granted a second method of achieving orgasm, in addition to sexual stimulation. You choose the way you'd like to be able to bring forth this orgasm. It can be by snapping your fingers, smacking your lips, stamping your feet, or any other nonsexual physical activity.

The idea in all of the preceding exercises is to have fun playing with these new ideas and each other. If you can't feel comfortable doing some silly little things like these, then putting spontaneity into your relationship is going to be a most difficult task.

The Mating Call

Invent a mutual mating call together. A sound or nonsense word that will let your partner know you are in the mood for love. This can be a fun-filled effort, but also can have a most useful function, particularly if either partner finds it difficult to let the other know when sexual desire is present. It is your secret signal, and you can have fun using it when others are present, since they won't know its special significance.

The Movie Musical

One night, decide you are going to do your love-making as a movie musical. You can rehearse it, or just let it happen. As you head toward each other in the bedroom, you might sing a line or two from an operetta, or a love song from the 1940s, or a new love ballad. Just sing the first line, or a few words from a song, as you feel it's appropriate. Remember, you're alone together, there's no audience, and it can get as naughty and silly as you like.

One couple reported going into hysterics when the woman gripped the man's penis and started singing, "What Is This Thing Called Love?"

Each partner can break into song at any moment, the more inappropriate the moment, the more fun you can have with it.

You might use physical actions to punctuate the songs.

Singing, "Five foot two, eyes of blue, kootchy, kootchy, kootchy, koo," you might tickle your partner in rhythm to the "kootchy, kootchy, kootchy, koo."

One man reported gently poking his wife's breasts to the tune of "Toot, Toot, Tootsie, Good-bye" with one poke for each "toot."

Body Labels

Using body paints or vegetable dye, you can try to label different parts of your partner's body with humorous signs. For instance:

Men Working
Out to Lunch
By Appointment Only
Fresh Paint
Curves Ahead
Proceed at Your Own Risk
Official Historical Site
Plan Ahead
May Be Hazardous to Your Health
Pass Go, Collect $200
Go to Jail
Don't Walk on the Grass

If you choose, you can just verbally describe your labels rather than actually writing them on the body.

As long as it's not overdone, humor can become a precious part of your sexual relationship. You can use it for creative expression, and as a way to relax and communicate your love feelings.

Try to think up your own ways of doing this. You may not think you have a sense of humor, but being silly doesn't mean you have to have a great comic inventiveness. Be able to remove sex from the sacrosanct place it enjoys in most relationships.

If you can't laugh together, you probably can't love together.

More things to have fun with:

Undressing Race

Have a race to see who can get undressed faster. A variation on this might be for you to undress each other.

New Uses for an Old Thing

Can you come up with new uses for your sex organs? Suggestions:

Penis: Flagpole
           Soup Temperature Tester
           Doughnut Holder
           Hand Warmer
Vagina: Grape Holder
           Finger Warmer
           Jar Opener

Decoration Day

Decide how you would like to decorate each other. Use whatever materials are handy. Ribbons. Whipped cream. Cake decorations. Christmas tree decorations.

Try working on each other separately and then simultaneously.

You might even want to record your efforts for posterity with a Polaroid picture.

The Obscene Phone Call

Whenever the mood strikes you, make an obscene phone call to your love-partner. Describe all the sexy things you're going to do together in very explicit terms. Try to be as shocking as possible.

Mock Rape

On occasion, each partner may pretend to rape the other. This can be played broadly and in the playful spirit of fun. Make sure that you don't use this to work off anger or aggression, at least not under the guise of a playful experience.

As you get into the swing of it, you'll be able to invent all kinds of games and fun things to do.

You have to have an attitude of trust and mutual respect before you are ready to bring this kind of adult playing into your relationship. As in all the things you do together, sharing your feelings, both negative and positive, can greatly enhance the experience.

It's a question of being able to say "You tickle my fancy, and I'll tickle yours."

Our false polarization of sex and love has interfered with our capacity to have fun. If you think that sex can be fun only in a casual sexual encounter, and that you have to be much more serious in a real love relationship, then you're in dangerous territory.

Real sexual fun can come only with the trust that accompanies a real love relationship. Letting go comes most easily in a safe atmosphere.

Prostitutes never have fun with sex. Overconcern with sexual technique can create this "whoredom boredom" in any love relationship.

Adding humor and fun to your sexual life can take it from the "worrying about doing it" kind of situation, and change it to a relaxed "doing it and enjoying it" experience.

Sexual expression can cover a variety of moods, and we limit ourselves when it is used only to express deep feelings of love. Having fun together is also loving.

You may be able to describe various sexual experiences as "moving," "full of love," "exciting," "really good," "warm and tender." But if you can't look at any of your sexual experience and say, "That was fun," you are missing something in life and love.

You may find it useful to explore where your conditioning came from in this area. Did your parents have fun during their sexual activity? The concept of sex as a dirty or forbidden thing necessitated that it contain as little pleasure as possible. Have you been incapacitated because of this inherited concept?

The only real way to overcome such conditioning is to practice putting more fun and spontaneity into your sexual activities.

Once you can easily laugh while making love, any negative conditioning is well on the way to oblivion.

Remember, too, that laughter is the one quality in love and sex that requires two people for expression. You may be able to love yourself, or sexually satisfy yourself, but it's pretty hard to add laughter to either of these while you're still alone.

Sex is fun, but not for one.

KEEPING THE WARMTH

The red is missing from our rainbow
I told you that
and quietly
you told me that
we would discuss it.
That was eighty hours ago
and now the yellow's missing.
                                    Judy Altura

There is a self-perpetuating myth most of us fall victim to. It says that love deteriorates, as do the American automobile, washing machines, and furniture. Like so much of the pervasive programming around us, in this age of instant information communication, if we believe the myth it becomes true for us.

Sociologists and anthropologists might have a field day examining why this is so. For our purposes, let's just briefly look at our own feelings and see how conditioned we may have become in this area.

Examine Yourself

Ask yourself these questions, and see if you can't meditate on each one for a few minutes. Look beyond your answer to how you first arrived at this conclusion. Was it through experience, or was it an opinion acquired from friends or family?

1. Do I believe that familiarity breeds contempt in a love relationship?
2. Is a love-partner less interesting and exciting a year or two after the beginning of the relationship?
3. Am I interested in involvements outside my primary relationship merely as a means to bring excitement back into my life and perhaps bring back some of the thrill that's now missing from the primary relationship?

One basic question is the root of all three of the above:

Do I believe that something goes out of a love relationship as time passes?

If you do believe that obsolescence is built into the love relationship you may be actively pursuing a self-fulfilling prophecy, and a self-defeating one as well.

Romantic Love Concept to Blame

The idea that love begins with a powerful explosion of emotion, great passion, overwhelming excitement, and constant "highs" is widely held and firmly subscribed to in films, plays, and books, which are responsible for many of our romantic concepts. Conversely, this idea usually brings with it the notion that this great passion, this great fire, cannot burn with the same intensity for very long. The notion that the most you can hope for is a pleasant lukewarm sensation. And many consider even this sensation an impossible dream.

How many stories have we read, and how many movies have we seen, that depict a man and woman meeting for the first time, exchanging little or no information with each other, and falling magically in love?

Love at first sight may not be impossible, but it may very well be extremely stupid. It also can stunt the growth of a potentially sound relationship.

Not that anyone is suggesting the abolition of romantic love, or completely removing the fantasies from the beginning stages of a relationship. In fact these fantasies can be very useful. But there is a happy medium somewhere between total fantasy and stark realism.

Love Fantasy

What is fantasy in a love relationship? One dictionary definition of the word itself says fantasy is a "supposition with no solid foundation." Let's simply say that anything happening at this moment is fact, anything that we imagine will happen in the future isn't true at this moment, and therefore can be designated as fantasy.

Much of this fantasy is unavoidable, and in fact desirable in the initial stages of a relationship. It is, after all, filling a vacuum. As psychotherapist Marta Vago puts it, "At the beginning of the relationship you don't have enough data. After one evening together, the information is extremely limited as compared to what you might know about each other a month or two later."

Marta Vago, M.S.W., is associate director of Laurel Institute, a counseling center in Philadelphia. She and Dr. Bart Knapp, a clinical psychologist and the institute's director, work extensively with couples, both privately and in group sessions.

Dr. Knapp feels the initial excitement in a love relationship is probably necessary, as he states, "to sort of glue the relationship together for a while. It's a temporary adhesive. The excitement greatly moves the relationship and gives it a ground in which it can develop."

Of prime importance, then, is bringing reality and fantasy into a very natural balance. No one is suggesting eliminating the high points that bring excitement at the beginning, but merely being aware of what is really happening and what is not. Extremes on either end can be harmful and get in the way of communication. Being open and enjoying the excitement of mutual exploration and discovery can allow you to easily replace the initial fantasy with actual factual material, without dulling or eliminating the highs.

Marta Vago states it very simply: "The highs, in the beginning, are based a great deal on fantasies, assumptions, hopes, and wishes. In other words, they're not really based on reality. While later on in the relationship that matures, the highs are woven into the fabric of the total relationship."

The mistake a lot of couples apparently make is in trying to build a foundation for the future out of these initial highs. These special moments of excitement should be enjoyed to the fullest, but never used to establish a norm. If you can keep it a "now" experience, you'll easily avoid that trap.

Which statement seems most realistic?

"Wow! This is it for me! Something this much fun and this exciting can't ever end. I can't imagine any better way to spend the rest of my life!"

Or:

"Wow! This feels great! I don't know how long this is going to last, but I'm going to enjoy every single moment of it!"

Do you see the difference?

Dr. Knapp says, "The highs provide a perspective of the potentials and the possibilities of the relationship rather than a standard or a consistent norm."

Marta Vago adds, "In a mature relationship, the highs are a confirmation of the present. They are neither reliving of the past nor a promise of the future."

When a relationship is based, as is usual in the beginning, more on fantasy than reality, the excitement is existent only in a very narrow framework. It can propel us forward and provide some momentum, but it doesn't really provide strength to help the relationship survive the upcoming hurdles and hassles.

Dr. Knapp also warns that, when holes in the relationship are filled with fantasy, there's no room for the real and necessary data. Furthermore, insistence on maintaining the fantasy can be highly destructive.

An example from Ms. Vago: "If I go out with a man, and I notice that he has five drinks before dinner and five drinks after dinner, and if I don't start wondering whether this man might have a drinking problem, then I'm really living in a fantasy world, and I'm not taking into account the data that's available to me."

It isn't always this easy and obvious, of course, to spot the fantasies. Part of the purpose of open and honest communication is to replace the fantasy with real data as quickly as possible.

In a relationship that is honest and growing, the passage of time only enhances and accentuates the joyful sense of wonder. When we attempt to soar above the merely superficial, we find that we are very complex creatures indeed, and it takes a long time really to get to know and understand one another. Actually, we can never really completely know another person. If that person is growing, he or she is forever adding new dimensions to the core personality: new experiences to react and respond to in new ways. It is possible for two people to be involved in individual growth and grow apart in the relationship as they may find they no longer fulfill each other's major needs. But is practically impossible for two aware, open, and growing love-partners to bore each other!

Where does that leave you? That's a question only you can answer, but there may be some guidelines.

One useful technique for self-examination in this area is to look at what turns you on about your love-partner, and see just how much of it is based on things you know and how much on things you hope or expect or assume.

Examining the Highs

List a few of the high points in your relationship. Try to determine how much of a role fantasy and reality played in making you feel good during the experience.

As one young man remembered one incident:

"It was our third date, the first one during the day, and we went to the beach. It was just one fun thing after another, and she really looked sexy in that bikini. I got so turned on when she had me putting suntan lotion on her shoulders that I could hardly speak. We had a great time in the water, a great time on the beach, and even up at the hotdog stand, where we found out we both like the same things on our hotdogs. Back at her apartment, she started to take a shower and called out for me to come into the bathroom. When I did, she was standing inside the shower stall, with her head peeking out, and said, 'Why don't you take off your suit and join me?' Later, laughing together, we went to her bed and made beautiful love. Afterward, I thought to myself, 'This is it!' and couldn't imagine ever having this much fun with anyone else. I thought back to the beach and how great it would be to spend my whole vacation with her, with every day a repetition of this one. I was so high I was floating. I pictured many more days like this one, stretching on nonstop. It was a mind-boggling experience."

There's no denying our young hero had a fantastic time. It was filled with many realistic highs. There was really no need for the fantasizing expedition into the future. But even with the fantasy, it was a most fulfilling day. The only problem would be in letting the fantasy dilute the reality. Starting to make the expectations overshadow what really was happening. The easiest way to avoid this is to recognize the fantasies, acknowledge them as fantasies, and concentrate instead on the realities.

As Marta Vago would define the realities of our sample situation:

"Super-now experiences based on all the richness of the relationship in the present."

Find Your Super-Now Experiences

Sit down with your love-partner and examine the high points together. Can you find these super-now experiences, ones in which what was exciting was what was happening at the moment rather than what you imagined it would lead to. Try to find at least two or three, and share your feelings at the time, as you remember them. Do you think it would have added to the experience if you had shared your feelings at the time?

Sharing Fantasies

Examine together some of the fantasy factors in one of your memorable experiences. Did you imagine some things were true about the other person that turned out not to be? Ask each other the following questions about this experience:

1. What one word would most describe how you felt at the time?
2. Was there something you didn't know for sure about me at the time that you thought you were learning from this experience?
3. Do you feel this indication or hint turned out to be true?
4. If not, does the fact that this expectation may not have been totally realized take anything away from the experience itself?
5. If you did have a fantasy about me that didn't turn out to be completely true, which do you remember most now, the actual experience or your disappointment later on?
6. If you had not had this fantasy expectation, would it have diminished in any way the experience itself?
7. Do you feel fantasy plays as big a part in our good experiences together now as it did at the beginning?
8. Do you enjoy the fantasies as much as the experience itself?

An Intentional Fantasy

Sit opposite each other, look into each other's eyes for a moment, and without talking close your eyes and imagine something you would like to do together. Spend about five minutes imagining actually doing it. Open your eyes and, one at a time, share the fantasy and what it generated in feelings.

A Fantasy Concept

A planned fantasy factor can often heighten the reality of an experience. There is one particular fantasy method that may help you focus on the present rather than the future. We could call it simply:

The End

As you do something together that you are both thoroughly enjoying, agree to try imagining that this is the last thing you will ever do together. Don't dwell on the sadness of this, since it isn't really happening, but on getting the most out of this final experience together. Share your feelings afterward and whether you think the method has any value for you.

The main premise of this chapter is:

THERE IS NO REASON FOR THE HIGHS TO SLOW DOWN AS THE RELATIONSHIP PROGRESSES, ESPECIALLY IF YOU OPENLY SHARE THE JOY OF DISCOVERY.

Merely communicating can eliminate a lot of the dull and dreary aspects from a relationship of some duration, but there are certain specific techniques that can act as "booster shots." A good many of these could involve the simple act of discovering something new together.

Harvey

For Harvey, something new meant someone new. As the young executive, married for eight years, told his psychologist:

"I first noticed Janis at the office when she started wearing very short skirts, and she seemed to be making a lot of eye contact with me. I avoided this for a while, but seeing her every day sort of stirred my blood up, and I began to imagine how an affair with her would turn out. I still wasn't intending to do anything about it, but we had lunch one day, and I found out she was really fun to be with. Then we had dinner one night, and one thing led to another and we ended up at her apartment. The funny thing is, though Janis was exciting and sexy and fun, she wasn't really as sexually satisfying as Sue. Well, after all, Sue and I had been sleeping together for eight years, so we pretty much knew each other's likes and dislikes. But Janis was different. She was into painting, and cooking odd gourmet dishes, and she had satin sheets. After having sex together, she'd bring me in something to eat, usually some exotic snack or dessert, and we'd have some wine. At times I felt silly. Other times, I found myself looking forward to the surprise snack more than the sex. Another thing that really turned me on happened before we'd go to sleep. Janis would ask me to help her brush her hair, or rub moistening lotion on her face, or share some other private act with her. It was exciting, but I didn't feel I was cheating on Sue, or that Janis ever really touched parts of me that belonged to Sue. In fact, I often wanted to share the fun parts of it with Sue, and even suggest that we try some of the things that Janis and I did together. I was afraid to, though, thinking she might somehow find out about the affair. Eventually, it just wasn't as exciting any more, and the fact the Janis didn't really sexually satisfy me became more and more important. We parted as friends, and still have a big 'Hello' for each other at the office. I think I appreciate Sue more now, though I must admit I still haven't had the nerve to suggest we try some of the things Janis and I did."

Harvey was lucky in that he had a relatively harmless affair, though repressing the truth may inhibit his communication with Sue. But no one has to have an affair to experience new things. In fact, they can be much richer when experienced with someone you have been already sharing experiences with. The sharing will take on greater depth.

In Harvey's case, it was really very simple things that provided the highs in his affair. Things that could easily have been shared with Sue if he had made the effort.

Sharing New Things

The best way to keep your love-partner interested and in love with you is to stay interested and in love with yourself and with life. There are incalculable advantages in making a determined effort to share new activities and new adventures together.

Here are some suggested new ways in which you can experience each other:

1. Sit down and have your partner lie down with his or her head in your lap. The back of the head should face the front of your body, with the legs stretched straight out. Simultaneously massage both your partner's ears with your fingers. Gentle kneading action. Slowly run your index fingers around the outer ear. Very slowly stick the tip of your index fingers into the ear channel, softly blocking off all sound. Close your eyes at this point and concentrate on the feeling. Keep your finger inserted for about one minute. Allow this to be a meditative moment for both of you. Remove your index fingers, slowly tracing your way back along the outer ear, massaging the back of the ear. Don't jump up after this and say "Your turn." Quietly share the experience nonver-

bally, and then change places. Allow each of you to experience fully the physical sensations and the feelings they generate. Afterward, share your feelings, both during the receiving and during the giving of this experience.

2. Shampoo your partner's hair. At one point, decide to try shampooing in different moods: Friendly. Loving, Angry. Zestful. Afraid. Silly. See if you can change the mood, and have your partner guess what it is. Try to come up with new ways to shampoo each other's hair. See how much fun and discovery you can bring to a normally mundane activity!
3. Smell your partner. All over.
4. Listen to each other's heartbeat.
5. Bite your partner somewhere that isn't terribly sensitive, doing it tenderly.
6. Dress each other from head to toe.
7. Women: Shave his face. Men: Shave her legs.
8. Read something to your love-partner.

To add a sense of spontaneity, experiment with variations on these and other sensitivity exercises. See if you can invent your own.

Even if only for a few seconds, see if you can't share some new experience, or an old one in a new way, each and every day you spend together!

Surprise of the Week

Here's a technique that can act as a booster shot for a relationship that seems healthy but not very exciting. The format can be changed to suit your individual needs and desires.

Alternating weekly, one love-partner plans a surprise of some kind for the other. You can also play some guessing games, but even without this it should be a lot of fun trying to decide what surprise you're going to get, and the following week trying to come up with a good surprise yourself.

The surprises can vary greatly, from the simple little acts of warmth we sometimes forget, to elaborate plans.

Some of the surprises thought up by couples trying the technique:

1. Invited an old friend of my husband's to dinner.
2. Had a picture blown up from our early days together.
3. We went to an amusement park and rode the rides together.
4. I bought my wife a pet kitten.
5. I had a trophy made up for the LOVE OF MY LIFE award.
6. I had a cake decorated with HAPPY EVERYDAY.
7. I wrote a poem for my love-partner.
8. I presented my wife with a certificate good for ten massages from me.

And the list goes on and on, but certainly you can do as well and probably better. You have the advantage of knowing your love-partner and both what would be a pleasant experience and what would be an unexpected act on your part for a real surprise.

One note worth keeping in mind: See how much time you spend anticipating the surprise and whether this might be more exciting than getting the surprise itself. This, again, is your fantasy capability coming into play. There's nothing wrong with this, especially if you understand it as fantasy and maybe wishful thinking. But see if you can't get to the point where you don't ever expect the surprise. That's the point where you receive the most pleasure from the surprise itself, and can most fully keep it a now adventure!

Sometimes we assume we know a lot more than we actually do know about our love-partner. As a relationship progresses, we assume there is nothing more to learn or discover. In a growing relationship this couldn't be further from the truth. The more actual data you have about your love-partner, the more positive interaction is possible. One useful way to check out very basic knowledge is to write the:

Love-Partner Biography

Write a biographical piece on your love-partner. Their accomplishments, their likes and dislikes, and whatever factual history you know. Then check out with each other the accuracy of your biographies. Even a paragraph or two about each other can prove valuable in this exercise. You might ask each other the following questions after writing the biographies:

1. Is there anything important that I've left out of your biography?
2. Is there any fact I've gotten totally or partially wrong?
3. If you didn't know me, would you think I was a fairly interesting person from the biography you just wrote?
4. Would you like people you know to read this biography?
5. If you were going to be in *Who's Who*, would you be willing to have this as your official biography?
   If not, what would you change, add, or subtract?

Learn Together

The growth experience is really a learning experience, and learning things together can be a valuable way to communicate and share new things.

Many couples find out that they can bring a new sense of pleasure and excitement into the relationship by going out and learning something neither ever knew before. Such as:

Chinese cooking skills.
A new sport.
Making pottery.
A new language.
A new dance.

Make your own list now. How many things can you think of that you might be able to learn together?

Sharing the joy of discovery is something we cannot help but enhance with someone we love and know well. It is something we can't do in quite the same way alone, or with someone we really haven't gotten to know yet.

Rekindling

For some couples, it may be worthwhile trying to go back to the beginning, when you had little or no actual data about each other, and, with a slightly different perspective, examine the feelings you evoked in each other. This sort of fantasy simulation works only if you both agree it might be useful to try it together.

Sit down apart from each other. Perhaps across a room from one another. Close your eyes and try to go back in time to a moment when you didn't know each other. Try to imagine you don't know each other now. For just this short period, see if you can avoid focusing on the feelings you now have for this person. Now, open your eyes and try to look at this other person as you would a stranger.

Examine each other closely.

What do you see?

What do you like?

One of you approach the other as if you were strangers, and start a conversation. See how much you have in common.

See whether you might like to get to know each other.

When you feel you have gone as far as you would like, or when either partner feels it's time to stop, end the exercise and start sharing the experience. You might ask the following questions:

1. What was your impression of me?
2. What were your feelings during the exercise?

3. Were you able to see me in a new way?

4. Can you use one word to describe me, not from the information you've had access to over the length of our relationship, but just from these few minutes of examining me?

5. Is there anything you'd like to know about my reaction to you during this exercise?

6. Is there anything else you'd like to share with me?

This and similar exercises can put us in touch with much information, including sometimes why we take each other for granted and how we might do something about it. After doing any exercise together, it may be useful to finish this sentence for each other:

"I think that I just learned that you ———."

A fantasy simulation such as the one you just tried doesn't always work. It is not an easy thing to do, to forget who you are and what your current depth of feeling is. Even if you only partially succeed, you can learn something from it.

By reading this book together and sharing some of the exercises, you probably already have noticed some changes in the way you relate to each other. They may not be major changes, but any new dimension you can add to give yourself new perspectives will prove a healthy and constructive process.

A Full-course Meal

While it's true that no single person can fulfill all of the needs of another person, there is a good chance that you can fulfill more of your love-partner's needs than you are now doing, and vice versa. Variety *is* the spice of life, and there is a superabundance of variation in each and every one of us, which is just waiting to pour forth. It is sad that so often we get tired of people we really know only in a very limited, superficial way. It is doubtful that any two people attracted to each other would be able to pursue all the avenues of mutual exploration and communication in a long lifetime together. The path isn't always an easy one, and sometimes it seems much simpler just to start with someone new. This can often lead to another superficial contact. It's almost like ordering all the appetizers on a menu without ever getting to the main course and dessert. The appetizers may be fun and exciting, even nutritious and satisfying, but just think of what you'd be missing. Pretty soon, you'd get tired of switching appetizers, no matter how different and exciting they were. The true gourmet knows how to savor a dish with all his senses. If we could learn to thus savor life, and thus know and experience our love-partners, the flame would rarely die, and our lives together would be fulfilling full-course meals.

TOGETHER THEN, TOGETHER NOW

Tomorrow
tonight is gone.
But all the day I will recall
how well you love me.
　　　　　Judy Altura

Living in the here and now doesn't mean totally forgetting all that has happened before. While it may be destructive to have the past as the primary focal point, remembering what was instead of enjoying what is, it can also be harmful and foolish to ignore the early experiences together. They may have much to say to you. If you have grown since the beginning of your relationship, then you may be able to learn more now from those early experiences than you did at the time.

There is a concept in most oriental philosophies that many of us can never fully understand. We sometimes call it total consciousness or "being in touch with the universe" or some other largely unsuccessful attempt to label something that really can't be labeled. One of the themes running all through these meditative philosophies and religions is one that says nothing we ever do is ever really wasted or lost. That life is like a great river that takes many twists and turns, but through it all there is a great sense of purpose. If we look at the love relationship in this context, we can realize how very narrow our normal viewpoint has been.

A good starting place can be to look at yourselves right now and imagine that you are strangers. This time from a different perspective than the one we used in the preceding chapter. Then we were examining how you would react to each other now if you were strangers. This time we want to examine how much of what you are now has to do with what you have shared in the past.

What's Missing?

So here you are. Two strangers. Really try to get into the feeling. You have wiped the blotter clean. The experiences you have shared together no longer exist. Ask yourselves the following questions:

1. What do I miss most of what we have had together, now that it's gone?
2. Do I miss the process of our growing together most, or the individual "things" we did together?
3. What don't I know about you as a stranger that I enjoyed knowing about you?
4. Can I care for you as much now that you are a stranger?
5. Do I find myself having less ambitious expectations of you as a stranger?

You may or may not learn anything from this type of exercise. You may already be totally in touch with your past history and have need to concentrate more on the now experiences. But reflection on the past is a part of human nature, and it can be useful to try making it a constructive process.

Remembering

Can you share again some of your early experiences together? You can take as much or as little time as you like to re-experience the following:

1. Your first meeting.
2. Your first impressions of each other.
3. Your first kiss.

4. The first movie you saw together.
5. The first meal you shared.
6. Your first sexual experience together.
7. Your first disagreement.

Some of these may be difficult to remember, depending on how long you've been together. You may even be able to have fun with the difficulty of remembering, or learn something from it. The ways in which you each remember certain things may not agree. You can do the remembering verbally, discussing your feelings at the time, and finding out how much you can recall of the mood at the time. Or you might try re-enacting some of the situations. Take a fantasy trip together by reliving something that was special.

Sense Memory

Many acting students study a process called "sense memory." To re-create certain emotions they will go back in their memories and remember something that really happened. This puts more reality into the performance. You can also take advantage of this ability we all have to re-create emotional experiences. You were just asked to re-create events. Now try to re-create some feelings you have had. Can you remember the first time, or some early time together, when your love-partner made you sad? Can you quietly re-create that situation in your own mind and re-create the feeling of sadness. It can be useful for the two of you to do this individually, but while being together physically. Without speaking, see if you can re-create some early emotions:

1. Sadness.
2. Anger.
3. Desire and Longing.
4. Love.

5. Joy.
6. Envy.
7. Hate.

Again, you may not be able to easily recall these emotions. Not all of them may have occurred. Don't turn it into a competitive exercise by saying things like, "You made me much sadder than I made you." But do share your feelings with each other. Share what you felt at the time. Share also what you feel now about re-creating the emotional experience.

Can you see where you have learned some good things from the past? Share them. Finish this sentence for each other: "I feel good about remembering ———."

All life is a learning process, as is all love. We can choose to ignore this, but we are missing much if we so choose. There is a texture and tone to each relationship. There is a path we travel together. Sometimes we grow into changing our path, but sometimes we merely wander off it. Only you can know which is true for you.

Your Movie

Imagine that a film is going to be made about your early times together, about the beginning of your relationship. Invent a title for this film. Do this separately and then share your titles. Can you now come up with a new title that will describe the film for both of you? You may even agree to keep one of your titles and discard the other. If both your titles were the same, then simply congratulate yourselves.

Now, again individually, write a brief synopsis of the plot of this movie. Again, share your plots and see if you can come up with one that describes both views.

Once you have your consensus title and plot, examine it. Is this a film you would enjoy seeing? You might discuss the casting. Who would each of you like to see cast as yourselves? As your love-partner?

Don't hesitate to have fun with this. Some couples working in an encounter group came up with the following titles:

The Lusty Innocents
Fools Rush In
Mary Poppins Meets King Kong
Love Over All
The Strong Ones
Ahead of the Game
Me and You Against Them

Imagine the movie's ending. Can you write a piece of
dialogue for yourself that will describe how you felt as your
relationship started to solidify? Share this and try to say
these lines to each other as you imagine they would be said
by the stars you picked to play each of you. One sentence
for each of you should be sufficient.

You can take this exercise a step further by bringing it
into the present. What kind of movie would you both choose
now? How would it be different? You can go through
the whole process again, but this time the movie reflects
where you are now in your relationship.

If we sometimes stop to realize how very much what and
where we are now is based on early experiences, emotions,
and impressions, we can also realize that, rather than having
lost anything, we have built on something. While it has
changed, the essence is still very much there. If we block
this sense of the continuity of it all, we bury the foundation
under a lot of emotional cobwebs. These can be swept clear
by, not only living in the here and now, but by bringing a
realistic sense of the past to the present.

What I Remember Most

To sort of bring it all together, imagine for a moment that
your relationship has just ended. Amiably but irrevocably,

and through mutual agreement. Take a moment to set the scene for yourself, then finish this sentence for each other:

"What I remember most about —— (love-partner's name) is ——."

This sentence can provide a lot of important information for both of you. Discuss your response to your partner's sentence. Were the sentences describing the relationship as a whole, the person involved, or something specific that happened? Did the answer reflect the relationship in its early stages, as it is now, or a combination of the two?

Remembering together can be fun and exciting and educational. It is harmful only when it gets in the way of living and growing and the creation of new memories together.

It can have a lot to do with your attitudes toward each other in the act of remembering.

Did the remembering make you sad and disappointed that the "good old days" are gone forever? Or did it make you realize that they are just as much here as they ever were, that everything that ever was can still be, if you really want it to be?

You can remember as much or as little as you want. You can live and love as little or as much as you want.

A sense of balance is necessary. When you honestly deal with feelings, both past and present, that balance will happen quite naturally. Past feelings can be useful and beautiful, but it is the current ones that are potent. Try to be aware that what you are feeling now can tell you the most about yourself and your relationship. But also be aware that what you have felt before has something to do with what you are feeling now.

Don't worship or mourn the past, but respect it. Much of it is still here.

ON YOUR OWN

I know a greater joy than then:
the joy of growing.
A saner love,
and closet space for people with possessions.
            Judy Altura

So, what do you do with it all? All the exercises, all the suggestions? How can you integrate them into your real relationship?

Let's first look at all the suggestions together, in the following list of general statements:

1. Expectations are harmful when they get in the way of the experience.
2. Sex is best as a true expression of feelings.
3. You have to take responsibility for yourself.
4. A healthy love relationship involves a sense of commitment to growth and honesty.
5. Being aware of feelings, and being able to express them, is the guide to real communication.
6. Motivation for being honest should have an underlying concept of caring concern for the other person.
7. You can achieve an ecstatic sense of release by letting yourself be vulnerable to another person.
8. Examining your priorities can help you understand whether you are trying to reach goals or fulfill real needs.
9. Fantasies can be used to avoid real feelings, or they can be used creatively to provide insight.
10. A strong self-image is the first prerequisite for a good love relationship.

11. Sharing yourself with another person may be fulfilling the strongest human need of all.
12. Many of the problems in a relationship are due to lack of information.
13. A love relationship is often more affected by what isn't said than by what is.
14. The more you say the hardest things to each other, the easier they become to say.
15. Saying "I love you" can often get in the way of the feeling.
16. You can create poetry merely by expressing honest love feelings.
17. You can be completely free in a relationship only when you have learned freely to use touch as a means of communication.
18. Letting go of conscious thought enhances your emotional experience.
19. Physical relaxation is a valuable prelude to love communication.
20. Learning to savor experience and removing unrealistic expectations can help us keep highs in a relationship well beyond the initial excitement period.
21. While living in the here and now is of prime importance, the past doesn't have to be totally ignored and can provide much useful information.
22. Making all your implicits explicit in a Relationship Contract increases your sense of freedom and your alternatives and communication in a love relationship.
23. Honest communication can facilitate a painless ending to a relationship.
24. Your competitiveness can be harnessed and used to enhance love feelings.
25. A childlike sense of playfulness can enrich your love and sex experiences.

This is by no means a final list or a definitive one.

You don't have to accept all of them in order to make use of some of them.

When Nena O'Neill was asked by the author if there was anything she wished she and Dr. O'Neill had stressed more in *Open Marriage*, she replied, "I think we would have

liked to have reiterated more frequently, or to have made
more emphatic, the fact that no one should expect to achieve
an *Open Marriage* instantly. *Open Marriage is a process that
one works towards. It is an ideal, a goal.* We could have included more often than we did that each person should select only the things that they feel they are ready for, and
not expect to go too fast."

Take it easy. The exercises in this book could provide a
very full year of experiences for a growing couple. There is
no final test. No trophy to be awarded if you finish first.

The best way to start using these techniques is to allow
yourself to experience them fully, not as an intellectual
exercise, but as an emotional experience. If you kiss someone, and start analyzing the why and how of this physical
act, and are thinking about where it's going to lead, you are
not going to be able to appreciate the kiss itself.

There is something else that can get in the way. Dr.
Freyda Zell, a New York clinical psychologist and co-director
of the Consultation Center for Women, makes this observa-
tion: "We come from a culture with a long history of saying,
'We suffer. We suffer.' 'Deprive Yourself.' 'Save.' 'Put off
gratification.' 'You must know the bad in order to enjoy the
good.' It's a whole tradition. When you have your mind set
that everything's a struggle and that it's difficult, it's very
hard to savor experience. You cut off a lot of the channels,
and try to not really look too hard at a lot of stuff. We've
only started very recently to talk about joy and ecstasy as a
scientific endeavor. We have to really tune into our experiences. If you tune into the physical events, the happenings in your body, if you get in touch with the flow of energy,
you can't help having some joyous experience. Even being
angry. Most people who tell you they were really enraged
during a therapy session add, 'But it felt so good,' because
everything's turned on, and that's a fine feeling."

If you try anything in this book and it becomes a chore or
duty, stop doing it. We often talk about "working hard" at
a relationship, but if we really define it as hard work it just

isn't going to be productive work. There has to be a sense of joy and pleasure and aliveness in the effort, a sense of closeness in the sharing of the effort. Without this, the effort is meaningless.

A Human Laboratory

A relationship is a wonderful opportunity. It is the finest laboratory ever created for the study and appreciation of human dynamics. As in any learning experience, you can just go through the motions, cramming in material without absorbing it, or you can really enjoy the learning itself. Furthermore, a relationship has the most chance for success when neither partner needs it to feel whole. While you may not share every activity, your commitment to the relationship, if you consider this other person a primary partner, must include as full a sharing of your feelings as you are capable of, and a sharing of the process that led to these feelings. You may each go out into the world separately at times, but you can bring your perceptions and responses back to the relationship laboratory, saying, in effect, "This is a place for me to let go. You become my alter ego, not by being with me every moment, but by allowing me to share all the important moments with you."

This sharing can eliminate the need for all our defensive postures, and we can stop the emotional armaments race.

The exercises and techniques are not designed merely to set up contrived situations, to simulate real life, but to teach you new ways of looking at life and experiencing it.

Modeling

We humans have some abilities and capacities that separate us from the animal kingdom, and give us much in the way of benefits, along with a lot of pain. One of these is the capacity of the human brain to model. The capacity of human beings to re-create certain situations in their imaginations, or to simulate certain situations, without actually experiencing them. This is invaluable in the pursuit of intellectual accomplishment. It means we can theorize and analyze a number of events without having to go to the trouble or through the danger of experiencing them firsthand. But this capacity is also responsible for almost all emotional pain and suffering. For we can also re-create in our minds the things that we fear, without actually experiencing them, and we can constantly repeat and relive these fear episodes. A positive way to use this modeling capacity is to set up simulated situations, under protective conditions, finding out we are capable of trusting and risking ourselves, and then automatically being able to adopt this in our real-life situations.

But before starting to use it all, you have to examine whether this is really where you want to go, and where your love-partner wants to go. You may not want to share all there is to share with this particular person at this particular time. Taking responsibility for yourself means being able to state this, in a forthright manner. And you have to check out your love-partner's willingness to explore any specific area, or to hear the results of your exploration. You have to be able to ask, "Are you willing to listen to me now?" and you have to be able to say, "I am not willing to hear that now."

The Dangers of Growth

There is a danger in all of this growing; it might even be called a paradox. Some people use the whole thing as an escape from the responsibility of being a human being. It is easy to misinterpret terms like "here and now" and "open and honest communication" so that there is no room left for warmth and compassion and real caring. The people who fall into this trap are very good at fooling themselves. They hoist the banners high, saying, "Look at me, I'm a growing person, and isn't life wonderful?" But you can notice something missing when you look into their eyes, and they may not even be able to make eye contact. They might have a set little smile that is gruesome in its rigidity. In the name of "here and nowism" their moods can change very strangely and suddenly. One day they might be proclaiming their love and affection, hugging and kissing and touching you, and the next day it somehow has all disappeared. In terms of being human, they've really died. The commitment to growth is merely, for them, a desperate intellectual grab for life, and some assurance that they're still human.

It's easy to blame humanistic psychology and the human potential movement for this reaction, this misuse of the techniques and jargon, but these are people who are not terribly stable and wouldn't have been in any event. The fantasy that they are growing people has quite possibly kept a few of them from really going off the deep end. So, when you see a group leader or therapist who cannot look you in the eye, or isn't projecting any warmth or tenderness at all, you may well question whether this is a whole and real person, and whether he or she has anything at all to offer you. The same is true in choosing friends and love-partners. Another advantage that increasing your own awareness and sensitivity has is to provide you with protection against these shallow creatures. Even if they come on with warmth and love, you'll soon learn to recognize real feelings. These growth parasites can also be recognized by the weakness they display in their necessity constantly to be surrounded by admirers and hangers-on. Strong people do not need constantly to surround themselves with weak people.

There is another negative aspect to growth, a sort of frenzied need to take it all in before it's too late. When you meet someone who's tried Gestalt Therapy, Transactional Analysis, The Primal Scream, Behavior Therapy, Dream Analysis, Bioenergetics, Rolfing, Reichian Therapy, Encounter, and all within the past six months or so, you know this is a sick person, looking for answers that will never be acknowledged even when they're found. These types aren't looking for growth, but for some affirmation that they're not sick, and they hear only what they want to hear, and are incapable of taking responsibility for their own actions. These dilettantes of the growth movement are a clannish breed at times, and other times very lonely people. They often can influence needy individuals with their apparent knowledge and glib chatter.

All of this is noted so that you will realize that *saying* you're a warm and open and honest and feeling person may not always be the same as *being* all of these things. Learning to look beyond the façade, to the motivation level, is the best way to understand whether the feelings are real and honest ones. This is as true of your own feelings and motivation as it is of someone else's.

Why did you buy this book? What did you hope to accomplish? Why do you want to accomplish it? These are the important questions.

Only you can really know if you are going to use these techniques at a feeling level, and only you can feel the feelings they will evoke. And only you can decide to share or not to share those feelings. You'll get out of this book what you honestly want to get out of it.

Though we talk mostly about one-to-one and primary relationships, you can use these methods at many other levels of intimacy. They can provide much information about someone you're seeing only casually, and can help either to deepen the relationship or make you aware that it should be ended. Many of the techniques can be used to foster good feelings in friendships, and between close relatives.

This isn't a book to be read and put back on the shelf. You may choose to try some of these things now, and not want to explore others for several months, or even several years. There is no rush, the process lasts a lifetime.

Love relationships are really human relations courses, and each new relationship brings us new information.

Love and Security

Man's constant awareness of his own mortality motivates him toward the seeking of some sort of roots. He therefore often looks to a relationship to provide this desired security, continuity, and stability. This can be a highly destructive effort, for no relationship is really permanent. Two people may stay together for a lifetime, but at the end of that lifetime they would be two different people. It doesn't really matter if you choose one partner now to spend the rest of your life with, or have a number of sequential relationships; the end result will be the same. You will be in a different relationship at the end than you were at the beginning.

A relationship can, however, help us find the stability and security we need. It's a question of saying to your love-partner:

"Every moment that we are together, I am learning something, and that knowledge becomes a permanent part of me. Everything we share and communicate becomes a permanent part of my growth process. Though my feelings will be different a year from now, or ten years from now, part of the difference is you. Because of you, I am a different person, and the person I will grow to become, with or without you by my side, will have gotten there partly because of you. If you were not in my life right now, I could not be who I am right now. Nor would I be growing in exactly the same way. Much of what I grow toward, and change within myself, has to do with what I respond to in you, what I learn from you, what I perceive about myself through you, and what I learn about my feelings in the dynamics of our relationship. I do not worry about our 'future together,' since we have already touched each other and affected each other's lives on so many levels that we can never be totally removed from each other's consciousness. A part of me will always be you, and a part of you will always be me. That much is certain, no matter what else happens."

And what are *you* feeling right now?

APPENDIX

PANEL: OPENING UP THE MAN–WOMAN RELATIONSHIP

The following discussion was conducted at the 1972 annual meeting of the Association for Humanistic Psychology in Honolulu, Hawaii.

Participants

Bart Knapp, Ph.D., Director, Laurel Institute, Philadelphia; Marta Vago, M.S.W., Associate Director, Laurel Institute; Jerry Gillies, Author.

BART: We've been doing a lot of talking about our positions in terms of the man–woman relationship. The ideas that we've developed, the concepts, our separate interests. There have been dialogues between George and Nena O'Neill and us, and we ended up with three different, although related, approaches, which really consider similar ideas and concerns. The O'Neills are coming from a social-anthropological research orientation. Marta and I have a concern with some of the theoretical issues, and the application of these in our own clinical practice, in our own working with couples. Jerry has a concern with the attitudes of man and woman within the relationship. One common thing is that we all share a concern with putting these notions and these ideas to work. So, in a real sense, we are action oriented. On the basis of these things that have happened between us, and what we were learning as we were exploring each other's ideas in terms of our own positions, Jerry proposed that we get together and have a panel discussion, in which the three approaches could be informally talked about. Our goal here is first to toss out some of our ideas, and hope there will be an interchange. We want to learn your ideas, and we hope that there can be a really synergistic outcome. With the O'Neills not being able to make it here to Hawaii because of other pressing commitments, this won't be the same thing that we had anticipated. On the other hand, we felt very strongly that, when we made the decision to go ahead with the panel with just the three of us, there could be some very worthwhile and very provocative things to come from it.

JERRY: I think we are all committed to the concept that the most satisfying and fulfilling experience in this life is to engage in a full, sharing love relationship. A primary relationship on a one-to-one basis. There are many ways to facilitate that. My approach is that each man and each woman in a relationship have a certain commitment to that relationship, a commitment to growth. Before you can have a commitment in the relationship, however, there is a need to understand what you each want. I think the best way to facilitate this is to have an explicit contract between the man and woman, outlining what you want from each other, and what you're willing to give. A contract that, of necessity, has to be open, so that you can modify it periodically. As you grow in a relationship, your needs and expectations and realizations will change. That's what growth is all about. Change really comes because we learn more about ourselves and what we want and what we need. This is the basic stimulus in any change that occurs in the human experience: learning more about ourselves, and so changing something about ourselves to more nearly meet our needs. This is, of course, most true in a relationship. The concept of a contract turns some people off. It sounds very contrived and structured. In reality, in practice, a contract opens up a relationship and allows more freedom. It gets a lot of the stuff out of the way that may be part of the growing pains of the relationship. That growing pain can sometimes get in the way and completely block a relationship. If, at the very beginning, you decide where you're at, and what you want at least from this point, and you open up a communication line (and that should be part of a contract: when you're going to discuss what's happening to you), you can avoid a lot of these growing pains.

In communication, the sexual aspect of a relationship should not be isolated, as it has been. Conditioning has forced us, in many instances, to take sex and put it in its own little area, so that some relationships stay in that area and they're just sexual relationships. Other relationships get very confused. The sexual relationship, to be the best that it can be, and this may be an ideal, should come because of natural feelings that are happening between the man and woman. The sexual aspect of the relationship then comes naturally with those feelings, and is much richer, a much fuller experience than when sex in a relationship becomes the means to an end. Then sex can distort and confuse the basic issue in a man–woman relationship, which is really that we all want to share ourselves with someone else. I think it's a deep need in the human psyche. To open ourselves up to another person and to be loved and to share and feel safe in sharing. And to foster that atmosphere of safety and trust, and caring and sharing, is basically why we're all here.

(In talking about her work with Bart Knapp, Marta Vago used a blackboard drawing of the Johari Window, a facilitative concept of group interaction, designed by Joseph Luft and Harry Ingham, two National Training Lab group leaders. It consists of a square divided into four smaller squares. These represent: 1. Things known to self and known to others. 2. Things known to others but not to self. 3. Things known to self but not known to others. 4. Things not known to self or to others.)

MARTA: In working with couples, we usually start by explaining one area in a relationship: "The things that I know about me, and the things that you know about me." Doing this for each individual. We work pretty much in the framework of making implicits explicit. There are a lot of things that we assume about ourselves, and a lot of things we assume about our partner, and a lot of things the partner assumes about us. A beginning effort, then, is to explore the areas that are quite overt, and yet they have either not been shared or they have not been made explicit. This provides pretty much a groundwork from which to grow. For example, beginning with a couples workshop, we'll spend a lot of time making implicits explicit, whether in terms of expectations or in terms of roles, desires, wants, and needs. Sometimes the couples are pretty much together. They have pretty full knowledge of each other's wants, needs, expectations. Other times, things may come as a total surprise. So we go with what is. We figure: Until you know where you are, how are you going to figure out where you're going to go?

Then we move into the areas of: "The things I don't know about myself that you do know." This is not done in terms of coming on with a whole heavy rap of "You're a terrible person, and this and that are wrong with you!" But rather, sharing perceptions, checking perceptions with one another. We move from the covert, the things we have not shared with the other person, perhaps because we were afraid to. In other words, if you have a lousy habit of squeezing the toothpaste out from the wrong end of the tube, and I've been afraid to tell you that because of what you might think of me and what it might do to our relationship, then these are the areas that we start moving into. I use the toothpaste example as a very bread-and-butter issue, but there are many other areas that are much more emotionally laden and can also be explored this way. If there are certain parts of me that I don't feel O.K. to experience or to act upon within the confines of a close relationship, not only will I not know that part of myself, but it's also an area that we won't be able to share with one another. If any one of us is locked into a role with all its ramifications and expectations, if a man cannot feel weak and dependent, if he cannot allow himself to cry, he will never know that part of himself. At the same time, he will never really understand and fully know those characteristics in his partner. So that getting out of the role confines is another way of moving the boundaries so that these areas shift in a dynamic kind of way.

"The things that I don't know about myself, and you don't know about me either" are dark areas, all the unconscious stuff. We propose that, as it becomes O.K. to talk about these other areas, as the defenses go down because there's a reduction of fear, there is a sharing, a communication, and we propose that this dark area will eventually be opened up. "The things about myself that I have repressed or suppressed" can then emerge because I feel safe, I feel I can trust you. As I'm able to accept parts of you, you will have certain parts of yourself come to the surface and be available, not as dark unknowns, but rather as part of a conscious feeling, thinking experience. What all of this assumes is communication. If you can't talk about these things, if there's no framework in which to share these things, if you don't have a common language, then this becomes very difficult to do. Without the communication skills, it will be very hard to open up these areas at all.

I think we'd now like to throw it open to you, and answer whatever questions you may have for any of us.

DR. A.: This is particularly directed to Jerry, but perhaps you'll all react. I'm especially put off by the idea of a contract. Contracts to me imply adversaries, and imply an attempt, in a way, to cool emotional interaction. I think of contracts as a way of resolving superficial issues, and usually I feel that when couples are fighting over issues they are not really fighting over the issue that seems to be fought over. If I can tell a story, maybe I can illustrate my point:

My practice is a partnership. It's been going now for thirteen years. Thirteen years ago we went to see a lawyer to get a contract written, and we made a couple of notes about what needed to be covered. And the lawyer said, "Oh, this won't do! You haven't considered any of the ways you can screw each other." This brief meeting turned into three long sessions, and this document grew into pages and pages and pages. Finally, we said to him, "Look, if we thought we were going to screw each other, we wouldn't go into business together." And he misunderstood our point, and said, "I'm glad you see the light. I've brought together many partnerships like this and they never work. All sorts of tensions develop. I wouldn't give you three months, and I'm glad you gave it up." We walked out of there thirteen years ago. We still don't have a written agreement. The way we've survived is, about every three months we lock ourselves in a room and scream at each other, and get out all our paranoid fantasies. My point is, I'm after commitment in a marriage, as you are. I don't think a contract gives commitment. I think there's an emotional agreement to stay in the ring and fight.

JERRY: I might comment that, in a Relationship Contract, you probably wouldn't be entering into the contract unless you did agree to screw each other. (Audience laughter.) The contract is not meant to set up your feelings, or get in the way of emotions. It's meant to clear a lot of the crap out of the way so you then can get to the feelings. In such a contract, we're talking about getting a lot of the superficial stuff out of the way to start with, so you don't have to spend that much time on it. It really opens up an opportunity to have this continuing dialogue.

BART: I'd like to respond to the question. How did you decide to meet every three months?

DR. A.: It isn't a set time. It's just that one of us looks at the other and says that it's time.

BART: When there's a need. I submit that you have a contract.

MARTA: Right on!

DR. A.: It's not an explicit contract, and it's changing and variable.

BART: Exactly, but you are aware that this is an expectation in the relationship. That when things get tight between Joe and me, we're going to go in a room and scream our bloody heads off until we get the shit out. And it modifies, it does change from time to time. The contract is not a static thing, it's a dynamic thing. But recognizing what the expectations are, recognizing the facets of the contract, enables you to change it without leaving the other person hanging.

MARTA: A point I'd like to make is that contracts make sense only in terms of the needs that they fulfill. What happens to people is that our needs change. And so, a need that you had two years ago might not be there any more. However, unless you've examined that to see what behaviors accrue around those needs, your partner could go along merrily, assuming that you still have that need, and never really have an opportunity to look at it and see if things need to change. So, what a contract does, it makes explicit whatever needs I have. And whatever needs you have. And how the two of us together or separately can meet them. And as our needs change, then we have something to talk about. And we can talk about behavioral changes, attitude changes, and so on.

DR. B.: It seems to me that you're saying a contract is not just a piece of paper but a process.

MARTA: It can be a piece of paper, and for some couples it's very important to have a piece of paper. We get some couples in our clinical practice who are practically killing each other, and sometimes the only way they can even talk to one another is by pre-arrangement. They know that, when the shit starts flying, they have a contract about what they're going to do about it. Sometimes it's as simple as deciding on a room in the house in which they're going to talk about these things. Or a time, or a time limit, or what have you. One of the things that contracts do foster is taking responsibility for yourself. And what the contracts do spell out is who's going to do what to whom, and when. If I have a difficulty in keeping to a contract, then I build in safeguards for myself to help myself not cop out. Contracts are pretty much taking responsibility for yourself, not for your mate.

DR. C.: Statistically, in one out of two marriages, there comes a time when the pleasant screwing stops and the unpleasant screwing starts, and the divorce proceeding comes. I was wondering to what extent you explored entering into an additional contract outlining how to terminate the relationship. In other words, covering property, the children, and so on.

MARTA: It seems to me that if you work pretty much in an open relationship, and there's a lot of communication going back and forth, and an examination of where you are, then terminations will be a natural and productive outcome. But again, if you don't know where you are and what's happening, then it's very hard to terminate gracefully.

BART: Incidentally, we're not limiting this to the marriage, we're talking about a relationship, whether it's married or unmarried. Hopefully, as they learn to work within the contract framework, if it comes to a point of dissolving, they already have developed the skills, so that at that time of stress the skills are present and they don't have to learn new ones.

JERRY: I don't think a termination contract or clause is necessary. I think what a contract quite often facilitates may well be termination of a relationship. When you see it in black and white, and you say "I can't live with this," very quickly you can realize that this person is not for you. A contract doesn't only promote and foster the relationship, it will end an undesirable relationship that isn't meeting either partner's expectations, or enough of the expectations to make it worthwhile exploring and growing further in the relationship.

MARTA: There's a whole business of belonging *to* a person, or belonging *with* a person. If you conceptualize yourself as belonging *to* someone, then the whole termination issue becomes a pretty hairy deal. But if you see yourself belonging *with* a person, you can say "I no longer belong with this person because my needs are no longer being met."

DR. D.: Would alternate relationships be part of the contract?

MARTA: It seems to me that the only way outside relationships can work is if the same openness that exists within the primary relationship exists in the outside relationships as well. If you can be open with only one other person, then what's going to happen is that, as you go to an outside relationship, the closeness or tightness of that relationship will eventually contaminate. If you have to start hiding certain parts of yourself, your desires, your concerns, your own personal issues, it's very hard to keep yourself in "this relationship" separate from yourself in "that relationship." If you can keep this thing going with the same kind of openness with more than one person at a time, more power to you. But let's recognize that it's hard enough to do it with one person alone. I think this is a problem a majority of the people are struggling with, how to make it with one person. This has been our clinical experience.

DR. D.: It sounds like your prognosis for this in contemporary America is sort of hesitant. You're saying this would really be a rough deal. Suppose, though, there is a possibility of two good relationships, having everybody know about everybody else, do you feel that one is necessarily primary and would tend to exclude the other after a while?

MARTA: I think in all relationships we're dealing with priorities, and I have not seen this kind of relationship, this ideal that you're talking about, where let's say four or six people can really live without any specific one-to-one primary commitment. I've not seen it. That doesn't mean it doesn't exist. Again, when it comes down to priorities, how are you going to set them? And on the basis of what? In other words, if you have only X number of hours in a day, how are you going to decide whom to spend them with? And what does that say about you and your feelings toward the other people?

DR. D.: This is where your contractual thing would come in, it would seem, almost as a necessity with any more than two parties, in order for all these people to be represented with all their needs.

MARTA: It's hard enough to deal with one person's needs, whether in terms of trying to meet them, or not trying to meet them. As you multiply by two it really mushrooms.

JERRY: In opening up a relationship to other possible partners, you run into several considerations, just as you do in getting into a relationship in the first place. The first consideration in getting into a relationship is really self-examination as to whether you are ready, willing, and able to get into a primary relationship. That's your first commitment, if that's what you want. If that is what you want, the primary relationship has to come first. There has to be a development stage. Too many people enter a primary relationship and decide they're going to open things up and bring in all kinds of other partners immediately, before they've even gotten to know where they're going in their primary relationship. That can be very dangerous, because it gets in the way of the natural development. It is very difficult to get into a primary relationship, a good one at least. My personal experience has been that anybody who's gotten into any kind of a group thing has done so because they did not have a happy, fulfilling primary relationship. A group relationship or multiple relationship is not a cure for your inability to get into a primary relationship, or the fact that you have not yet found a person with whom you can get into a primary relationship. I think all relationships have to be on a one-to-one level, even additional ones. If you want to get a group thing going, that's fine, but if you don't have the one-to-one relationship before the group thing gets going, it's not going to work or last. And you may not want it to last. You could choose to get into things that aren't going to last. A lot of people do, it's sort of a self-destruct mechanism. They get into a relationship they know is not going to last, and do things to continue the temporary status. I think a contract is necessary in every relationship, whether verbal or on paper. Even additional auxiliary relationships. There has to be a contract between you and your primary partner as to what you're willing to accept from each other in external relationships. And there has to be a checking-out, I think, in each individual situation. A primary relationship may be threatened by one alternate relationship and not by another. If you check it out, and you say, "I am very sexually attracted to so and so, I would like to pursue that," and your primary partner says "That would be very threatening to me, and very painful for me," you then have to decide your priorities. You've been warned. You've been told that your primary partner would not take it lightly, is not willing for you to go into that, is not giving you carte blanche. And then you have to really decide. And sometimes that can bring you to a decision as to what your primary partnership means to you. When you get closed in, when you're trapped or feel trapped, you tend to think you need more extra relationships than you do. Once you have the freedom to explore other relationships, you may find you're not exercising that freedom as much as you thought you would be.

DR. E.: Could Bart and Marta give us a sample of their contract?

MARTA: This is a very simple contract. If we get into an argument, either person can say "I want to stop at this point, because I just don't feel I can handle this." And at that point we set up an appointment as to when we are going to handle it. And the other person has the commitment to not push the person who wants to stop, respecting their need to stop.

DR. E.: Well, I'd like to see what areas most couples cover.

BART: It's actually impossible to give the full contract, without sitting down and doing a tremendous amount of work. While much of it is explicit, it covers most areas of the relationship, and it may cover very superficially those areas where there's no disagreement or just a small problem. Other areas, there's a great deal of work. This clause of breaking off an argument that Marta described, and what it means to me, and what it means to Marta, took a great deal of working through.

MARTA: We have two friends who live in a nonmarriage situation. Every six months they sit down for a state of union discussion, and every six months they decide if they're going to be together for another six months. At that point they share their feelings about how the last six months have been, what it is that has been working well, what they have to work on further. Their commitment is always negotiable, at six months' intervals. That's a much broader contract than the one we just gave on how we handle arguments.

There's a whole business of choice. Very often couples come to us because they feel they have no choice. They feel locked in, and as they begin to clarify their relationship, the issue of choice becomes very central: "I can choose to do this by myself. I can choose to do this with you. We can choose to do these things together or not do them together. I can choose to meet this need in you, or I can choose not to, and that's O.K., too." In other words, the whole business of living up to another person's expectations becomes almost a moot point, because there's a whole element of choice involved. When that's true, you can say "I don't feel coerced. I don't feel that you're going to make me feel guilty if I don't do this to you or for you."

Another thing I'd like to bring up in terms of contracts is that there's been a lot of work recently, I guess stimulated by Dr. George Bach, on fight training. While I think that fight training is valuable in and of itself, I tend to feel that, unless the issues that you're fighting about are clarified, you're going to fight like crazy, with wonderful positive resolutions, except the issues will still remain the same. So that, for our purposes, we clarify the relationship first, and then we help couples learn mechanisms to deal with the issues, and the fights that arouse around the issues. Clarifying the nature of the relationship is a preamble for learning conflict-resolution skills. If you only learn conflict-resolution skills, but you don't look at the relationship, you really fight good, but about what? For example, a couple could have tremendous fights over who's going to do what, and they can draw up very elaborate contracts with "I do the dishes, and you do this" and so on and so forth, but what they're not talking about is roles and role flexibility. What are the assumptions that we have made about our relationship in terms of roles? The implicit assumptions that we kind of fell into backward. Just to have a contract about who's going to do dishes doesn't really address itself to the issue of what our role expectations of each other are, and how we are boxing ourselves into that.

DR. F.: You talk about a third person coming in and possibly muddying up the waters of a primary relationship, but what about children? I see children as possibly primary in another way. And children are often there and I feel a tremendous responsibility to them. It's not like a third party, where I can say "O.K., this is where I am right now." You can't do that with kids. In my personal experience the water isn't clear between my partner and me all the time because there are three other little bodies who are there, and want to be in on the contracts.

MARTA: Just off the top of my head, if you look at the relationship again as a closed one, belonging to someone, then it's awfully hard to make room for anybody else. It's the whole business of personal identity versus the couple-front. If you start giving up your own self and your own personhood to become part of this kind of a block called a couple, then any outside person, whether it be a friend or any new children coming along, will have a tremendously difficult time breaking into that. So, the whole business of identity gets very, very important. Your own personhood. Has the relationship become 50–50, where I'll give up 50 per cent of my needs, and you'll give up 50 per cent of your needs? Or is each of us going to bring 100 per cent of ourselves into the relationship, with very open boundaries that can then be open to children, family, friends, the community, social causes, what have you? The concept of a couple-front is that there's only so much love to go around, and there's only one person to share it with, and anybody else coming in is going to mean a reduction of love for that one person.

BART: It seems to me that, in a relationship where the implicit has been made explicit and the expectations are out in the open, where you do have an open relationship and there is a contract which is subject to renegotiation, then as any crucial event occurs, like a child, or financial catastrophe, or change in any form, it is able to be handled by the skills and processes that you have developed beforehand.

JERRY: The happiest family relationships that I've seen are those that do have a contract with the children. A contract, for example, that every evening from seven to eight the whole family will sit down and have a discussion of what's been going on that day, and what the children would like to see happen, what they want. Children can understand much more than we give them credit for understanding. I have friends who sit down and tell their children that there's a private time for mom and dad, in which the children, unless its important, are not to intrude. Children can respect that, as long as they know they are getting their time, too, and that their time will not be intruded on either. I don't think the freewheeling parent–child relationship is as effective as one where there are some basic premises set up, some basic contractual commitments set up. They should be flexible, of course, I'm not talking about running a military establishment. But there should certainly be a time for communication. That's one of the most important things in any contract, a communication clause: "On so much notice, you and I will sit down and talk. You won't give me that excuse that you have to go play golf, and I won't give you the excuse that I have a beauty parlor appointment." Children should also know that they have that kind of call on you.

DR. G.: What is the stage of relationship at which this is helpful? My own bias is that I shudder at the idea of people jumping in too early and trying to specify their role expectations and things of that kind.

JERRY: You are starting an implicit contract anytime you are starting a relationship. From the first time you make eye contact with that person, that can be a contract that you're going to explore something further. And each additional meeting is a contract, and each time you make plans to see each other again, or understand that you are going to see each other again. The contractual process is continuing. The time you actually start to put it down in writing, I think, is when you have to decide whether that person and you are in a relationship that you want to continue and grow. When you both have pretty well decided you want to explore it further than just casual dating or just casual sex, or whatever that relationship has constituted. I think it starts to come naturally once you sit down and start talking about a contract. Now, it's very unlikely that both of you are going to be as willling to enter into a contract. There's usually going to be one partner who thinks more of the idea, or suggests it first. You may have to get to a place where you understand that the other person may have been adamantly opposed to a contract, and you have to approach that. That has to take place in negotiations. That's one of the first big hurdles, the agreement that you are both willing to sit down and have a contract. Again, it's a question of priorities. Is the relationship worth making the effort?

MARTA: In response to the question "How early?" one of the things that Bart and I would really like to get into more is workshops for couples that are really prophylactic in nature. This is fostered by an experience that we just had. We had a couples group with the couples in various stages of togetherness or difficulty, and one couple came in in the throes of love. They'd been together for about four months, and they thought that there was just absolutely nothing that was closed between them. But they both had been married before, and that's a more and more common occurrence, and they were really afraid that they were going to bring a lot of past baggage with them into the relationship, and start making the very same mistakes that they made before. They really wanted to come in on terms of working on things now, before they became crucial issues, and exploring things like roles, expectations, what does it mean to be a couple, how's my identity related to this couple relationship, what is our commitment to one another? What they found out very quickly was that there were already batches of things that they had swept under the rug. And they were so high that you had to sort of tug at the balloon every few minutes to make sure they were still there. They were so high, and yet already there were areas that they had started closing off, and there were already things that they had stopped saying to one another, there were already fears creeping in. They were really, really glad to catch them at a time when they were not in difficulty, a time when they were just at the peak of the first few months of the relationship. And we feel that there may be a lot of merit in couples coming in early, not in terms of fixing difficulties, but learning skills to handle whatever difficulties might come up in the future.

DR. G.: Well, then, don't you think it's at least good that they had at least four months without a contract, without being that explicit, to allow themselves to get carried away a bit and get a little irrational?

MARTA: I really don't know. There's just no way of knowing that.

BART: It's very easy at the start of a relationship to be carried away and think that everything is going to be great. The point at which you begin to explore the nature of the contract is probably the point at which you feel it necessary and advisable to do it, and this may vary from couple to couple. The awareness that this is available as a process is a very important one, and I would expect that each couple would go into this at their own pace.

DR. H.: Is there anything harmful about making contracts? Does it cut some processes off?

JERRY: My feeling is that, if a relationship cannot survive a contract, it never should have started or should be ended immediately, if the euphoria is so flimsy. Drawing up the contract can be exciting and full of love and sharing. It can be a way to add to the excitement.

DR. I.: Are the people you have in mind so mature that they can really cross this difficult bridge, or are they so naïve that they need this? I never know what kind of people you address yourself to. Are they so naïve that they can't communicate and this contract will help them, or are they so mature that they can work this out?

JERRY: Making a contract is universal. For those who are naïve, it will help them. For those who are mature, it will help them foster that, and share that maturity.

DR. I.: You're a true believer.

JERRY: I'm a true believer. I think the contract concept is one that is almost foolproof, and is never harmful to a real sharing relationship, if the feeling is really there. What it will do, it will cut off some of the pleasant high feelings of a relationship that wasn't meant to be. A euphoria that may have lasted four months instead of two, but still would have busted up, maybe with more bitterness. It will end some relationships that should have been ended sooner, and may end some of them sooner than you may like them to end.

DR. I.: Life usually takes care of that without a contract.

JERRY: Yes, but with a lot of unhappiness for a lot of people. Most people aren't very happy with the way their relationships end. And a lot of people feel they waste a lot of time in relationships that they might have ended if they had only known more about where it was going and what they were expecting from each other. They might have had time to get into a more fulfilling relationship. We are limited in the time we have on this earth. To a great extent, you can avoid and eliminate wasting time in a relationship where you're going to be running into expectations that are going to be tossed at you after things have really moved pretty far along, and finding something coming up that you've never dealt with.

BART: I feel very strongly that the contract we're talking about is not an artificial device. It's not an intellectual device. It's a way of conceptualizing the sort of agreements that are implicit in the relationship. And I submit that these agreements and expectations are present very, very early in the relationship, from "Wow, would I like to ball her," to "We could make beautiful music together," or "She'd be a great mother," or whatever.

DR. J.:   When is the best time to make the implicits explicit?

MARTA: I think the best time to really get a handle on implicit contracts is during fights. One of the things we have done, both with ourselves and with the couples that we've worked with, is that, after a fight is over, whatever resolution came out of it, we go back and look at the process. What happened? What did I assume about you? What did you assume about me? What kind of needs was I expecting you to meet in me? What kind of needs were you expecting me to meet in you? People fight because there's a conflict, a conflict of interests, a conflict of needs, a conflict of expectations, and it seems to me that one of the best times to process things, in making implicits explicit, is at the resolution of a fight. I think perhaps some people tend to think of a contract as a static, rigid thing. Like anything else in a relationship, it is a process, and as the relationship moves, as the people within it move, these things change and develop in ways that we just cannot anticipate.

DR. K.:   Isn't it a contract when a penis will enter a vagina to say that the woman will have an orgasm?

BART: That sounds like an expectation.

JERRY: Most couples have never sat down and discussed whether they're both expecting an orgasm. A woman would like to know the expectation of the man, and he would like to know her expectation, but they rarely talk about it. Putting something like that into a contract could be suitable, even if it's a verbal contract: "What do I expect from you sexually?" and "What am I giving you sexually?" It's all well and good to say "Well, it's flowing naturally and it's beautiful," but if you start examining it, you'll find that there may be some other things you would like to happen. This is why so many American women are reported as having faked an orgasm at one time or another. This was an assumed expectation. It may not have been a real expectation on the part of the man. Maybe he didn't expect or even care if the woman had an orgasm, and of course faking an orgasm may get in the way of a real orgasm. This is an area that should be explored and discussed. A contract can merely be an agreement to discuss some of these things, not necessarily during

(Audience laughter.) or right before or right after, but maybe the next morning.

DR. K.:   But you can discuss this without a contract?

JERRY: You can discuss it without a contract, but just agreeing on what you expect from each other would be a contract to some extent. You can choose not to put any of this in writing. It can be little episodes that occur, and little agreements that you make. Putting it in writing sometimes clears it up, and makes it a little more easy to refer back to when you want to see whether you are going off the line you want to stay on.

DR. L.:   Where are some areas of troubled waters you may have experienced in writing a relationship contract?

JERRY: There are times in any relationship when you are really not willing to make a commitment. Being able to say "No, I'm not willing to agree to this" I think is important in contract negotiation. Saying "I'm not willing to give up that much of my privacy. I'm not willing to set a time to communicate with you twice a week, I think it's too arbitrary, I think we should just give each other a signal when we want to communicate." What you are willing to commit to the relationship, that's where you run into trouble, because again you run into the same things that the contract is meant to solve: the expectations. You have expectations as to what a contract is going to do, and *they* can be unrealistic. Again, there is the fear of risking losing something you are enjoying, so you may choose to give in to something your partner wants, when you really don't feel deep down that you want to give in on that, and you don't want to confront it, and the unwillingness to confront it then, at the beginning of the contract, leads to trouble later, because you're going to feel trapped. A contract can be manipulated by one or the other partner into a trap situation. I think the open communication almost has to come in a relationship before you're really ready for an explicit contract. When you ask about timing, you're ready for a contract when you're ready for honest communication with each other. If you're not, then the contract is meaningless, as worthless as the piece of paper it's written on.

DR. M.:   How do you help people become aware enough to make it work?

BART: In our workshops, initially this is a very highly structured experience. Working first on what they both know about each other, and sharing and clarifying it, so that it is in the public domain and out for discussion. Then gradually working over into the sharing more of oneself, "What more I'm now willing to tell you about me," again getting in touch with the expectations. "And as I build up trust in you, I'm willing to share more of what and who I am. I'm also willing to listen and to respect your perceptions of me, your understandings of me, and build on those."

MARTA: Our experience in working with couples is that the self-awareness issue is not that great. People are pretty much self-aware. The difficulty comes in talking about it in an atmosphere of trust and safety. That when there is an atmosphere of acceptance, "When I can accept your feelings, I don't have to like them, but I can accept them," when there is a framework in which to share these things, we have not had difficulty in people coming in and not knowing what they wanted. Of course, our experience is limited to the two of us, and the people we work with. I don't think that self-awareness per se is the biggest stumbling block, I think it's the sharing of these awarenesses with a partner that's very difficult. We don't believe in letting it all hang out in a workshop situation. "I'm going to tell you all the things I hate about you, and you're going to tell me all the things you hate about me, and then we'll start working." No. It's step by step. Kind of pushing the boundaries gradually in an atmosphere of safety.

JERRY: I think Marta just touched on an issue that is really a primary one in this whole humanistic movement. What happens if someone comes to a panel like this, or an experimental workshop, and then goes back to their partner, who hasn't been attending, and tries to relate what's been happening. Letting it all hang out can be a very forceful manipulative act on the part of one partner, to be used against the other partner. Bluntness and opening up your guts can be a very useful thing sometimes, but it really has to be a mutual thing, and the motivation has to be clear. What, for instance, is our motivation in entering in a contract? Do we want to possess this person? Do we want to guarantee our own security and safety? This really isn't the reason for a contract. A contract can certainly be as misused as any other tool that's used to facilitate understanding and trust. I've seen this happen so many times. Someone will learn to do a little more sharing of themselves, and they'll demand that their partner open up as much as they feel they've opened up. "You should open up and communicate with me, and let me know everything you're feeling right now." That's sort of a ridiculous demand,

and is using the opening up for a purpose totally opposed to really opening up: to make demands on another person the other person isn't willing to meet. One of the clauses I had in a relationship contract was "I will no longer say you should do this to make our relationship a happy one. I will tell you what I would like you to do, and then you can tell me whether you're willing to do it." In coming up with theories and attitudes about what makes a good relationship, we're not trying to say that all of these are going to be true in every instance, or that you need all of them to be completely fulfilled.

DR. N.: I question the assumption of this panel that a one-to-one relationship is the ideal situation.

MARTA: It's not an assumption, it's simply what people seem to do. Even in communes there is a lot of bonding, which leads us to suspect there is something in a one-to-one relationship that people need. Whether this is ideal or not, we're not prepared to say.

DR. N.: It could be that people keep regressing to this because of the fantasy that it is going to meet their infantile needs, and they are repeatedly frustrated in this area because it never can be this ideal infantile mother–infant bond.

MARTA: I feel uncomfortable putting such valuations or labels on anything, whether it's a one-to-one relationship or a group relationship, I just don't think we know.

DR. N.: But just because people keep doing this, I don't think is evidence that it's the best thing. We keep having wars, and we keep doing a lot of other things. . . .

MARTA: I think that all we're saying is that, given the facts that most people seem to want a one-to-one relationship, our concern is how we can facilitate that relationship, and make it open enough so that the couples are not locked into each other because that's the only thing in the world they can seem to do.

BART: We are not saying in any sense that this is *the* way, that this is the right way. All we're saying is that, in our experience, limited as it is, we're finding that this is an effective concept, one that people can work with. It's not dogma. It's not enlightenment. It's not *The True Way*. And I'm certain that there are other ways. This is a way that we're comfortable with in our relationship. And we found that it makes sense to other people, not everybody, but a number of other people.

DR. O.: What about the differences in people? Some people prefer implicit communication. They may not like to talk about certain things, or may not be as articulate as their partner, or may not like to plan. They may like the spontaneity.

JERRY: Well, I can talk from my own experience. No one likes a surprise more than I do. I don't even like to know what I'm eating for dinner on any particular day, as long as it's not chicken. I think it would be hard to find a person who was unwilling to communicate and who could still form a synergistic relationship with a person willing to communicate. There has to be a two-way flow. If one person really has a need to share, and the other person is unwilling to share because of shyness or fear or whatever, I think the relationship is in trouble before you even get to the contract-writing stage.

MARTA: I consider, and many others consider, these so-called instinctual characteristics as not instinctual at all, but as learned. You learned to be a certain way because that's the way you learned to operate and survive in this world. If you're more withdrawn, it's probably because of your upbringing, and the kind of signals that your parents or significant others sent out to you about: Is it O.K. to talk, or is it better to shut up? If you look at characteristics as learned behaviors, then there's an implicit assumption there that they can be either unlearned or that other learned behaviors can be added to them. And I think that one of the central things that Bart and I try to do in working with couples is to help them learn new behaviors. Not necessarily eliminate behaviors that they already have, unless they want to get rid of them and they're dysfunctional or counter-productive, but to help them learn new alternatives. If you can only be one way, then you really don't have much choice. If you can be different ways, then at least you can choose among them. At times you might want to withdraw. At times you might want to retire in a psychological/emotional sense. But then you know that you also have the capability to come out and to talk and to be a little more extroverted. Looking at these things as learned behaviors, reinforced by parental or outside forces, can really help in looking at the whole situation a little differently.

JERRY: There's a lot of talk about male–female consciousness raising. I think that when we talk about consciousness, we find that a man or a woman is able to expand his or her consciousness as much as they want to. All of us are able to expand and go much further. I think we're limiting ourselves to say that we cannot still have that sense of surprise and excitement while we're dealing with deeper issues and confronting deeper realities. Sitting down once a week to discuss what's happening can be a surprise. You don't know what's going to come up at that meeting. You can use these things to add to the sense of joy and surprise in a relationship. If you're saying to yourself "My contract is going to eliminate all the joy and surprise, all the spontaneity," then it probably will, becoming another self-fulfilling prophecy. If you believe a contract will add to the adventure of a relationship, it will do that.

ANNOTATED BIBLIOGRAPHY

Author's Note:

Most of the research for this book was in the form of experiential workshops, discussions, and interviews with psychologists, psychiatrists, social workers, and group leaders.

The books listed here aren't the only ones I've read on these subjects, but they are the ones that really made an emotional impact. This is a very personal list, and I am pleased to be able to share it with you. I urge you to consider all ten books listed here as a good beginning.

OPEN MARRIAGE. Nena and Dr. George O'Neill (New York: M. Evans and Company, Inc., 1972)

This is one of the most important books ever written on interpersonal relations. It should be mandatory reading for anyone interested in love relationships and making them work. The research is impeccable, the reasoning superb, and the O'Neills scholarly approach does not dilute their sense of humanity. It is perhaps ironic that two anthropologists have done the best job in describing and defining so many of the principles of humanistic psychology. Their concept of synergy as applied to relationships is a valid and important one. Though the freedom they espouse as options within relationships may threaten or frighten some people, those reading the book will realize that the O'Neills are not suggesting or recommending that multiple relationships become an indication of freedom and openness. You may not care to adapt all of the concepts outlined in this book, but you can't help but gain some new insights from it, and some new areas to explore.

TOTAL SEX. Dr. Herbert A. Otto and Roberta Otto (New York: Peter Wyden, Inc., 1972)

This book evolved out of the many classes and workshops conducted by the Ottos, considered pioneers in the human potential movement. Its main premise is that we all operate at pitifully low sexual potential, and that this potential can be greatly increased by a holistic program of sexual development that covers all aspects of life: physical, emotional, spiritual. This involves everything from examining your sexual fears and taboos to understanding more about your sexual organs and how they function, and practicing a wide variety of new sexual experiences. It is a "how to" book in the best sense of the word. Even if you feel you have a happy and fulfilling sex life, there is bound to be something you can learn from this book.

MAKING FRIENDS WITH THE OPPOSITE SEX. Emily Coleman (Los Angeles: Nash Publishing Corporation, 1972)

This can be a highly informative and entertaining book. Emily describes herself as a "gutsy lady" and proceeds to prove it. She has some especially good advice for the woman who wants to start exploring growth, though this is a book for men and women. It conveys a lot of Emily's vitality, and is the next best thing to being in a group with her. Social nudity is explored here, with both a full explanation of how this can free you and an examination of the fears that might prevent you from trying it. Emily Coleman has that unique talent of making people feel better about themselves, and much of this comes through here.

SENSE RELAXATION. Bernard Gunther (New York: The Macmillan Company, 1968)
WHAT TO DO TILL THE MESSIAH COMES. Bernard Gunther (New York: The Macmillan Company, 1971)

This is a double feature of awareness experiences, all developed by this pioneer in sensitivity training at Esalen Institute. Bernie Gunther is a group leader who manages to bring a sense of life and warmth to his workshops, and he has managed here to adapt this to the printed page, with the help of some beautiful photography by Paul Fusco. Just looking at the expressions on some of the faces can inspire you to try the experiences.

AWARENESS. John O. Stevens (Lafayette, California: Real People Press, 1971)

More than a hundred in-depth experiences are included in this volume. What makes this book unique is the careful explanation given by the author, so that you know exactly why you are trying a particular exercise, and what it's meant to show you. It's written very conversationally, and the instructions are precise and comprehensive. John Stevens has a lot to say about feelings, trust, and love, and he says it well. His chapter on leading groups is a masterpiece, and a must for anyone ever interested in conducting workshops involving interaction. This is one of those rare books that makes you want to sit down and have a conversation with the author after it's all over.

BECOMING PARTNERS: MARRIAGE AND ITS ALTERNATIVES. Carl R. Rogers
    (Delacorte Press, New York, 1972)

This is an intensive examination of some actual relationships, the struggles and pains, and the joys of exploring growth together. Dr. Rogers does an excellent job of conducting a perceptive dialogue with the individuals involved, and this is a valuable subjective look at the love relationship. Dr. Rogers also generously shares some of his own personal experiences in love and marriage. There is little exposition here, but he does manage to get his important points across. The annotated bibliography is worth noting for its completeness, and will be a good one to check out if you're finding this one too limited in the numbers of books involved.

NOTES TO MYSELF. Hugh Prather (Lafayette, California: Real People
    Press, 1970)
I TOUCH THE EARTH, THE EARTH TOUCHES ME. Hugh Prather (Garden City, New York: Doubleday & Company, Inc., 1972)

Both these volumes are filled with precious feelings and honest exercises in self-observation. It would be hard for anyone to read through them without coming across something that evokes an emotional response. They can be particularly valuable if you want to start a Love Journal or daily record of your feelings. Hugh Prather shares not only his hopes and fears and expectations and realizations, but even his doubts as to whether he should be sharing all of these things. They are poetic personal documents, and meant to be read at leisure. You might find the best way to enjoy them is to read just a page or two at a time. These are beautiful books to share with your love-partner, and can help you articulate some of your own feelings.

BIOFEEDBACK: TURNING ON THE POWER OF YOUR MIND. Marvin Karlins and Lewis M. Andrews (New York: J. B. Lippincott Company, 1972)

This book covers the wide range of possibilities in biofeedback training and research, and shows how this new science may provide the means to fight the psychological dehumanizers who wish technologically to castrate mankind by benevolently conditioning all his responses. Very humanistically oriented, the authors nonetheless provide an excellent portrait of the research going on, and the speculations for the future. Particularly impressive is the philosophical chapter on biofreedom. This is a must book for anyone interested in exploring biofeedback. The bibliography is annotated and exhaustive.